AFTERMATH

The kitchen was a wasteland. A dozen pairs of booted feet had left indelible marks in black on the sanded oak of the floor. The rugs in the living room were beyond repair. The stairs looked as if someone had fallen at least once, on the way up or the way down and used the banisters as a crash barrier on the way to the floor. The bedroom, predictably, was a cave. A windowless, airless, smog-filled pit. And dark. So very, very dark. A dark that sucked. Took the torchlight and swallowed it whole and gave out sounds in its place. Soft. Hidden. Painful. The final keenings of heat-tortured wood. The whispers of falling plaster. The guttered groans of timbers shifting suddenly in the roof space. This place has stood for nearly three hundred years. Generations have lived here and died here and the cottage has never changed. It doesn't like the intrusion of fire. It hates the intrusion of men afterwards. The air held something close to loathing about it.

Fine fingers of fear traced their way up my spine and squeezed tight in my throat. . . .

NIGHT MARES

MANDA SCOTT

BANTAM BOOKS
New York   Toronto   London   Sydney   Auckland

There is a vet school in Glasgow and it is in the middle of the Garscube Estate, more or less as described. This is as far as the facts go in this novel. Every other detail, every clinical case, every clinician, every particle of the landscape is a product of the author's imagination. None of them has any basis in fact whatsoever.

The author gratefully acknowledges the financial assistance of the Eastern Arts Council in the writing of this book.

NIGHT MARES

A Bantam Crime Line Book / published by arrangement with
Headline Book Publishing

PUBLISHING HISTORY
Headline trade edition published 1998
Bantam paperback edition / July 1999

Crime Line and the portrayal of a boxed "cl" are trademarks of
Bantam Books, a division of Random House, Inc.

ISBN 0-553-57968-1

Published simultaneously in the United States and Canada

Bantam Books are published by Bantam Books, a division of Random
House, Inc. Its trademark, consisting of the words "Bantam Books" and the
portrayal of a rooster, is Registered in U.S. Patent and Trademark Office
and in other countries. Marca Registrada. Bantam Books, 1540 Broadway,
New York, New York 10036.

PRINTED IN THE UNITED STATES OF AMERICA

OPM 10 9 8 7 6 5 4 3 2 1

For Hester

Acknowledgments

The number of people who contribute to the writing of any novel is immense. In this case, however, there are a well-defined few who made *Night Mares* what it is. Jane, my agent, is clearly well on the way to sainthood, and Anne and Victoria at Headline have kept remarkable good humour in the face of hard-pressed deadlines.

On the veterinary side, I would like to thank Hester for some serious input on imaging and general veterinary common sense, Pat and Sean for digging up details of the pathogenesis and pathology of endotoxaemia, Warren for reminders on surgical technique and Shane for help with a certain feline forelimb fracture. On the medical front, my thanks to Dr Charles McAllister for help with the human anaesthesia and the intensive care protocols.

Night Mares was written largely under the influence of Dublin Vet School and while I would like to make it clear that not one single bit of the content reflects on that remarkable and very wonderful institution, it would have been a great deal harder to write had I not been there. My thanks, therefore, to all of the clinical staff and final year students, specifically to Eilis, Deirdre, Mary and Cliona for being there, to Maureen P., for not being there when it mattered, to Warren for remembering and, with Niamh and Shane, for making the department such a rewarding place to work. Thanks also to Hester for opening her home, hearth, and wordprocessor to a wandering anaesthetist and, in England, to Betty and Joe, the world's most patient neighbours, for taking care of cottage, cat and the essentials of life while I was travelling. Finally, thanks to my family, as ever, for keeping faith.

NIGHT MARES

Prologue

The world is blue. Pale and oddly translucent. Like the sky over Skye. Some cretin with a sense of humour has painted the ceiling in pharmacy blue. Because they could. And so the world is blue with magnolia walls.

There's a fat, bloated sun floating somewhere in the back of the blue. Above and to the right. Miles out of reach. It's a drip bag. Fat and overfilled and yellow like flat Lucozade. The yellow is pentobarbitone. There's enough in there to kill a horse. Several horses. I know. I put it there. I took every drop we had in the dangerous drugs cupboard, signed it all out and pumped it into a 500 ml bag of dextrose-saline. That bit was easy. It was getting the catheter in that was hard. I need to use a catheter. I'm not about to fuck up again. But it's more difficult than I thought. I don't have veins like a horse. And there's only one vein on my left arm that's worth going for. All the rest were shot to bits *after* last time. I used a 23 gauge cat catheter because I thought it would be easier to get in. Even so, it took me two tries. The bruising hurts more than I remember. It doesn't matter, but it's making things more difficult.

I hooked up the drip to the catheter and turned it on, full bore. It's slow, though. I forget how slowly things go through small catheters. Agonisingly slow. I can count the drops as they spill through the giving set. Small yellow doses of death falling like lethal, linear rain, back lit against the blue of the sky.

I keep counting. It is important to count. To count the seconds between one drop and the next. Between one breath and the next. The breaths will end before the drops. I know this. I have been here before. The blue will expand outwards, filling the world and the magnolia will fade to nothing. The drops will keep flowing but I will stop counting. I will stop trying to work out how much time I have left. I will have no time left.

There may be dreams. I worry most about the dreams. Last time there were dreams but then last time I woke up and had to remember. This time I won't wake up. And if there are dreams, they will be dreams of another space and another time and they could not possibly be worse than the nightmare of the here and now.

'It's just pentobarb in the drip? On its own? Nothing else?'

'Yes.'

'But you used ketamine with it last time. And morphine.'

'I know. And I fucked up.'

'So it isn't last time?'

'No. It's this time. It's now. Soon.'

'Do you want that?'

'No. Not now.'

'But, in the dream, do you want it?'

'No. I don't want it. But, in the dream, I have no choice. I can feel it coming, sucking me in. Like gravity. I can't fight gravity, there's no point. So I don't try. I just sit there and watch it happening. And, in the end, I don't care. I really don't care at all.'

'And now? How do you feel about it now?'

'I'm too tired to feel anything, Kellen. I don't want to feel anything. I can't cope as it is. There's too much going wrong that I don't know how to handle. Too many nightmares coming true.'

'Could you take a break from work?'

'And leave Steff with a surgical ward full of dying patients? I don't think so.'

'Does she know?'

'About the dreams? Yes.'

'And Matt?'

'Matt's always known.'

'So you have two people who can help you. Use them.'

The air is still. Some ideas need a long time to take root.

'I'll try.'

We need more than that.

'Nina, I want you to promise me that you won't do anything . . . permanent . . . without calling me first. Will you do that? *Can* you do that?'

A long pause. As if she is weighing her integrity against the pull of gravity and there is precious little to choose between them.

'Yes. I promise.'

'Thank you.'

She gets up to leave. At the door, she thinks of something new.

'You won't tell anyone, Kellen?'

'Never. I can't. You know that.'

And besides, who in the world would want to know?

I counted seven magpies in the morning.

Seven. All brilliant blue on black, sharp-edged against the raw white of the last frost of spring. The first six were spread out down the lane between the barn and the far paddock. One on the gate, one on the fence, one on the hawthorn hedge, three, all in a row on the fallen beech that bridges the stream. For a while, I thought that was the lot and warmed the morning with gentle fantasies of gold.

The seventh hid at the back of the field, digging something bright from beneath a mound of horse dung. He saw me coming and fled to the beech wood, cursing me to a summer full of other people's secrets. Gold, at least, would have had some novelty to it.

I thought of them lazily throughout the day, in between clients. A kind of visual mantra, useful in keeping

the tangles of one session from weaving their way into
the next.

I thought of them quite pointedly at six o'clock when
Nina Crawford was late for her evening appointment
without calling to let me know. Some people are late out
of habit. Quite a few manage to 'forget' whenever they
think things are running too close to the bone. Nina
misses about one session in five simply because she is
still in theatre with an unplanned emergency. But she
has never yet forgotten to call. Not once in the last seven
and a half years.

Magpies loomed rather larger than I would have
liked for the rest of the barren hour. Magpies and the
pull of gravity. At half past, I pawned the car out of the
car park and headed for home; out along Great Western
Road, up through Anniesland Cross and over the switchback towards Milngavie. At the last moment, I turned
right, across the dual carriageway and down into the
gateway of Garscube Estate.

You can ignore magpies for the rest of your life and
get away with it.

I'm not so sure about gravity.

███

Dr Nina Crawford, senior lecturer in equine surgery at
the University of Glasgow Veterinary Teaching Hospital
lives on the job, for the job and through the job. When
she's not performing acts of veterinary heroism with her
scalpel or leading her corps of students through the
minefield of surgical anatomy, she lives in an ageing cottage in the grounds of Garscube Estate. The place was
originally built for one of the farm workers in the days
when the vast majority of farm workers were being piled
on to sailing ships bound for Canada and only the lucky
few were kept back to herd the sheep. Shepherds were

not, I would say, expected to live long nor to enjoy the experience.

It is pleasant to live in a home with a history. It is less amusing when that history prevents any kind of rational redevelopment. They let her put in electricity because the place was deemed uninhabitable without. They didn't go for the double glazing, though, and I have been there on mornings in February when the condensation was frozen to the inside of the window and we had to break the ice in the cistern before it was possible to flush the loo. I have suggested once or twice that she might consider living somewhere with, say, central heating, as an optional extra. She counters with the fact that this is the only place within the boundaries of Greater Glasgow where the trees are thick enough to screen the traffic noise, where she can look out of her back door and see a heron standing on the river in the mornings and where she can listen to the toads mating at night. All of this may be true but it is also entirely spurious and we both know it. The real reason she doesn't move is because the cottage is within a short sprint of the operating theatre and even if something goes into cardiac arrest on the table at two in the morning, she can be there before the attending clinician calls the time of death. This is the kind of drive that has taken her to the top and kept her there when anyone else would have been happy with a steady rung on the ladder.

The back door to the cottage was unlocked when I got there but that in itself is nothing new. For a Glaswegian, Nina Crawford has a shocking disregard for the fundamentals of personal security. There were no letters in the basket beneath the letter box but that meant nothing either. This is a woman who lives on the wrong end of

her e-mail account. The only genuine pen-on-paper letters she gets these days are from her mother and that's
only twice a year.

I let myself in and did a quick tour of the kitchen.
Let me rephrase that. I turned in a circle without moving
my feet and was thereby able to investigate every surface.
You could swing a cat in Nina's kitchen, but only if it
was less than eight weeks old. The door to the oven
collides with the one to the fridge and both of them
block the way to the sink. The kettle sits, unplugged, on
top of the bread bin, which is, in its turn, pushed back
into a corner to make way for a basket of crinkle-
skinned apples.

I checked them all out. The kettle was almost empty
and the water covering the element was cold. The bread
in the bin was hard. The grapes in the bowl on the hob
had a two-day coating of grey mould. A rim of congealed
bacon fat lined the washing-up bowl and a single plate
lay untouched beneath a layer of scummy water. Nobody home. Nobody, at least, with any interest in clean-
ing up.

Ominous.

Nina is ordered by habit. It goes with the territory.

There isn't really any division between the rooms on
the ground floor of the cottage. The kitchen area is
bounded by a half-height barrier and leads into a kind of
open-plan lounge/dining room, which I know from experience has sufficient floor space for one tallish woman
with a sleeping bag—provided you move one of the hal-
ogen uprights away from the corner opposite the television and shove a pine blanket box out of the way into
the space under the stairs. The rest of the furniture stays
where it is and gathers dust. Only visitors use the lounge
in this place—the ones who watch television and need to
sit at a table to eat their dinner. Nina sits on the staircase

to drink her coffee and the rest of us tend to eat our breakfast sitting on the low stone wall of the garden on the grounds that it's warmer than staying inside. All of which means that I would be hard pushed to say if there was anything seriously out of place in the living room, but there were magazines where you would expect to find magazines and no one had taken the flex from the standard lamp to string themselves up from the ceiling, which was good enough to be going on with.

I took a minute or two for a full look round and then elbowed my way past a pile of unironed laundry and scrambled up the near-vertical flight of stairs. I made that journey downwards once while drunk and nearly died in the process. In daylight, sober, it was easier.

The main bedroom is on the right at the top of the stairs. A rounded stone from the river propped open the door and a shifting breeze pulled at the curtain hanging beside the open window on the far side of the room. A one-eyed bruiser of a black and white tomcat lay on the bed and glared at me with the venom of old acquaintance. The pattern of dips in the duvet told tales of undisturbed catnaps stretching back for several days. No sign of a human nap at all.

Across the landing, her 'office' was knee-high in Xeroxed research papers and back copies of the *Veterinary Record*. The computer was dead to the world and the coffee half filling the mug was as old as all the rest of the food. A '1471' on the phone said that a number with an Edinburgh dialling code had called yesterday at 22:47 and that if I wanted to return the call, I should press 3. I considered it for a moment, thought better of it and wrote the number on the back of my hand instead. Her mother lives in Edinburgh. But then so does the other half of the Scottish veterinary academic community—the ones who don't work in Glasgow—and I wouldn't know

most of them from Adam. Or Eve. Time to find out later.
If it matters.

There's a loft space, with access from the landing,
which has more or less enough room to lie down in
between the box files and old lecture notes. I found the
pen torch in its usual place and flashed it once in a wide
arc. Lots of dust and enough notes to bury a horse. No
signs of human intrusion this side of Christmas. No
body lying with a drip in one arm waiting for the count-
down to zero. Oddly, it didn't make me feel any more
secure.

I was back in the office checking dates on the papers
when I heard the back door open downstairs. The stairs,
in daylight and sober, are lethal if taken at speed. I lost
my footing midway down and landed in a mess at the
bottom.

Nina Crawford stood in the doorway. Or rather, a
tousled mess of humanity that bore passing resemblance
to Nina Crawford stood in the doorway, staring at me in
the way any ghost might look at the living.

'What the bloody hell are you doing here?'

'You missed your appointment. I came to check that
you weren't dangling from a light fitting.'

She grinned tightly, like a skull. All bone-white lips
and no humour. Not pleasant.

'You're early. Come back in an hour. At least you'll
know not to bother with the ambulance.'

'Very funny. Are you as bad as you look?'

'I don't know.' She rocked back against the doorframe and tried to lever off her wellingtons, the toe of
one braced against the heel of the other. 'How bad do I
look?'

'Pretty bad.' Like an angular, ascetic, wire-haired
scarecrow that's been left out in the field over winter.

Except that scarecrows don't smell that bad. Not the ones I've met. 'Have you been bathing in horseshit?'

'Only by default.' She failed on the first boot and slid down the wall to a more stable position on the floor. 'If you make me something decent to drink, I promise I'll go and have a shower. How does that sound?'

'Delightful.'

Essential, in fact. And soon. The smell was marching across the room towards me like a column of starving soldier ants. Thick, gassy waves of it. The basic, organic stench of horse manure run through with nasty toxic lowlights. It smelled very much like the day Gordon Galbraith's slurry tank caved in and the whole ten thousand gallons of liquid pig manure flowed out on to the high land above the village. The difference being that I wasn't required to sit in a kitchen the size of a small telephone box with Gordon or any of his lads afterwards.

I filled up the kettle and then moved back to sit on the stairs, as far out of olfactory range as possible while still keeping within reasonable conversational distance. Not that there was any significant amount of conversation. For a while, the only significant sound was the rising hush of the kettle and a string of single-syllable curses emanating from the floor as Dr Nina Crawford, a woman with more letters after her name than in it, sat on the sanded oak floor of her kitchen and did her best to remove her own boot.

Last time I tried it wasn't that hard. I curled up my feet in the corner of the stairwell and watched for a while, trying to work out how much of the chaos was on the surface and how much was coming from further inside.

It's not easy to tell that kind of thing with Nina. More than most folk, there's a difference between interior and exterior. What you see is very rarely what you get.

She's not beautiful, Nina, not on the outside. She's too angular to be beautiful, too asymmetric, too scarred in places that show. But when she's well, she radiates the kind of magnetism that keeps her residents running round the clock because they'd rather run themselves into the ground than let her down. And even when she's been up all night with a colic and spent all day in theatre with the students, she still manages a brilliant combination of the quick, quirked smile and the tilt of the head with its tousled mess of hair that grows on you within the first five minutes of meeting.

The odd thing is, in all the time I've known her, I've never seen her filthy before. Untidy, perhaps. Wild, frequently. Tangled, often, mostly by intent. But never filthy. Particularly her hair. She's got a thing about hair, like a second millennium Samson except that in Nina's case, Delilah was some bitch of a nurse in the intensive care ward at the Western who shaved it all off for a scan in the late-night panic after the first time the lass tried to kill herself.

To the best of my knowledge, there is no real need to shave anyone's scalp for any kind of scan and I never found out exactly who did it or why, but it made one hell of an impact on the girl's psyche. It was short, apparently, before they took her into hospital. Short and curled and wild. Afterwards, she let it grow longer. It took almost two years to grow out to a length she was happy with. Somewhere around the time it passed her ears, she turned it a deep, henna red and has kept it that way ever since. Part of the mask that stops the world from seeing too much of the real woman underneath. The real woman has hair the colour of horse chestnuts straight from the shell and with the same kind of shine. Henna is not what it needs but I am hardly the person to tell her that.

Either way, she has cut it a bit shorter now so that
the terrier-curls make a dark, shining halo around her
head. And it does shine. Every time I've seen her,
straight out of the operating theatre, straight out of a
consultation or straight out of bed, it has shone.

Except now. The woman who sat on the floor in
front of me wrestling with her boot had hair clogged
with sweat and wood shavings and other unnamed, un-
speakable bits of animal debris as if taking care of herself
had somehow dropped off the list of personal priorities.

Not a good sign.

The hush of the kettle rose to a boil and failed to
stop when it should have done. I leaned over the counter
and switched it off at the plug. The woman on the floor
showed no sign of having heard. She wasn't showing
much awareness of anything beyond her footwear. I sat
back on the staircase and reached out, prodding her with
my toe.

'Nina, what's going on?'

'I don't know.'

She won the war with the boot. It spun across the
floor, spewing fragments of wood shavings and straw in
its wake. She scooped at them half-heartedly with the
edge of her hand and then gave up and leant back
against the doorframe. 'I guess I'm cracking up. Had to
happen sometime.'

Maybe.

I needed to look at her eyes to know for sure and she
wasn't about to let me.

Nina's eyes, when she is not driven by the nightmares, are a shade deeper than her hair; more walnut
than chestnut, and with that rare glitter of real intelli-
gence that takes her beyond the masses even in a profes-
sion where they think they're all beyond the masses
anyway. When she is living in the nightmares, her eyes

change first. If I were thinking in medical terms, I would
know all about the size of her pupils and the effect of
altered blood flow on the iris. Since I do my best not to
think in medical terms unless I have to, all I know is that
the shade of her eyes changes as she walks closer to the
depths of her own private hell and the darker they get,
the worse it is. She knows this and she knows that I
know. And the times when she avoids eye contact are
the times when she thinks things are bad.

Sitting there watching her undress on her kitchen
floor, I realised that I hadn't seen her eyes since the
moment I slid down the stairs into the living room.
Which meant things were worse than bad.

'Do you want to talk about it?'

'Not really.' She stood up, slowly, using the doorframe for leverage. 'But I probably should.' The other
boot came off without resistance. Suddenly and with a
soft, unpleasant, sucking noise. Her foot and the leg of
her overalls were wet with fresh blood.

She saw me looking and lifted one shoulder apolo-
getically. 'It's not mine.' Her second shoulder joined the
first. 'We had a nose bleed.'

'We?'

'Me and Steff. We were tubing the horse. Nasogastric
tube. To decompress the stomach. Caught a vessel on the
way in.'

I don't think I want to know.

'I came in for a shower.' She said it more to herself
than to me. 'Coffee and a shower.' She looked at me,
almost directly. 'Coffee in the shower?'

I think she just might. 'Coffee *after* the shower,' I
said. 'And you tell me what's happening.'

The bathroom in the cottage is of relatively recent
origin but it still manages to conform to house style in
terms of its furnishings: there is no heater, the bath takes

over an hour to fill, the white tiles on the wall grow green mould in three days if you don't wash them and the lino on the floor has ripples cunningly placed to stub the toes of the unwary.

The only new addition to the entire ensemble is the shower, put in by Nina on the very reasonable grounds that anyone who comes home covered in blood and gastric contents at two in the morning after a late-night colic needs to be sure there'll be enough hot water to get clean before morning. She got the lads from the engineering department to put in something industrial with the jet pressure of a power hose, and standing underneath it for any length of time does terrible things to your skin.

By the time I was ready with two cups of coffee, the place was full of pine-flavoured steam, there was condensation running down the walls and a force four gale angled in from the open window above the sink. The offending overalls were soaking in a bucket of water near the door. The smell barely penetrated the fog.

I dried off the lid of the toilet with a spare hand towel and sat down out of the draught. The steam acquired a new flavour. A kind of odd, citrus mix of lemongrass and ginger but without the culinary overtones. It's Nina's smell, at least at the times when she doesn't stink of horse excreta. A signature scent. Something to do with what she uses to wash her hair although I've never found out what it is. The smell of it filled the room, billowing out of the open window. Oddly peaceful for someone who spends their life in such turmoil.

The coffee began to cool. I pulled the cord twice, flicking the lights on and off to let her know I was there. 'Coffee,' I said, above the noise of the shower. 'You want to come out while it's still hot?'

'Sure.' The noise of the water slammed off and a hand emerged from behind the plastic screen. 'Towel?'

'Here.' I threw her a towel from the rail beside me
and heard her mutter further small curses at her hair.
She emerged faster than I'd expected, with the towel
wrapped round her head and the rest of her dripping
wet. Naked, she looked more vulnerable than before.
Everyone looks disarmed when they're unclothed but in
Nina's case it was the towel on her head that made the
difference. Red hair and vulnerable don't go together
even if it's not a real red. With her hair covered and the
colour gone, she looked smaller; thinner, more exhausted. The scars on her neck stood out whiter against
the faded tan of her skin: two arrow-headed vampire
bites where they ran the drip lines into her jugulars because they couldn't find any veins left on her arms that
worked. The time she grew her hair long, it was specifically to cover the scars. It took the best part of five years
in therapy before she came round to the idea that people
see the woman first and the scars second. Her entire
wardrobe changed in the months after that. Polo necks
to open shirts in the space of one season. It took longer
to get her to give up on long sleeves but then the scar on
her arm is altogether more spectacular than the ones on
her neck; a long albino snake coiling up and around
from wrist to elbow, the remnant of four hours in theatre
with the Western Infirmary's top reconstructive team trying to rebuild something useful from the mess left by the
pentobarbitone she'd put in her death-wish cocktail.

It was the pentobarbitone that did the most obvious
damage, at the start. They put horses down with
pentobarb. It's not meant to go in human arms, espe-
cially not outside the vein. The ambulance team did
what they could with subcutaneous injections of normal
saline but the damage was done by then. In the twenty-
four hours it took them to get her stable, the skin had
sloughed off her forearm and the muscles beneath had

turned to molten cheese. A reconstructive nightmare.
She's lucky to have an arm at all and the fact that she can
make a living as a surgeon is the kind of miracle that
goes a long way to restoring my faith in modern medicine.

If they could have repaired the damage to her mind
at the same time, I would live the rest of my life a be-
liever. But it took a lot longer than a month in intensive
care to patch up the holes left by the ketamine, and
hospital doctors aren't really cut out for that kind of
thing, even the ones with psychiatric leanings. And so,
when they let her out of hospital, they sent her to me; an
ex-medic turned therapist with connections in all the
right places. She was the first of my die-hard suicides.
And the last.

It's nasty stuff, ketamine. I've no idea what made her slip
it in the bag except that it was there when she opened
the drug cupboard and there's nothing wrong with a bit
of overkill when you're desperate. Either way, it saved
her life. Hit her brain before the barbiturate and triggered a series of twitching convulsions that were enough
to jerk the catheter from the vein.

The gods balance these things. Give life with one
hand and take sanity with the other. For a long time it
seemed she was never again going to have both together.
When we first started together, an hour in session with
Nina felt like a month in a war zone and I went home to
Bridget in desperate need of emotional resuscitation afterwards. It blows open the doorways to your unconscious, ketamine, and that's not a kind thing to do to
anyone.

For the best part of four years after they let her out of
hospital, Nina lived in a world haunted by the dark,

tangled monsters from the depths of her own private
hell. Things that stalked her days and made massacres of
her nights long after the pentobarb and the morphine
worked their way out of her veins and her liver. It was
hell. Every step of the way was hell and there were times
when both of us thought she was going right off the rails.
But even so, she got her act together and worked her
way through a Masters and a PhD and picked up the
exams she needed to become a surgeon and there was a
day, nearly five years after we first started work, when
she stood in the doorway of my office and told me she
had just slept a whole week of nights without a single
solitary nightmare. We went out for a drink to celebrate
that night and to hell with the proprieties of professional
and client. We thought we had it cracked, both of us.
And we carried on believing it. Until last September,
when the whole bloody cycle started again.

    That's the thing about nightmares. Like gravity, they
never really go away.

                          ▆▆▆▆▆▆

She caught me staring vacantly into space and slid another towel off the rail beside her.

    'If you tell me I've lost weight,' she said, 'I'll throw
you out.'

    'Hardly.' I wouldn't dream of it. 'I'll wait until you've
finished telling me what's going on down at the ranch.
Then I'll throw myself out and let you get some sleep.'

    She wrapped the towel round at arm-pit level and sat
down on the edge of the bath.

    'If I knew what was happening, Kellen, I'd be out
there doing something about it.' For someone on the
edge of crisis, she sounded uncommonly stable.

    I handed her the coffee. 'So tell me the basics,' I said.
    'Oh God, I don't know.' She sunk half a mug and

then started rubbing absently at her hair with her free hand, as if sitting still had become impossible. 'The horses are still dying, Kellen. There's one in the end box now. We cut him on Monday morning. He keeled over Tuesday night and he'll be dead by tomorrow, barring miracles. He came in for a tie-back. Ordinary, straight-forward elective surgery. Nothing that couldn't have been done in general practice except that the owner's one of the staff and so the practitioner fought shy of the anaesthesia, wanted somebody else to take the risks. There shouldn't have been any risks. He should have been home by now, bumbling around in his paddock with nothing better to do than decide on the best patch of grass to mow next.'

'But he isn't?'

'No, he isn't. He's flat out in the ICU box with a wire in every orifice and a desperate look in his eye that knows death is coming and wants to know what's keep-ing it away.'

'And you're the one keeping it away?'

'I am. I've had the gun in my hand twice now and not used it.'

'Because?'

'Because I don't know what's going on. Because I don't want to admit defeat. Because this is the third one to go the same way since Christmas and there were an-other four before that and we still don't have a handle on what the hell is happening. I've been in there since he went down, Kellen. That's two days and two nights watching him die, trying to find out what's going on and all that's happened is that I can't walk straight, I can't think straight and I don't know if it's better to slug him with something else out of pharmacy or walk across the corridor, pick up the gun and give him the peace he needs.'

She ran out of steam suddenly, like a car without fuel. She took a long drink of coffee, chewed at her bottom lip, stared hard at a fixed spot on the wall. 'What would you do?' she asked. As if I could possibly know anything she didn't.

'I'd go to bed and get some sleep and let someone who knows what day it is make the decisions,' I said.

'I don't want to sleep, Kellen. Really. There are more dead horses in my sleep than there are in the wards.' She put her mug on the floor and devoted both hands to drying her hair. Coiled springs of it leaked from the enfolding towel, spiralling darkly around her fingers. 'I only came back to have a shower and get a decent cup of coffee. The crap they make over there is undrinkable.'

Anything's undrinkable if you drink it for three days in a row.

'Nina,' I asked, 'what day is it?'

'I don't know.' She reached up to a cupboard over the sink and pulled out a small electric hair dryer. The kind that should never, ever be used in damp, mouldy bathrooms. 'Thursday?' she offered.

'It's Friday,' I said. 'Seven o'clock. P.M., not A.M. And you're telling me you haven't moved out of that box except to pee, shit and make coffee since Tuesday night. That's three days, Nina. Not two. No one can make rational decisions on seventy-two hours without sleep.' I took the dryer from her hand and led the way back into the safety and relative warmth of the kitchen.

She followed me through, leaving wet footprints on the clay tiles of the floor. 'Hospital doctors do it all the time,' she said. 'Staying up all weekend without sleep and then writing out prescriptions on Monday morning.' She cocked her head at what was supposed to be an appealing angle. 'I know, you told me all about it.'

Very funny.

'I was an intern, not a consultant surgeon. That's what juniors are for. Get some sleep, Dr Crawford. Leave it to the resident. Steff will shoot your horse if he needs shooting. She'll dope him if he needs doping. She'll throw the entire contents of pharmacy at him if that's what she thinks he needs. That's what she's here for. She's the gopher, you're the boss. Just get on the phone and pretend that you're a real consultant . . .'

'Thanks.'

'. . . and then dry your hair and go to bed. I'll get someone to wake you up sometime next week. Later if it's all still peaceful.'

2

Dr Stephanie Foster, DVM, is tall—taller than most of the men she works with—and she has bright blonde hair cut into spikes that add another two inches to her height. Underneath that she has the kind of lean, square-edged features that never give yes for an answer and diamond-grey eyes that tell you attack is the best form of defence. A silver nose-stud glitters aggression in one nostril and there are two or three hoops in different shades of gold ranged up each ear. And she has a Chicago accent which does nothing to soften the impact.

The first time I met her in person was at Nina and Matt's engagement party when the vet school's new super-star resident had just walked off the plane from the States and was busy telling the world how much better they did things in Madison, Wisconsin, where everything was smarter, shinier, bigger, brighter and more expensive and where the veterinary technology made everything in Scotland look like it had oozed from the primordial swamp.

For a newcomer expecting to spend three years in a foreign country, she seemed hellbent on unmaking friends, and by half an hour into the bash, no one was going to step out of their way to disappoint her. By half-way through the evening, she had one corner of the buffet table all to herself and when she ordered a taxi back to the vet school long before the party ended, there wasn't a single volunteer offering to show her the way to the residents' quarters.

For the last two and a half years, I have listened to weekly bulletins of Steff and her impact on the vet school hierarchy, which was not unlike the effect of rubbing carborundum paper briskly across an endless series of matchheads. In due course of time, when all the fires died down, the world was divided into two groups of people: those who thought she should be forcibly placed on the next plane back to Chicago and those who believed that she was one of the best things to happen to the clinical department in years. Fortunately for Dr Foster, Nina was of the latter group and Nina was the boss which meant that the lass got to stay. I don't imagine she's had a particularly easy time of it, however.

I found her in the horse ward down at the foot of the hill beyond the operating theatres and the small animal unit.

The place was oddly quiet. I've been into the vet school clinic three times as a client of Nina's since she first came to see me for therapy. It's not exactly orthodox and it made for an odd reversing of roles but, on the other hand, we didn't have many alternatives. She's the senior surgeon—at times, the only surgeon—at the clinic. I own a farm with upwards of twenty horses, an uncountable number of free-range cats and a dog. Sim-

ple law of averages says that at least one of them will
need specialist attention every once in a while. In basic
terms, there were only two other things we could have
done: she could have changed therapists, or I could have
sent Sandy in with the animals. Neither of us wanted to
do that and so we settled on the principle that, on my
territory, she was my client, while on her territory, I was
hers.

It has worked so far. In the first year, I brought Midnight in with a surgical colic that kept her in the horse
ward for two weeks. Three years after that, I brought a
cat that had complex surgery for a femoral fracture and
then, two months later, he went for a sprint in the
orchard and managed to break the implant. It took almost six months for that one to heal and I was on first-
name terms with everyone from the nurses through the
canteen staff to the security guards by the time he was
finally discharged.

In all that time, I have never seen either of the wards
without at least a couple of long-stay patients to keep the
yard staff and the nurses happy on their triple time. Even
at Christmas they had a goat with a fractured metacarpus
and a couple of chronic diabetics taking up room just in
case anyone thought they might otherwise go home
early. This time, I walked into a building that wasn't just
devoid of life, it was swept out and scrubbed clean.
From the calf pens by the doors to the big stallion boxes
at the far end, there wasn't a single wisp of straw. Not
one solitary flake of wood. Nothing. I was walking
through a ghost ward, denuded even of ghosts.

I found Steff in the end, by following the smell. Like
Nina's overalls but with the toxic bite of the disinfectant
rather stronger than was healthy. She was in a foaling
box down at the far end of the barn that had 'ICU'
etched on a copper plaque on the door. A handwritten

note stuck to the wall with zinc oxide tape warned: 'ISO-LATION—TREAT AS INFECTIOUS' and below it a rack of overboots and a tray of milky white disinfectant of-fered ostensible protection against whatever nasties lurked inside.

There were three of them inside the box: two hu-mans and a horse. Steff sat, fast asleep, propped up against the wall beneath the manger; a spiked blonde replica of Nina down to the smell and the blood on her overalls. The student—only a student would wear a white coat in a box with a diarrhoeic horse—was, quite simply, comatose and could easily have been dead for all the movement he made. Which meant that when I pulled on the overshoes and swished my feet around in the foul phenol of the disinfectant, it was only the horse who was awake enough to take any notice.

He was a nice horse. A big, raw-boned chestnut with a white snip to his nose and the scars of old saddle sores lined up along his back. He lay calmly in the straw, with his legs curled under him in the way a dog would lie beside a fire. Even like that, he took up most of the box, his head near the door, his tail in the far corner opposite the hay rack. Sixteen hands, easily. Possibly more. He raised his head slightly as I looked in over the half-door and, even with a stomach tube blocking one nostril, he still managed a small, deflated huff of greeting.

There is a rule of thumb in the ICU that says the likelihood of coming out of the ward alive is inversely proportional to the number of drip sets, wires and tubes attaching the patient to the machines. In human medi-cine, the cut-off number is five. Below that and you're probably OK. Above it and you're in deep water. On the line is evens. I have no idea if the same applies to horses but if it does, this one was way over the odds. Four separate drip lines flooded different kinds of fluids into

catheters in both jugulars and the tangled wires of a
multi-lead ECG lay draped across him like a damp cob-
web sending erratic signals to a bank of monitors high
up on the wall. Other probes in his rectum and clipped
to his nostrils fed temperature, respiratory rate and arterial oxygen tension in to the other boxes of tricks. The
whole bank of monitor screens pulsed with livid streaks
of electric light; greens and ambers and a cold, unpas-
sioned blue. A stomach tube emerged from his left nostril, ran up the front of his face and was taped in place
across the poll of his head collar with more of the ubiquitous zinc oxide tape. Suddenly, and very horribly, he
looked not at all unlike Nina on the first day I met her.

I hope to God she doesn't know.

It seemed important, then, to know his name. His case
notes were leant up against the wall near the door. I slid
back the bolt and let myself into the box. He huffed
again as I crouched down by his head.

'Hey, son. What's up?'

He didn't say much but he blinked a couple of times
to show that he knew I was there and the anxious wrinkles deepened in the hollows above his upper eyelids. I
moved back to pick up the case notes and the look in his
eyes as he watched me walk past was anything but
peaceful. Nina was right. He wanted death and he
wanted it very badly. If I was her, I doubt if I would have
held off with the gun.

The case notes carried his basic details in computer
type: 'Branding Iron', property of one Mrs Campbell of
Stewarton. An eleven-year-old thoroughbred gelding, ex-
racehorse, ex-eventer, ex-show jumper with a future as a
hunter if the surgeon could fix his larynx. The surgeon,
had, by all accounts, fixed his larynx. Details of the sur-

gery were recorded in a rounded longhand in the pages that followed and the line of a neat, new scar, four inches long, ran along the side of his throat still with the nylon sutures holding it shut. As Nina said, he should have been home enjoying the springtime. Except that there were liquid faeces running out from under his tail and the blood oozing out round the stomach tube was darker than anything I've ever seen in any living thing, human or otherwise.

There was movement in the straw across the box and a voice said: 'Kellen?'

A Chicago accent, with just a touch of Glaswegian. I looked up. Steff hadn't moved but her eyes were open and she was doing her best to focus in my direction. 'What the hell are you doing here?'

Twice in one day. It's so nice to feel welcome.

'Guess,' I said.

She sat up and started to run her hand through her hair then realised she still had her rectal gloves on and thought better of it. 'You've seen the boss?' she asked.

'I just suggested she took a month or so in bed. You don't look any better. What's going on?'

'Pass.' She smiled the same kind of hard-pushed, baring-of-teeth as her boss and shook her head. The hoops in her ears flickered in the green and amber glow from the monitors. 'The devil has come to stay in the large animal ward and we can't persuade him to move on.'

'And the horse?'

She shrugged. An expressive all-encompassing shrug that spanned the entire contents of the box. 'The horse is dying. He's been dying since he hit the floor on Tuesday night. He's only alive now because Nina doesn't want to let him go.'

That's not quite the way I heard it.

'Is she getting overinvolved with the patients?'

The silver stud at her nose flickered as she smiled. 'Nina's always overinvolved with the patients. You know that . . . This time I would say she was obsessed.' She stood up and stripped off her gloves, tying them absently in a series of intricate knots. 'And—this time—she's not the only one.'

'You?'

She pursed her lips ruefully. 'Me, the yard staff, the students—except Dominic,' she nodded in the direction of the barely moving white coat on the floor, 'who hasn't noticed that there's a crisis on—the anaesthetists, the secretaries, the librarian, the guy who comes in every other afternoon to refill the coffee machine . . . We're all "overinvolved".' Her gaze ran round the monitors on the wall and she winced slightly at the news they carried. 'I'd get out while the going's good if I was you, Dr Stewart. Unless you want to be the next one on the bandwagon.'

Too late for that. I was on the bandwagon from the night the first one died. The night Nina Crawford turned up after hours and stood in the doorway to my consulting room asking for an emergency consultation. That was over six months ago.

A monitor warning alarm bleeped suddenly at the other side of the room. Like an electric alarm clock but with an undulating rhythm carefully selected to drive you mad if you don't do something serious in the space of ten seconds. Steff reached over and jabbed a finger at the cancel button.

'Stupid effing machine.' She swears like her boss. Semi-controlled bad language as if the rest of us might be offended by the real thing. She fiddled at the back of the monitor for a second and the amber blip threading its way across the screen settled back into the double notch of an arterial pressure trace. She watched it for a screen or two, pressed a couple of buttons and swore again, more seriously.

'Something wrong?'

'Brainless bloody thing thinks his pressure's falling.'

'Do you believe it?'

'Might do.' She shrugged. 'He lost a bit of blood when we tubed him.' She knelt down by the horse, ran her fingers along his back, pinched his skin, looked in his eyes. All the kind of things I would have done if I'd had a machine telling me lies about a patient. They do that all the time, machines; tell lies. It's part of the programming. Stops the clinicians from becoming complacent.

I watched one of the four drip bags run its last few mls of fluid into a giving set. The final drop hovered, shivering, in the plastic column far above eye level.

'You could do with some more fluids up.'

I said it carefully. Not everyone appreciates other folk intruding on their cases.

Steff is not, apparently, as touchy as her reputation suggests. She looked up at the bag, nodded once and then looked down at her sleeping student. She smiled again, a broad smile this time, more real and laced with late-night acid. The silver in her nose flashed brightly.

'Time for sleeping beauty here to do something useful.'

He looked too peaceful to disturb for something that trivial.

'Leave him be. It'll take longer to wake him up than it will to get the stuff. I'll do it.'

She looked at me sideways. 'You sure?'

I nodded. It's a long time since I did anything

clinical. It was fun once. Before the politics overtook the medicine.

'OK,' she said, 'if you're sure . . .' She checked her watch. 'We may as well do his eight o'clock treatment while we're at it.' She lifted the clipboard from the hook on the wall and ran her thumb down the treatment page. 'There are five-litre bags of Hartmann's in the cupboard behind the door in the drug store. Stick one of them in the microwave and get it up to blood heat. I'll get everything else.'

Five-litre bags are huge and they take a good five minutes, even on full power, to come anywhere near body temperature. Most of the other drugs had gone in by the time it was ready. I carried the bag back to the box and knelt by the horse, hugging the bulk of it to my chest like an oversized hot-water bottle while Steff unhooked the old drip, flushed the catheter and reconnected the giving set with the kind of practised rhythm that said she could have done it in her sleep if I hadn't been there. She has an odd kind of grace for someone so tall. A careful economy of movement. A reining-in of power as if the world is made of eggshells and she has broken them once too often.

She finished connecting up the drips and knelt by the horse, weaving the new piece of plastic tubing into his mane. He bent his neck and nuzzled at her pocket, carefully because he had a stomach tube taped to his nose and however stoic you are, it still hurts like hell if you move a nasal tube. She played with him for a moment, scratching the itch at the back of his ears where the sweat dried under the headcollar and then she started clearing the debris.

I looked at the growing pile of discarded empties. It costs me somewhere near a weekend's takings to have Ruaridh Innes come out and spend half a night putting a

single drip into one of the horses. More than that if he
has to pile in more than fluids. Even more if he uses
drugs that aren't on the daily-use list. Penicillin and bute
come cheap. Everything else costs more than the bank
manager wants me to imagine. I looked at the empty
vials of third-generation cephalosporins and the part-
used bottles of non-steroidals and the half-litre bottles of
intralipid and tried to imagine the possible cost. More
than I could ever afford for a horse.

'Is Mrs Campbell paying for all this?' I asked.

She snorted, like the horse but with less energy.
'You're kidding? "Mrs Campbell" wasn't even paying for
the surgery. That's Maureen. Mo. Was Maureen Flanagan
till she married one of the guys from final year. You'll
have met her here, somewhere along the line; she's been
around for years.'

I remembered. A dark, slim-built lass with an Irish
sense of humour and her countryman's way with horses.
'The head nurse?'

'Right.' She crouched down with a sharps box and
began to strip needles from syringes. 'So she knows what
we're up against, as much as anyone does. She's been in
charge of this end of the clean-up programme. She
brought in laddie-boy here for us to run through to
make sure theatre was clean. Kind of an act of faith to
show the boss we all believed in her . . . "I hereby lay
before you my first born and most beloved on the altar
of Almighty Surgery." Because we knew, we all knew,
that there couldn't be any infection left. Not a single
effing microbe in the whole of the godforsaken large animal hospital . . .'

She stopped, reining in the irony and the anger in
much the same way she reined in everything else, and
stood up to check the pressure monitor. It blipped
peaceably to itself. A nice, regular, healthy rhythm, aes-

thetically synchronised with the other blips ranged along
the wall. All of them whispered peace. None of them
said it was going to last. She sat down in the straw by the
horse, resting her back against his shoulder and reached
up to scratch the spot behind his ears. He leant back
against her, angling his head against the push of her
fingers. The yellowing light from the single strip in the
ceiling merged with the fluorescent greens and ambers
from the monitors to turn her hair the same shade of
green-white gold as the hay in the rack. Her face caught
in a patchwork of shadows, turned harlequin-smooth,
washed free of the need for sleep. An ageless doll in the
age of technology.

She pressed the heels of her hands into her eyes and
shivered once, violently, the way a horse shakes off flies.
'I guess this is the good news,' she said. 'If it was anyone
but Mo we'd have the lawyers camping outside the box
by now.'

'So where is she now?' I asked. 'Maureen?'

'Home with the kids. We sent her off on Wednesday
when it really got rough. Didn't seem much point in her
staying to watch the execution.'

'Is she the reason you're holding off with the gun?'

'Partly . . . No . . .' She stopped to think, curling
a strand of straw round her fingers. '. . . We're holding
off because the boss thinks that if we can get him
through the acute phase with fluids and intravenous
feeding then we might bring him out in one piece.' She
bit on her bottom lip and turned to look at the horse.
The horse turned his head to stare at the wall. The anxious wrinkles over his eyes deepened.

'And you? What do you think?'

'Me?' There was a long pause. She found a sweet spot
on the horse's neck and scratched round and round in a

circle. 'I'm not paid to think. I'm just paid to get on with the treatments.'

Very likely.

'And off the record . . . ?'

'Off the record? We're fucked, Kellen. We've done everything there is to do and we still haven't beaten it. There's nowhere left to go.'

'They're dying. The horses are dying. They're in theatre, most of them. On the table. Draped up, anaesthetised. Just like the real thing. I lift the blade and start to cut and Steff's there, or Mo or one of the students, swabbing the blood away from the wound edges, passing me the scissors, or the retractors or the arthroscope. Everything's so totally normal. I don't notice at first that the bleeding doesn't stop. Not until I'm deep down into the wound and the abdomen's filling with blood and the suction jars keep overflowing and then suddenly it's not Mo or Steff on the other side, it's Matt and he's telling me that the horse is dying, showing me the monitors with all the lines going haywire. The giving sets are pouring in blood but never fast enough to stop it flooding out of the hole that I've made. Then the horse wakes up and turns round and starts to scream at me that it's all my fault. It always ends with the horses screaming and it's always my fault. I make the wound and I don't stop it bleeding. I do

*everything there is to do and they don't get better. There's
nothing left to do.*

━━━━━

'How much of this is the dream and how much is happening in reality?'

'Most of it's real. Except the horses don't scream at
me. They just lie there, wanting to die. No one else
screams at me either. But they know it's my fault.'

'How is it your fault?'

'I'm the surgeon. If I wasn't there to cut them, they
wouldn't be in the ward. If they weren't in the ward, they
wouldn't be dying.'

'There are other surgeons in the world. If it wasn't
you, it would be someone else.'

'No one else has their cases dying like flies.'

'Do you know what it is that's killing them?'

'They bleed to death. I told you. Blood. I'm drowning
in blood.'

'But in reality, not in the dreams. What is it kills
them for real?'

'Infection. A simple, straightforward E. coli. Except
this one's vicious and armour-plated. We can't find anything that kills it and it's set up home somewhere in the
large animal theatre. Our surgical risk statistics have just
gone through the roof. That is, my surgical statistics have
just gone through the roof. Steff gelded one of the farm
ponies last week and it's bouncing round the paddock,
fitter than all the rest put together.'

'Maybe it's got local immunity.'

'Maybe.'

'So what can you do?'

'About the rest? Close theatre. Bomb it. Scrub it.
Sterilise it. Do whatever it takes to exterminate every
bloody microbe in the whole sodding place. I'll autoclave

the straw if I have to. I won't cut another horse until Bacteriology give me a form signed in blood saying every square inch is sterile.'

'Will that work?'

'It'll have to work, Kellen. There's nothing else left we can do.'

It was warm, sitting there with the horse. Warm and peaceful. The smell seemed less pungent than when I'd first arrived. More horse-breath and hay and less phenol and flatulence. I settled back against the wall near the door and listened to the gentle flow of breathing. The horse, the student. Steff. Steff sitting half-awake, twisting straw between her fingers, filling in a history I already knew. A tally of deaths that should never have happened. A cleaning-up process that left even the drains coming up sterile on tests. You could have built microchips in the hay barn by the time they'd finished and they would have come out pristine.

'What are you going to do now?'

'I don't know.'

'Did Nina call you before she went to bed?'

'Sure. About five minutes before you turned up. She handed over clinical control. He's my case now.' The straw twisted tighter. 'Yesterday I wanted to shoot him.'

'And today?'

'Today I think we might make it if we keep going with the fluids and the parenteral feeding.' She kept her eyes on the horse, not on me. 'Interesting, isn't it, what responsibility does to your sense of perspective?'

Footsteps sounded down the corridor; a long stride with a soft, steady tread.

'Steff? Is that you . . . ?' A voice in the dark outside the box. A male voice. Coming closer. Over the box

door. 'Christ, woman. Have you any idea how bad it
smells in there?' A warm, soft-edged voice, leavened with
the worn-down remnants of a Morningside accent. A
voice run through with the time of night and the day of
the week and the clinical wreckage of the box. A voice
that held on to the familiar sharp bite of irony. A dark,
tousled head framed against the upturned collar of a
white clinical coat leaned in over the top of the door.
Red gold glimmered on the little finger of the hand laid
on the latch. I would know that hand anywhere.

'Hello, Matt.'

'Kellen!' A new thread ran through the voice then.
'Christ. What in God's name are you doing here?'

'Finding out if Steff dreams of dying horses too.'

'Don't you start. One of them going over the edge is
quite enough.' He passed the soles of his shoes over the
top of the disinfectant, let himself into the box and
crouched down to examine the horse. He checked the
stomach tube, lifted the eyelid, looked under the lips. He
flattened the ears, pressed at the eye to make the third
eyelid pop out. He pursed his lips, frowning and stood
up to check over the monitors. He used to be an anaesthetist, Matt. Did his PhD and got his exams and then
moved, with the zeal of the converted, to surgery. He
knows more about the high-technology of intensive care
than anyone else in the hospital. When he's in a good
frame of mind, he can lift his students to the stars. When
he isn't, he can cut them to shreds. I gather that much
the same applies to the residents.

He spent a good five minutes flicking through the
channels on the machines, reading trends and patterns
from the past day and beyond. Then he turned his back
to the screens and he looked down at Steff as she sat
curled in the warm curve of the horse's side.

The atmosphere prickled. He is leader of the group

that wants her to take the first plane back to where she came from. She knows it. They don't get on.

There was a sharp, static moment when he thought of commenting on the read-out from the monitors and she thought of telling him where to go and then both of them looked at me and thought better of it.

The moment passed.

Matt found a clean section of wall and leant back, hands in pockets. 'Where's Herself?' he asked quietly.

'Kellen made her go to bed.'

'Did she, by God?' He thought that was funny. 'Well, I'm glad someone has what it takes. Just a pity it wasn't one of us. Next thing you know she'll be going part time and the world will be perfect for all of us.' He turned to me, smiling the kind of smile that has had over a year to get used to not being the Betrothed but still hasn't quite made it. 'What about Steff?' he asked. 'Can you do the same for her?'

When she's just found out what it is to have sole responsibility? I doubt it.

'Who's going to look after the horse if I go?' Steff rolled the whites of her eyes at the figure on the floor. 'Dominic?'

'Shouldn't think so.' Matt shook his head. 'Dominic's coming with me. We've got a German shepherd coming in from Maryhill. Road traffic accident. Major haemorrhage. Comminuted forelimb fracture. Possible ruptured spleen. Probable fractured pelvis. Sorry.' And that, after all, was why he'd come. To pick up his student and drop his piece of news.

Steff isn't the kind to leap for the chance of late-night heroism if it isn't strictly necessary. She counted to ten as the news sank in and then nodded, took a deep breath and pushed herself up to her feet. For the first time, the lack of sleep showed in her voice as much as her eyes. 'Do you need a hand?' she asked.

'No.' He shook his head. He is not, whatever else, without compassion. 'Nice idea but I think you need to cover for Nina till this is over and then you need to get to bed. All I want is one of the duty students to scrub in for the surgery. Lucy's still sitting with the wolfhound from this afternoon and Aiden's stuck with an oncology disaster that will apparently fall apart if he moves from its side. That leaves Mr Motivation down there.' He looked down at the body curled up in the straw. 'Is he with us?'

'As much as he ever is.' She leaned over and prodded the white coat somewhere around chest level. 'Come on, get up. Spring is here. You can go back into hibernation after the finals.'

It took them a long time to wake him up and longer than that to get him on his feet and walking. Steff got him a black coffee from the machine outside the drug store and made him drink half of it before he left. It smelt foul. Acidic and meaty. As if the Bovril in the next compartment had leaked across to mingle with the hot water. Still, it got him moving and more or less capable of speech. I sat with Steff in the doorway to the box and together we watched him trudge off down the corridor in the wake of his surgeon.

'The boy's got narcolepsy at the very least.' She sounded way past caring. 'He's failed every exam he's ever sat. It took him three tries to get through Pathology. If he bombs this time round, they'll throw him out for good. You'd think he'd have learned not to wind up the surgeons by now.'

There are things in life that I worry about. The pass rate of final year veterinary students is not one of them.

The failing health of my client's main source of support, however, could worry me quite a lot.

'When were you planning to get some sleep?' I asked.

'Whenever there's not someone here to keep me awake.' She settled back, pointedly, into the curved space of the horse's side.

Branding Iron closed his eyes and the wrinkles above them smoothed out. Like that, he looked a great deal less as if he wanted to die. Very peaceful, the two of them.

'OK.' I stood up. 'I'll leave you to it.' I pulled off the overshoes and dropped them in the yellow waste bag to the side. A quick search of my pockets turned up an old till receipt. I scribbled my home number on it and clipped it to the case notes before I hung them back on the wall. 'If there's anything I can do, you give me a ring, huh?'

'Sure.' She was already half asleep.

I pulled the door closed and swung the latch over as quietly as it would go.

3

Outside, it was raining. Slow, heavy drops spattered from a heavy cloud layer that promised real rain later. The bright white of the security lights reflected down off the sky and my shadow skipped over the embryonic puddles that formed on the Tarmac ahead of me as I crossed the car park. Behind me, Matt Hendon and his spaced-out assistant unloaded something large and unwieldy from the back of a mud-spattered Four Trak. The night's surgery. Rather them than me.

Out on the switchback, the mid-evening traffic had all but disappeared and the journey home took half the time it would have done if I hadn't called in to see Nina. Still, it was close to nine o'clock by the time I drove through the village and turned down the lane to the farm. I steered round the potholes by sheer force of habit, with my brain in late-evening neutral, pondering magpies and gravity and dying horses and wondering, not for the first time, just how far Nina Crawford could push herself before she went right out over the edge. At the end of the lane, the gate had been left open for me and I coasted to a halt in the yard, secure in the knowledge that the ponies had been fed and that there was a fair chance Sandy might have brought them in when he realised I was going to be late home. He's like that, Sandy. He thinks ahead, he has the initiative to act on the results and he is one of the best business partners you could ever hope to have.

He is, in fact, one of the few reliable features of my life. One of those gifts the gods produce every once in a while to remind me that life is not all bad.

He turned up the spring after Bridget died, on a wild, wet Saturday morning, a week or two before the trekking season was due to start. I was mucking out the ponies, all eight of them, on my own. Immersing myself in work as the best way to avoid having to think. Not that there was a great deal to think about. The when and the how of selling them, possibly, rather than the if or the why.

The rain drove in from the north east. Long horizontal sheets of it that seemed to curl over the brow of the hill and angle up under the pantiles on the barn roof, lifting them up, and driving in through the half-dozen sizeable gaps that I had successfully spent all winter ignoring. Rainwater ran in rivers down the walls and splashed from the beams on to the concrete of the passage and the bedding of the loose boxes. The noise of it would have driven me mad if I could have heard it over the thrumming howl of the wind. The entire barn smelt of wet wood and soaked straw.

The ponies muttered comments to each other and shoved against me as I entered the boxes. They could find better shelter outside in the field. And then wouldn't be standing in on wet straw. Fresh hay and a quick brush-over is not fair exchange for fresh air and daylight. And they knew I was going to send them away. I could feel it.

Even the dog was on their side. Normally she would have followed me from box to box, standing guard in the doorway in case I might need her for something urgent. A stowaway mouse in a hay-net perhaps, or an unexpected insurgence of rabbits breaking in through tunnels in the floor. Anything to make the day worthwhile for a hard-bred hunting collie. Except this morning, of all mornings, when she chose to keep her own counsel. Found herself a dry space on the bottom layer of straw bales and curled up, a white-with-tan mass of hairy judgement watching me through odd-caste eyes that said with certainty that the ponies were in the right, that I was the under-scum of Hades and that the rain, which was ruining the hunting, was, indeed, my fault.

Only Rain, the dun Connemara filly in the end box, seemed happy to see me. But then I had spent the best part of the winter in a carefully planned friendship campaign, trying to persuade her that people, if not necessarily her first choice of company, were none the less an extraordinarily reliable source of Polo mints. As long as you made the effort to walk across the box. Or to trot across the field. Or to canter all the way down from the hill when you heard the right whistle. By late March, she wasn't about to miss the chance to frisk my pockets for the sake of a bit of damp bedding. And besides, her box wasn't under any of the drips.

I was grovelling in the straw, picking the packed faeces from her feet, when the gods' gift turned up.

'It's not the best of weather,' observed a voice outside the door. 'Were you wanting a hand to finish the feeding?'

It was a low, melodious voice, with the rounded vowels and soft, chopped consonants of the West Highlands. A voice that could ooze patience and serenity, even on the wrong end of a handgun; one of the few voices whose arrival in the yard didn't, at that point, signal any kind of crisis or catastrophe. Inspector Stewart MacDonald, senior officer of the Strathclyde Central Constabulary. If I'd been half switched on, I would have known he was around the moment the dog abandoned her seat of judgement on the bales and took herself out for a run in the rain.

I didn't bother to stand up. 'You can tie up the hay-nets on the far side if you like. The one soaking in the water tub's for Balder. His breathing's gone bad again.' I shouted it above the hammering of the gale, saw him nod and listened to the solid tread of size twelve Doc Martens receding down the corridor.

'You should get them turned out if you want to stop his cough,' said another, altogether different, voice. 'You'll not do anything with soaking the hay, just.'

I jerked upright and spun round.

Nobody.

'Stewart?'

A figure stepped out from behind the half-door of the loose box. 'No, no. He's away off down to see to the hay. The name's Sandy. Sandy Logan.' It held out a hand. 'Pleased to meet you.'

It was a gnome. I swear it was a gnome. A wee, scrunched-up gnome, with a head that didn't quite reach to the top of the half-door, a face like a crinkled prune and a fuzzed halo of white hair that poked out from under a flat oilskin cap. It grinned a broad grin that flashed no teeth at all in the top row of incisors and it proffered a hand so twisted that it could have been carved from old hawthorn roots.

'You'll be the Dr Stewart,' it said. The grip was warm and dry and solid and did nothing whatsoever to invoke any sense of reality.

'Ahhh . . . Yes . . . I expect I will.' There was a blank pause where my brain failed utterly to deal with the unexpected. 'And this is Rain,' I said, to fill the gap. 'Named for her predecessor, not the weather.' And then, because he seemed to see it as an invitation: 'But she's not that keen on people.'

'Aye?' He didn't believe me. He just nodded and stepped past me into the box with the pony. And she, having spent the winter swearing to me that she loathed the entire human race, nuzzled his shoulder and tried to edge off his cap with her teeth.

Definitely a gnome.

He ran his cramped, arthritic fingers across her withers and down her back. She stood still, like the granite out on the hill, and arced her neck like a show pony. 'Aye, she's fine, the wee filly,' he said, as he reached her tail. 'What makes you think she's no' friendly?'

'Someone fired a gun by her ear a month or two back,' said Inspector MacDonald from the doorway. 'Now she thinks every man and his wife carries a Colt 45 in their armpit.'

'No. She just knows that you do.' I turned back from the pony. MacDonald was leaning against the door. He smiled and it told me nothing. With MacDonald, it never does.

I returned the favour.

'Are you going to tell me what's going on or do I have to guess?'

'Nothing's going on,' he said, and the top edge of both his salted grey eyebrows blended with the flop of whiter hair falling down from his brow, as if a tall frown somehow added plausibility. 'It's a filthy wet day and I thought you'd be here on your own with the ponies. I just thought me and Sandy here could give you a hand for a while and then you could make us a coffee and a quick bite to eat.'

Really?

MacDonald never 'just' did anything in his life. He doesn't even go out for a walk with the dog without an ulterior motive.

'That's very kind,' I said, 'but I started early. There's only the hay-nets left to do. Unless you wanted to have a go at mending the roof?'

He considered it briefly and the gnome Sandy stopped fussing my favourite pony long enough to cast an appraising eye at the drips raining down into the next box. Their eyes met and the gnome sucked the air through the gap in his teeth in the way of a mechanic who has just viewed the steaming engine of my car. Just for a moment I thought he was going to say something smart. Just for a moment, so did he. MacDonald's eyes widened ever so slightly and his head twitched a faint half-inch to the left. So the silence stretched a little longer and the gnome swallowed whatever it was that was about to come out and, instead, he just kept on sucking in and sucking in until he'd grown at least an inch taller and then he let it all out again in one big, untoothed grin. 'Maybe no' just now,' he said. And he was thereby not ejected from the barn.

And so it wasn't, after all that, me that made the lunch. Sandy Logan seemed uncommonly interested in meeting the rest of the ponies and so I introduced him, one at a time, to the remaining seven. Don't ask me why. I don't usually introduce my string to complete strangers. Particularly not in the middle of March. Granted, none of them is as flighty as Rain; trekking ponies can't afford to be flighty, but they're never overfond of visitors in the holidays and they were definitely well pissed off with being kept inside. They took to him well enough though—even Midnight, who was through her colic surgery by then and was more than a touch cranky with strangers.

MacDonald had no real need to meet the ponies afresh. He spent half the winter after Bridget died helping me to muck out and he knew the farm as well as I did, possibly better. There were still parts of the hills I hadn't ever explored. He saved them for me like treats for a child and took me out on the days when he thought I needed cheering up. There had been a fair few of those after that Christmas.

It's not that he was ever specifically invited, you understand, and equally, he had never asked if he could come. He just turned up once in a while when he had some time off and took the dog out ferreting or helped me stack the bales that had just come in off the lorry or built up the fire while I was on the phone to Galbraith's, wheedling down the cost of another month's feed for the ponies. It worked well enough. It still does. He's there when he's wanted and he's not when he's not. On the whole.

So he knew me well enough to look in the Rayburn for the potatoes, to rescue them before they turned into small lumps of charcoal and then to rake through the debris in the fridge and the larder to produce something approaching an edible meal. When he was ready, he banged a wooden spoon on the back of a metal tray and the sound carried, just about, above the noise of the rain.

I heard it before the gnome did. He was standing with his ear to Balder's left nostril, listening to the crackles of the big bay's breathing in much the same way the rest of us would listen to the sound of an engine firing on three cylinders.

'It's better when he's out in the paddock, aye?' he asked.

'Yes.' Naturally. That's a feature of airborne allergies: remove the allergen and the condition improves. Out in the paddock equals no more hay. No more hay means no more spores to breathe in. No more spores, no more cough. Simple. Except when it's raining. And I didn't make it rain.

The tea-tray rattle carried across the yard for a second time.

'I think that's MacDonald,' I said. 'We should . . .'

The little man was looking upwards, pensive. Scanning the barn, skirting round the area where the whitewash of the walls meets the tiles of the roof. His eyes narrowed. There were cobwebs. There have always been cobwebs. Even in the four years when Bridget was in charge, there were cobwebs. It's simply that I don't normally look up at the eaves and count them.

'Look,' I tried again. 'We really ought to . . .'

'Prevailing wind's from the west, isn't it?' he asked. 'From over the village?'

What? 'Yes, I think so. Why?'

'You could open up the brickwork,' he said. 'Up there, see?' He nodded upwards, jutting up with the peak of his cap like a duck grabbing bread. 'Put in some ventilation tiles. With baffles on them on the western side. It wouldn't stop it, mind, but it would help the old lad's breathing.' He rubbed the big horse on the muzzle and Balder, knowing that the gnome was absolutely not responsible for the rain, shoved his nose gently into the crook of his arm. 'See? He thinks it's a good idea.'

Oh good. That's it settled then. What more could we possibly ask?

'We'll start work in the morning,' I said, without

pausing to consider whether gnomes understand the meaning of irony.

'No, no,' he shook his head. 'After the weekend will do.' He smiled his gap-smile and patted me on the shoulder in a paternal fashion and pointed again with his cap, this time in the direction of the house from which the clatter of the tea-tray sounded for a third time. 'I think we're being called inside,' he said.

The kitchen smelt warm. MacDonald had banked up the fire and hung his jacket across a chair back in front of it. The filter of peat-smoke met with the steam of the wool and both wove in with the cacophony of food smells coming from the far side of the room. Two full plates sat on the breakfast bar and the kettle hissed quiet curses to itself amidst a clutter of cats on the Rayburn. MacDonald sat in one of the two big armchairs by the fire with his feet up on a low stool, a copy of the *Scotsman* spread out on his knee and his plate balanced on the arm of his chair. Two of the younger kittens lay on the floor and tied knots in his laces. The dog lay peacefully at his feet. Very domestic.

I like the farm. It has a sense of belonging that the flat off Byres Road never had. I spent four years living in town and it was one of the bigger mistakes in my life. There wasn't a day when I didn't miss the farm and the woman I had shared it with and now, even with her gone, I don't often pass through the back door without a sense of relief at being back home again.

But I don't have visitors often. Not new ones, at any rate, and so the gnome's entrance into my domain had a fair degree of novelty value. I found myself looking at the place with a stranger's eyes and, like the cobwebs in the barn, patches of grime on the windowledge suddenly

came to light. There were fingerprints on the window,
too. The small leaded one above the sink that looks out
over the duck pond. I tend to throw the remains of the
morning toast to the birds and must, on occasion, have
the odd bit of butter on a finger. There were more cat-
hairs, too, than I would have thought likely. Random
clumps of grey and orange, tawny and white hairs were
scattered on the chair backs, on the cushions, on the
windowledges and in small piles in the corners. And
there were cobwebs, of course. There are always cobwebs somewhere if you look for them.

It shouldn't be too surprising. Nobody expects a
working farmhouse to be perfect. Not one this old. The
place that is now my home is older than Nina's cottage
by a couple of centuries, and although Bridget and I did
a frantic round of decorating when we first moved in, I'd
left before it was time for a second round and no one else
had thought to do it instead. The day Sandy Logan came
to visit, it needed a fresh coat of paint in much the same
way that the barn needed a fresh set of tiles but I'd been
back home for less than six months by then and I had
better things to do with the intervening time than watch
paint dry on the walls.

MacDonald looked up as we entered, his mouth full.
He waved a fork at the plates and went back to his
reading of the paper. 'You don't mind me starting without you?' he asked and then, not to me: 'Majesty Blaze
came in at 7 to 1 at Newark.'

'Aye, I saw.' The gnome took the plate I offered him
and settled, without being asked, in the second of the
two big chairs by the fire. I am used to MacDonald treat-
ing my home as his own. It was a little unsettling to
watch somebody else do the same. I took my own plate
and sat on one of the high stools by the breakfast bar
where I could keep an eye on both of them and try to

figure out what was going on. Why, for instance, Mac-Donald should suddenly evolve so unlikely an interest in racing. I'd known him for nearly half a year by then and in all of that time, I'd never seen him show the slightest interest in the back pages of the papers.

'Sandy's dad was a trainer,' said MacDonald. 'In Ayrshire.'

The man reads minds. It's one of his less endearing features.

'Archie Logan,' said the gnome, and they both looked at me as if I was supposed to say something.

I took a mouthful of baked potato and said nothing at all.

'He trained the 1959 Derby winner,' said MacDonald. 'You might have heard of him.'

You have to be joking.

I refuse to choke on my meal just to satisfy this man's warped sense of the ridiculous.

I bit down hard on a fragment of overdone skin and did my best to stare him down. MacDonald absorbed the look with complete equanimity and let his eyebrows drift upwards for the second time in one day.

I wasn't in the best frame of mind to play games. 'I wasn't born in 1959, Inspector,' I said. 'And I wouldn't remember the Derby winner if I was.'

I haven't called him Inspector since the night he shot the man who was trying to kill me. It made the point well enough. He grinned peaceably and withdrew from the field of battle.

The gnome carried on the charge.

'Are you as young as that?' he asked, with some semblance of awe. 'You don't look it, right enough.' He grinned his faerie, gap-toothed smile.

I really don't like playing games. I like it even less when I'm the ball.

'Do you want to tell me,' I asked carefully, 'exactly why you're here?'

MacDonald knows me well enough to see when he's reached the limit. I've never thrown him off the premises yet, but that doesn't mean I won't if I have to. He put his plate on the floor and, with it, laid down the various layers of dissemblance.

'Has the lassie changed her mind?' he asked.

'Caroline? No. Of course not. She won't.' She has no reason to. And she's not being unreasonable. Or even illogical. She just wants a life of her own. I may not like it, but I can hardly argue against it.

He smiled thinly and nodded as if all of this was somehow relevant. 'So are you still going to sell the ponies?'

'Yes. I don't have any choice, Stewart. We've been through this before. Several times.' Almost daily, in fact, since the day after Christmas when Caroline Leader broke it to me that she couldn't handle the myriad ghosts of the farm and she wanted to sell her half of the business so that she could move back to her old life in the West End. She didn't mention that she was taking Elspeth with her, of course, but it became apparent very shortly afterwards.

I shook my head. 'Nothing has changed.' And I don't particularly want to air my personal crises in public, thank you.

He heard what he was supposed to hear and ignored it anyway. 'Sandy here's got a wee bit of a proposal for you,' he said.

A proposal. Has he indeed? If MacDonald is old enough to be my father, then this man is old enough to be my grandfather. Easily.

The mind boggles.

Stability suddenly seemed more prudent than height.

I slid down off the stool and sat on the floor. 'What kind of proposal?' I asked.

And so they told me.

The gnome's father trained racehorses in Ayr and Sandy started off life as a stable lad with plans to be Champion Jockey, at least in the UK, if not internationally, by the time he was twenty-one. Fate and better riders stopped that one in its tracks and the young Sandy, never one to be second grade at anything, took to farriery instead. A heaven-sent decision if there ever was one. In shoeing horses, he found his forte. He set up shop in Newmarket and made serious money getting up at four in the morning and travelling round the racing yards shoeing and reshoeing before the early gallops. He would probably have spent the rest of his life there if a well-placed kick from a particularly scatty two-year-old hadn't shattered his lumbar spine and put him in the orthopaedic ward at Addenbrooke's for the best part of the next twenty-four months. By the time they let him out and taught him how to walk again, his juniors had the business well in hand and Sandy had realised there was more to life than horseshoes. His fingers were swollen with arthritis and his back was too sore to be worth bending over for six straight hours a day, however much money he was making. And, besides, he was homesick. He wanted to spend his winter years in the place he'd grown up. Somewhere with hills instead of the endless flat fens of East Anglia where the closest things to a mountain is the half-mile of one-in-ten slope that makes up the training run of Newmarket Heath.

So he sold the farriery business and all the goodwill that went with it to the people who had been doing the job so well without him and headed back home to Scotland to spend his fortune breeding the perfect racehorse.

That was it. They sat there in their armchairs on

either side of the fire and waited for me to look suitably impressed.

The gnome laid his plate on the floor and took off his cap. He's bald on top—completely, shiningly bald with a rim of white fuzzed hair flaring out just above ear height. There is no good reason why being bald should render a man more human, but it did. One simple movement and suddenly I was not sitting with a gnome at all. Simply an old man with crippling arthritis and a lot of time on his hands. And a lifetime's worth of horselore that he didn't want to lose.

'I still don't understand the offer,' I said.

'He wants to buy into the business,' said MacDonald, patiently from his side of the fire. 'So you don't have to sell the ponies.'

If only.

'The money's only half the problem, Stewart,' I said. 'You know that. Even with the cash, I can't manage the business on my own.'

'So then, you need a partner. Someone you can trust. Someone who knows horses and has the time to spend looking after them. You have the farm and the horses and the land. Sandy here has the time.'

Segments of my life drifted urgently across my field of vision.

'I'm not selling the farm,' I said. 'Not until I absolutely have to.'

The old man leaned over and laid his hand on my arm. 'I'm not offering to buy the farm, lass,' he said gently, and his voice had lost the sing-song lilt it took on when he was telling his story. 'Just the business. Not the land, or the barn or the house or the ponies. Just the business itself.'

'But I've got no idea what it's worth. We could take months sorting it out. I haven't got that kind of time.'

'I've got a lawyer who'll do it over the weekend,' said
the gnome. 'If you don't like the answer, you can find
someone else.'

I could. But Bridget used to be my lawyer. I know
too much about the inside workings of the legal profes-
sion to trust many of them after that. 'No,' I said. 'Yours
will do as good as any. If I really don't like the numbers,
you and I can argue it out without the sharks making a
killing from both of us.'

The gnome spat on his hand and held it out. Foul
habit. Can't imagine that goes down too well in the high-
bred stables of Newmarket. 'So it's a deal?' he offered.

'What's all the hurry?' I asked.

'Trekking season starts in three weeks. The barn
needs a lot of work before we start having folk running
through it for the summer. You'll need the cash to get it
fixed,' said MacDonald.

'The breeding season's gone three months in,' said
Sandy Logan. 'I've a mare I've got my eye on and I want
her in foal before the month's out.'

Of the two, the latter seemed by far the more rational
reason to hurry.

I took his hand, ignored the sliding sensation as I
gripped his palm. 'Deal,' I said.

Oddly enough, it has worked. It's not perfect, but it's
a great deal better than it could have been.

Without Sandy, I'd be back in a flat in the West End
by now, and bitter into the bargain. As it is, three years
down the line, I have the farmhouse to myself, a thriving
business, a handful of yard lads and lasses—most of
whom seem to harbour ambitions to be Champion
Jockey one day (and who am I to disillusion them?)—
and a field at the back of the hill that is quite clearly
lodged at the end of some horse-loving leprechaun's
rainbow. The first crop of foals raced as two-year-olds

last season and, of the seven, we had three placed, including one group winner, which is better than most make in a lifetime. We even have our own small-scale pony-breeding programme, designed to produce the best trekking ponies seen this side of the Highland line. Sandy Logan never does anything that's not going to be a winner.

And so on this particular Friday evening, somewhere towards the middle of April, I made my way across the yard in the dark and the wet, and the only real problem in my life was that Gordon had dropped off the next week's sack of potatoes after Sandy went home and it was sitting just outside the back door getting wet. I heaved it into the porch and then spent a peaceful half-hour feeding the dog and clearing up the debris left by the cats and dithering over whether or not to bother lighting a fire, and so it was later than it should have been when I found the note that Sandy had left wedged under the kettle. That, in itself, was odd. Odd enough to make me stop and read it through when I might otherwise have carried on playing with the fire. I don't get notes often from Sandy. He doesn't write much if he can help it. The joints in his right hand get worse with each passing winter and holding a pen is difficult to the point of impossibility.

The words smudged across the paper, all sharp angles and painful curves.

Friday 6:15

Sorry. Got to go. Rain's off her food. Could be foaling. Not milked up yet. Not straining. Keep an eye on her. West Acre Paddock. S.

Rain. My Rain, blossomed now from shy filly to strong-minded, full-bellied, maiden mare. She was ten days over dates by then but maidens go over all the time. I learned that the first year when I stayed up with the first one of Sandy's maidens, watching her hourly through the nights for close to two weeks. She dropped her foal at four o'clock in the afternoon while I was at work and it took me a week of early nights to catch up on the lost sleep. After that, I stopped worrying about first-foaling mares, even Rain.

And so I did, after all, take the time to build up the fire and to make a sandwich and to sneak a quick look at the headlines while I ate it and it was somewhere after ten o'clock when I finally pulled on a jacket and dug the big torch from the cupboard under the stairs and forayed out into the wild and the wet to see if Rain had dropped for Sandy the filly he wanted.

4

Each of us has our own nightmare. This is mine.

It is cold and it is dark and it is wet. Very wet. The world is awash with water. Rain soaks steadily through jeans and fleece and trainers. Arcing jets of it bounce off beech leaves on to the small, unprotected patches of skin at my ankles and wrists. The smell of it rising from the sodden turf almost covers the other smells of sweat and rancid faeces. The crash of the river spinning down over the shallows at the side of the field hushes all other noises to nothing. If I look anywhere away from the limmering pool of torchlight, all I can see is the sheen of the rain and the odd splash of foam from the burn.

If, instead, I choose to look down into the torchlight, there is a small, dun pony mare, stretched out on her side in the grass with her head heavy on my knees, her eyes dull with drugs and her twitching feet periodically smashing grass into mud.

If I look a fraction beyond that, there is a man; a short, compact man, lying face down in the dirt with his shirt off, his free hand clenched tight in a fistful of grass by way of an anchor and his face locked hard in concentration.

As I watch, he slithers backwards and kneels up, peeling the plastic rectal glove from his arm. The skin beneath is laced with a network of livid, red creases from the pressure. At least it's clean, the arm. The rest of him is not clean. If he had kept his shirt on, it would be wrecked. Because he didn't, his chest is awash with the mud and the blood and clinging fragments of grass, his right cheek the same. The torchlight makes comet trails of the smears on his glasses. He takes them off to wipe them clean and I can see his eyes even if he can't quite focus on mine. They are brown and wide, and they struggle with something hard that goes beyond the lateness of the hour. They don't tell me anything I don't already know. I did what I could of a full clinical exam before the man ever arrived. Horses aren't that different to people. And it doesn't take a medic to spot a bad foaling from across the field.

The mare snores, in the way that a whale snores on surfacing and her feet smash the turf near his hand. Ruaridh Innes edges backwards and feels around in his case for the bottle of dope that will slow her back into sleep. He nods at me to tip the torchlight to her jugular, then slips the needle in the vein with the smooth practice of the addict. Blood swirls black in the body of the syringe and he shoots the load home.

I run my hand forward along the line of her jaw. The mare snores again and twists her head round to look at me. The whites of her eyes glisten oddly in the torchlight and her nostrils flare red. Her pulse hammers under my fingers and then calms as the drug takes hold. Her eyes glaze and fix on another reality, away from the cold and the rain and the pain in her guts. All I can smell now is the metallic bite of her sweat. It smells of death.

Ruaridh dumps his drugs in the box and reaches for the blood tube leaning up against the lid. He squints at it in the torchlight and reads it as a teller reads the dregs of the tea. What he sees doesn't make him any happier but he still doesn't look as if he's about to break into speech. He's not one for unnecessary rhetoric, our Ruaridh.

'And?' I ask. 'What's happening inside?'

He shrugs. 'Not a lot,' he says. 'A lot less than there ought to be.'

'Is it a breech?'

'One of them is.'

One. *One?* Dear God. 'She's got twins?'

'I'd say so. I can feel three joints and all of them are knees so either you have one foal with three front legs or else you have two foals.' There is a pause while he fits his glasses back on. The smears are now pleasingly concentric. He tightens his lips and runs his cleaner hand across what is left of the hair on his head.

'That's not the worst of it,' he says. 'She's ruptured, Kellen. There's a whacking great tear in her uterus where one of them's put a foot through. She needs surgery and she needs it now. If she stays as she is, they'll all three be dead before morning and it'll not be a pretty way to go.'

That's what I like about Ruaridh. He saves his sentiment for small children and pocket pets. Adults are granted the dignity of adults.

He waits while the news sinks home, rummaging in his box for a towel and his shirt as if either are likely to be dry.

'Edinburgh's the closest,' he says. 'But that's two hours away. Three if we drive at a sensible speed. Plus whatever it takes to get her into the box. I wouldn't like to say she'd live that far. There aren't too many other options.'

'Are there any?'

'I've got the gun in the car,' he says. 'We can give her a clean ending at least.'

No. Not yet. I owe her more than that.

'What's wrong with Garscube?' I ask. 'We took Midnight and she did fine. It's ten minutes down the road. Less if you put your foot down.'

I exaggerate; it's half an hour, even on a good day. But that's not the point.

'No deal.' He reaches back into the box and loads another dose of happy juice into a clean syringe. 'They've had a bunch of infected horses die after surgery. They've closed all the theatres while they get their act together and clean the place up. You won't get a horse in there for love nor money.'

Oh, I think I might.

I reach in my back pocket, pull out the mobile phone and begin to key through the directory for the right number. 'It's worth a try, though, wouldn't you say?'

The mare sighs as the pain pushes through the barrier of the drug. The man takes off his glasses and bites his lip. The full syringe balances in the palm of one hand and this time his attention is on me. This close, even without his glasses, his focus is sharper.

'The gun would be kinder, Kellen.'

Maybe. But this is Rain. Who is my friend. And I have the key that unlocks the doors to theatre.

Magpies. And their secrets.

I spend my life working in other people's nightmares. It seemed perfectly reasonable, just this once, to ask someone else to work in mine.

I have no good memories of theatre. If asked, I would
have said I had no memories of theatre at all although I
would have been lying, and wilfully so.

There was a time, in early studenthood when I believed, like all the rest, that the healing blade was the
only way forward in modern medicine. I grew out of that
one long before we were ever allowed to set foot in the
hallowed spaces of the scrub room, and when I was finally old enough to experience the sacred art at first
hand, the cloud of it cast a shadow well into my adult
life.

They don't like students in theatre, not in human
theatres, anyway. They're not overkeen on junior clinicians either, particularly not the ones who have already
thrown in their hand with the physicians. I spent six
months as a junior surgical intern in the general surgery
unit of the Western Infirmary and my memories are,
without exception, of being in the wrong place at the
wrong time, locked in a circle of sterile space with a
consultant surgeon whose prowess in the dissection of
living house officers ran way ahead of his world-wide
fame in hepatic and renal transplant techniques.

I don't know, I never have known, the order of ves-
sels leaving the vena cava from the diaphragm downwards. I have no memory, if I ever knew it at all, of the
course of the pancreatic duct or the precise location of its
opening into the proximal duodenum. I don't even remember the number of lobes in the liver although I believe that I did remember it at the time. All of these I can
forget. And I can forget that I forgot them. I could probably, if I had to, watch an entire kidney transplant on
video and tell myself I had never taken part in the real
thing.

Being inside theatre though, is different. In theatre, there are triggers more powerful than sight and sound. In theatre, there is the smell and smell is the arch-traitor. The one sense you can't obliterate. The oldest. The earliest. The first to be formed and the last to leave. Ontogeny repeats phylogeny. The blind and deaf predecessors to the dinosaurs hunted their way up the evolutionary tree by smell. Everything else grew in as added luxuries. And so the olfactory lobes reside in the paleocortex, the oldest and earliest portions of the brain. Long before there are wrinkles in the hemispheres, the olfactory bulb is there, picking up the scents of the uterine fluid. Which means that smell survives when all the other senses have succumbed to the lure of the dream. In sleep, in unconsciousness, under general anaesthesia, it's the smell that sinks in and lingers. People will remember what they smelt long after they remember what they heard and they remember a frighteningly large amount of what they hear while they're under anaesthesia. Wise anaesthetists play music to their sleeping patients. Some of them have been known to play prerecorded messages of healing and thereby speed up the recovery rates of their cases in the post-surgical period. The rest let their subjects hear the consultant's description of their internal pathology to the gathered throng and then wonder why they don't recover as well as expected afterwards.

For those of us who passed through theatre without the balm of unconsciousness, the clatter of a scalpel blade on a steel tray or the wheeze of a ventilator or the whistle of the oxygen alarm on an anaesthetic machine can trigger sudden twinges of primal fear. A sense of dry-mouthed anxiety without any real understanding of its source. But it is the smell alone that has the power to open the floodgates to memory, to take the twisting spirals of the nightmare and twist them tighter still.

Except, of course, I didn't know this until it was too late.

Until the horse, who was my horse, lay on her back, unconscious, on the operating table with no music playing in her ears.

Until the surgeon, who was my friend and my client and who should, if the world were sane, have been in bed sleeping the sleep of the blessed, was gloved and gowned and ready to cut; glowing with the kind of radiant luminescence that one sees only in the truly driven.

Until the nurse, whose horse was dying in the barn, had laid out the trolley with an array of instruments that could just as easily have been there for a liver transplant.

Until the resident, who was taller than I remembered, even with the surgical cap flattening the spikes of her hair, had spread the spirit on the shaved patch of skin and laid out the drapes in the precise, retentive rectangle that defines the surgical field.

Until the surgeon, anonymous now behind surgical mask and tight-tied paper cap, called for a blade and a swab and ran her thumb along the line of the incision and turned to the anaesthetist, who is also a surgeon and who was once her lover and asked, in time-honoured fashion: 'OK to cut?' and received a short, preoccupied nod in reply.

Only then was it obvious that this was not the right place for me to be.

And by then it was a long, long way too late.

![divider]

There was blood on the wall.

A thin, punctate, crimson line arced across the sterile white of the tiles. The hot, metallic smell of it filled the room, masking, just in that moment, the rest: the surgical spirit, the volatile anaesthetic, the hibitane. Then they were through the skin and into the abdominal cavity and the smell of that covered everything else. A warm, enveloping, new-hay smell spiked with silage and with something else sharper but still not unpleasant. I wasn't expecting that. In all the shifting timeframes of the nightmare, I was not expecting the abdomen to smell so relatively unputrid. Human abdomens do not smell of new hay and fermented grasses. They smell of old sewage and rancid gall and the reek of it clings in your hair for hours after the last suture has been tied and the patient is back in the recovery ward. Or the mortuary.

I had braced myself for that smell, promised myself that I was not going to be sick. The unexpectedness of what came in its stead did odd things to my sense of reality.

'Clip.'

'Clip.'

'Get that bleeder.'

'Got it.'

The blood stopped. Cut off at the height of its arc. A final full stop in red. I hadn't realised I was using it as an index of life. She could have died then and I would never have known.

Except the ECG carried on. And the arterial pressure wave. And the myriad other electronic miracles that monitored the life of my horse.

There were more lines here connecting the living mare to the machines than there had been in the ICU box where the technology was monitoring the slow progression to death.

I would rather not to think about that.

If I keep my eyes on the screens, I could believe myself a decade younger, locked back in the hellhole of surgery.

If I look instead at the vastness of the ventilator, or
the diameter of the endotracheal tube, or the sheer size
of the patient under the drapes, the extraordinary warp-
ing of scale will send me screaming over the edge. I am
Alice and I have eaten in the company of the White
Rabbit and the world has lost all sense of perspective.

Alternatively, it is half two in the morning and it's a
long, long time since I last worked straight through the
night. Nothing is supposed to make sense at a time like
this.

'Scissors.'

'Scissors.'

'Retractors.'

'Which ones?'

'Whatever you've got. I don't care. Just get her
opened wide so I can see what's going on in here.'

Real surgeons don't talk like that. Real surgeons give
precise orders in clipped monosyllables and expect them
to be carried out without comment.

But this is Nina and the assistant on the other side of
the drapes is Steff and I would trust either one of them
with my life.

'Hold that.'

'Good . . . get the uterus up where we can see
it . . . there's the tear . . .'

'Shit . . . she's bled some . . .'

'Leave it. She'll be fine. We'll get the kids out
first . . . Blade.'

'Blade.'

'Scissors.'

'Scissors . . . I've got the hock . . .'

'Good. Lift him up . . . Oh. No. Not a him. It's a
her. Kellen, you've got a filly. A dun filly. Magic. Image
of her mum. That's it . . . lift her up. OK, guys, first
one's on her way out. Get going with the suction.'

And suddenly I am not alone in my space on the white-tiled floor. There is a lank-legged foal; a glowing, moon-gold dun with a dark mane and tail and a long dark eelstripe down her back and a faint spray of white-on-pink between her nostrils; an exact replica of her dam, sopping wet and coated from nostrils to tail with the slimed membranes of her failed birth. She is inert, unbreathing. Her heart thumps visibly through the barred cage of her ribs. I put my hand over it, to be sure, and feel the first attempt at a breath. It fails. The membranes are tight around her nose and mouth; all she can do is snore.

But Maureen is there with the suction catheter, sliding it deep, down each nostril, slurping noisily at the thick fluid in her airways, clearing a path for the breath. She passes me a wad of drapes, as if I am part of this team and, because it is expected of me and because I have been at enough foalings by now, I rub briskly in fast lung-thumping spirals, drying her off, scraping away the membranes from her eyes and her ears and her skin, rubbing dried whorls into the damp buckskin of her coat. She has to breathe. If she doesn't breathe, she will never live. I stop for a moment to look. Her tongue protrudes from the side of her mouth; a dark, ugly purple. Her eyes are closed but when I touch them, there is a movement; a crinkling of the damp skin of her eyelid, a withdrawing, a gasp of pretended breath. Maureen is at her head now, kneeling, with her mouth to the foal's nose, blowing in lungfuls of air. The filly twitches her head, knocking it free. She doesn't want someone else breathing for her like that.

And then Matt is there. Matt, who should be concentrating on his anaesthetic, is there with a tracheal tube and an oxygen cylinder and together they run the tube up along her nose and into her larynx and then they squeeze the bag and push the oxygen into her lungs. To persuade her to breathe, to bring her into the land of the living.

An eye opens. A dark, lucid pool of night-time.

She looks at me and I am lost.

Every foal born is the most wonderful being that ever lived. This is the one to die for.

'Check her pulse.' Matt. To me.

I slide my hand round under her hind leg and feel for the femoral pulse. It's there. Regular. Weak, but regular.

'Got it?' He doesn't look at me, he's too busy trying to persuade my foal to breathe.

'Yes.'

'Good. Tell me if it stops . . . Mo, get the Dopram . . . Nina, how's the mare?'

'She's fine. Second foal's on the way . . . It's a red colt, Kells. God, he's gorgeous. You've got non-identical twins. This is the one that was jammed in the pelvis. Heart's still going strong. All you have to do is get him breathing. Matt, we're starting on the uterus. You can hit the mare with the oxytocin any time you like.'

And suddenly I am alone with the filly. Matt is drawing up drugs for the mare. My mare. And Maureen is waiting for the colt, weighed down like a midwife with a fresh set of drapes. 'It's OK, Kellen. I'll get this one. The girl's yours. Keep ventilating. Tell Matt if you run into trouble.'

The colt appeared; a bright, shining chestnut with shock-white socks on three of his legs and a spectacular, perfect new moon set between his eyes. I watched them lower him on to the bed of green cotton drapes, watched Maureen clear the mucus from his nose, watched the colt, with a prayer to gods I had forgotten existed, take a single strong breath and shake his head. Saw him kicking to live. A fighter born, that one. One to stare death in the eyes and dare him to move.

And then I turned back to the filly and saw her change.

There's an odd space, halfway between living and dying and she was there. When I turned away, I was pushing breath into a foal with light in her eyes. When I turned back, the shine was already turning dull.

I let go of the oxygen bag and felt for her pulse.

Nothing.

I don't believe this.

I felt for her heart.

Still nothing.

I touched her eye. Right on the eyeball. Nothing at all.

'Matt! She's gone.'

He was injecting something into the drip bag running into the mare. He turned and looked, not at me but at the clock on the wall above my head. 'OK, we've got an arrest. Keep ventilating . . . Mo, can you leave the colt?'

She didn't look up. 'Not if you want him to live.'

'Fine.' He dropped his syringe on the edge of the table and dragged a red plastic box from the shelf on the anaesthetic machine. 'Can you do cardiac compressions?'

'I don't know.'

'OK, I'll do it.' He knelt by the foal and leant over it, pushing his weight on her chest. The classic cardiopulmonary arrest protocol. A burst of short, sharp shoves, pause to feel the pulse, then back to the heart.

Three times he went through it. Push the heart. Ten compressions. Check the pulse. Nothing. Back to the heart. Push and push and push and the room didn't reek any more of surgical spirit and volatile anaesthetics. The

air buzzed with the musk of male sweat and the salt-in-
honey smell of placental fluid.

On the third try, we got Maureen. 'Colt's breathing
fine. What do you need?'

'Adrenaline. And keep your finger on the facial artery. Tell me if you get a pulse.'

'OK . . . Nothing so far.'

The last time I saw anyone draw up a vial of adrenaline one-handed was in the ICU at the Western. It's not a
skill most of us need to learn. I watched Maureen snap
the top off a succession of vials and draw up 5 cc of
adrenaline left-handed with her free hand on the artery
as if she did it on a daily basis.

'Still nothing. There's no pulse . . . wait a bit . . .
you got one there . . . Nope . . . Gone again . . .
OK, Adrenaline's ready.'

'Go for it.'

They did go for it.

Half a dozen times they went for it. They pulled the
ECG from the mare and clipped it on to the fine buckskin of the foal's chest to check that she wasn't fibrillat-
ing and when all the machine could give them was a
single, flat line, still they went for it again.

I knelt on the wet tiles of the floor, squeezing my
oxygen bag as if it was my life that depended on it and
watched her eye grow more dull, saw the skin around
her lids begin to slacken and begged all of the gods that
looked over the colt to turn their gaze back to the filly.

They didn't.

Or they did and she still chose not to live.

█████

We had been going for fifteen minutes, apparently, when
Matt called the time of death. I believe him, because he
was the one who had the sense to look at the clock when

it started. But it didn't feel like that. It felt like eternity. Or a fraction of a heartbeat.

I sat, numb, on the floor while Maureen closed my filly's eyes and pulled a half-dry drape across her head.

The colt whinnied from the far side of the room. A call to a mother who lay asleep on an operating table with two surgeons tying sutures in her uterus. Or a call to a sister, lately gone. Or simply a demand for food. There was milk ready, in a bowl on the side. Steff milked the mare out before they put her under. The kind of thing you do as routine when your patients start dying unexpectedly.

Maureen brought me the bowl and a calf-bottle, together. 'He's hungry, the wee lamb. D'you want to feed him?'

'No.' I stood up, feeling the thin cotton of the scrub suit cling wetly to my legs. 'Can you do it? I think I need some fresh air.'

'Are you sure?' She looked doubtful, as if a therapist ought to know better than to run from the site of death and defeat.

'I'm sure.'

I changed in the staff changing room (female), a small shoebox of a room that smelled of old rubber and wet clothes. Most of the wet clothes were mine. The ones I was wearing and the ones I had left hanging on the peg by the door. The only difference was that the scrub suit I had on was warmer.

A set of shelves along one wall held spare sets of dry scrubs. Short-sleeved tops on the left. Trousers on the right. Green for the surgeons. Navy blue for the nurses. One of each if you're cold and wet and neither a surgeon nor a nurse. I wrapped my rain-sodden fleece round my shoulders in honour of the rain and went outside to find someone to talk to who knew nothing of foals.

If you believe Schrödinger's theorem, the cat in the box is not dead until the observer opens the lid to check. If the same applies to horses then it is possible that, had I not decided to go for a walk in the ward, Branding Iron might have lived for an hour or two longer. It doesn't seem very likely. If theoretical physicists spent more of their time in hospital wards and less of it in the laboratory, they would know that people die all the time with no one in attendance. Horses are not so very different. And, in any case, he was dying long before I got there.

I heard the shattering crack of a shod hoof striking wood as I slid in through the side door of the horse ward. In the time it took me to sprint the full length of the barn, he hit the walls three more times. If it had been the box door it would never have held. As it was, the oak planking of the partition between his box and the next held long and ragged scores that stretched from eye height down to the floor and the monitor nearest the manger hung over the edge of the rack with its screen imploded and a crescent-shaped dent in the steel of the case.

The horse lay on his side; rigid, neck stretched out, nostrils flared, feet flailing, running, racing, fleeing. Anything, but not lying still with the pain. His eyes showed white along the entirety of their rims. His lips snarled back over gums the colour of dead fish. Blood ran from both nostrils. Not the bright jet of a good, honest nosebleed, just a thin, steady stream of dark liquid washing his life down the drain. In those first few moments, the smell of horse-sweat and blood obliterated the stench from the rest of the box.

He shuddered, once, as I watched and the frantic paddling slowed suddenly, as if the race was won. Only his breathing didn't slow. His lips rolled tighter. His nostrils widened. He drew in one single, sucking, ear-tearing breath. The indrawn air-hunger of a drowning man magnified and multiplied. His body shook with the effort of it. And the next one. And the one after that. Each one followed the last by a longer and longer interval in a pattern that cut grooves somewhere near my kidneys. Agonal gasping. The final goodbye. The closing motor reflexes of that last section of brain to die. It happens in people too, sometimes, and you draw the curtains and move the visitors out of the ward and do anything you possibly can to make sure that the relatives aren't there to see it.

If anything, I'd say it's worse in horses.

I opened the box door and went in then, laying a hand on his neck. Not because there was anything left I could do, but because I was there and I didn't want him to die alone. I knelt at his side, feeling the warm bulk of his body shudder against my knees, closed my hand over eyes that no longer knew the difference between night and day, talked irrelevant horse-talk into ears already deaf and stroked again and again down sweat-sodden withers, feeling skin that had lost all sense of touch. And I wept. Silent, unsqueezed tears. Not for him particularly, but for the night and the nightmares and everything ahead that I could feel in my guts but couldn't see.

I stayed there a long time when it was over. I could have gone back inside but walking back into a sterile surgical suite from the death-mire of a toxic horse is not one of life's brighter moves. Steff showered twice, washed her hair with hibitane and changed all her clothes before they let her near the scrub room and still she double-gloved. Besides, Maureen was still in the theatre and I may be a therapist but I have yet to find a good way of looking someone in the eye and telling

them that their best friend is dead. So I knelt against the
great bulk of his body, feeling it slowly cool against my
knees and I thought of the filly foal lying dead in the
theatre and the mare lying fast asleep on the table and I
did my best not to remember the one, single unspoken
rule of medicine: the rule of three.

Three. Death comes in threes. It's the last thing they
don't tell you in lectures and the first thing you learn
when you start on the wards. People can die one at a
time, with a decent interval between and you don't need
to start counting. But when the shit hits the fan, when
everything is falling apart, when the world is turning
itself upside down, then you know that death's on a roll
and that he always takes them three at a time.

'Kellen? Are you all right?'

It was Steff, leaning over me. Steff with her hair wet
with sweat and the rain and flattened to her scalp by the
surgical cap. Steff, wide awake and dressed for the
weather in a clean set of overalls and someone else's
body-warmer that cut in under her armpits and barely
covered her kidneys. Steff, clearly unhappy.

Three.

I tried to stand, faster than I should have done and
ended up half sitting on the dead body of the horse with
my head spinning and my mouth full of bile.

'The mare?' I asked and she managed to smile. A
smile free of jewellery so that the small, punctate hole at
the side of her nostril stretched briefly to oval.

'She's fine. They're both fine,' she said. And then: 'I
thought he'd crushed you.'

'Sorry.' I stood up straight, feeling my joints crack.
The horse was still warm but his back, when I put my
hand to it, was hard, like the wood of the walls. 'I
just . . . thought he needed company.'

'I guess he did.' Her eyes roamed the box. Broken

drip sets hung from the ceiling. Fractured ECG lines lay
knotted in the far corner. The dead monitor still tipped
at a dangerous angle over the edge of the rack. The horse
took up most of the box. In death, he looked bigger than
he had in life. Seventeen hands. Maybe more.

'How in heaven's name are we going to get him out
of the door?' I asked.

'There's a winch on the back of the flat-bed.' She
wasn't looking at me. She was looking at the chunks of
timber missing from the far wall as if they were the last
letter from a departed lover. She chewed her lower lip,
painfully hard. 'Mo's gone home,' she said. 'At least she
won't be here when the boss decides to do a post-
mortem.'

'At half four in the morning?' I asked. 'Is that likely?'

'In the frame of mind she's in tonight? I'd have said it
was guaranteed.' She turned with that tight-reined, sam-
urai grace and dipped her boots, one at a time, in the
disinfectant at the door. 'After all,' she said, 'she's the one
who's had some sleep.'

5

Dawn came at ten to five that morning. I know, I sat on the threshold of the post-mortem room and watched it happen. Saw the burned edge of the sun knife its way up over the edge of the Parasitology block, saw the mist rise slowly off the river, heard the mutter of a tractor and the random calls of ewes to lambs and lambs to ewes as the morning feeding started in the fields beyond the bridge; heard, somewhere close by, the whicker of mare to foal and a brief, high-pitched answer.

My mare. Her foal. Both of them alive.

The sound carried past me, in through the open door, to where Branding Iron hung suspended in the centre of the room. A half-inch steel chain attached to a two-tonne electric hoist held his right hock somewhere up near the ceiling. His nose and both forefeet dangled a foot off the floor. A long, linear cut from pelvis to sternum opened him up, showing the empty cave of his abdominal cavity. All that had been inside lay in white plastic tubs underneath: liver and kidneys in one, guts and spleen in the other. A fire hose played gently over the surface of his intestines, running rivers of red water into the drain in the floor.

Nina stood in front of him, her knife in one hand, a waterproof writing pad in the other, reading unspoken pathological truths from the patterns on the surface of his diaphragm.

The foal whinnied again, demanding attention.

Nina looked past the horse to where I was sitting in the doorway. 'You can shower in the changing rooms next to the small animal ward if you want to go and see them, you know,' she said. 'Just don't go straight from here. Your foal's got no immune system yet. I don't think we should take any chances on contagion from this one.'

'I know. I'm not in any hurry. I'll give them a few more hours to settle.'

'So then go home, Kellen. You're as bad as Steff. I can do this on my own. Really. I don't need a chaperone for a basic post-mortem.'

'I know. I heard.' I heard Matt and Steff both try to argue to the contrary and heard them both fail. She's very single-minded when she's had some sleep. And a surgical success.

I watched the heron fly in to its stand under the alders. The wind, warm now and coming from the south, shivered through the trailing leaves. A bank of solid cloud gathered just above the dawn line promising rain later. It always rains in April in Glasgow. But the dawns are usually bright. It makes up for a lot.

'I'll go home in a bit,' I said. 'I'm just building up courage for the lorry.' Under normal circumstances, I'm quite fond of my lorry. She's a challenge. Defective power steering and the acceleration of a slug. Just at that particular moment, I didn't need any extra challenges.

'Well then, go outside.' Nina slid the knife into the belt loop of her rubber apron and crossed the room towards me. 'Kellen, if you go any whiter, you'll vanish into the walls. Go outside, get some fresh air, get a coffee and go home.'

'Not yet.' The angled steel of the doorframe dug into my spine as I stood upright. 'I've never seen the insides of a horse before. I might not get another chance.'

She looked at me carefully. Her brows are much darker than her hair, almost black. Her eyes were level and clear. No nightmares in sight. Just the familiar quirked smile. And more understanding than I would have expected.

'There wasn't anything you could have done, Kellen,' she said.

'I could have called you.'

'He was infected. I wouldn't have come.'

'Somebody would have done.'

'The only one who was free was Mo.' She tipped her head to one side. 'I don't think she needed to be there.'

'No.' *You do anything you possibly can to make sure that the relatives aren't there to see it.* 'No. She didn't need to be there.'

Nina hefted her knife again, considering. 'If you want to drive home,' she said, 'I'll lend you my car.'

'I don't want to go home.' Not yet. I don't want to have to explain to Sandy Logan that we lost the filly he spent the last eleven months planning for. A few hours more and he'll be out with the horses. Then I can simply go home and go to bed.

'If you say so.' She held out the writing pad. 'In that case why don't you put on an apron and come and help scribe. If you really want a close-up view of horse guts, you won't get a better chance than this.'

The post-mortem room is white-tiled and sterile, not unlike theatre. Unlike the theatre, it smells of formalin and glutaraldehyde and death which, oddly, made it easier to handle. I have no hidden memories of autopsies past and, in any case, there are no similarities at all between the delicate art of a human forensic dissection and its veterinary equivalent except possibly the endless rows of specimen jars and the pathological need to label every tissue sample in tedious, repetitive detail.

Veterinary pathology is educated butchery, pure and simple. One step up from the Middle Ages when the kill was paunched before they slung it between two ponies and carried it home. The only difference between then and now is the technology available for the paunching. They still use a knife to open into the abdomen and free up the intestines like they always did but now they have a circular bone saw to slice through the sternum.

I stood well out of the way while Nina Crawford, a surgeon who lectures students annually on the necessity of careful tissue handling, power-cut a line down the breastbone and then angled inwards across the left side of the rib cage. Fragments of bone dust and liquefied particles of intercostal muscle sprayed finely out over a radius of about four feet. When she had finished, a neat rectangle of thoracic wall toppled out into the tub at her feet.

She discarded the power tools in favour of the knife, reached her hand in through the gap in the chest wall and drew an organ up to the surface. 'OK, this is what we're after.' She made a long, linear cut the way one would open a melon and peered closely at the results. 'Heart. Left ventricle: congested. Petechiation on both surfaces.'

I wrote to her dictation. When I looked up, she was holding out an offering on the point of her knife. I caught the small cube of tissue in a jar, flooded it with formalin and wrote the label. 'That doesn't sound too healthy.'

'It's not. It's classic, non-specific endotoxaemia, just like all the rest.' She handed me a syringe full of blood, the needle bent over near the hub to form a temporary seal. 'That's from the right ventricle. Keep half for culture, half for routine bloods. Unless this is some wild freak of nature, the path lab will come back with a diagnosis of peracute cardiac arrest with circulating endotoxins and then the cretins in Microbiology will run every test they've got and tell me there are no pathogenic microorganisms.'

'You mean there is no E. coli?'

'No. I mean our micro crew have two neurones to share between them and they don't synapse often. It's there. No question. I have horses dying of endotoxic shock. And the endotoxins all type for a pathogenic E. coli. We just can't find it. We can't find anything that kills it, either.' She stuck her knife into the thorax and left it standing there. 'Bastards.'

I wouldn't want to be a microbiologist if the cultures came up negative on Monday morning.

Bacteriology was never my strong point. The bits I remembered were not entirely comforting. 'Nina . . . ?'

'Mmm?' She had turned back to the open thorax.

'This is beginning to sound unpleasantly like the veterinary equivalent of MRSA.'

'Not far off.' She nodded, distantly. 'Except this one's specific to the surgery department. To me.'

'Oh. Good.'

I don't think so. MRSA is not the kind of thing you would choose to say out loud in a hospital, even as a joke. MRSA. Methicillin-resistant staphylococcus aureus. Staph. aureus is ubiquitous. Everyone carries it. You can grow it off your skin if you feel so inclined. Most of the time it's pretty harmless. It's only vicious when you take it into a hospital and feed it up on every antibiotic you've got until it can eat each and every one of them for breakfast. Then it kills people. Fast. They close down entire hospitals for this sort of thing.

And this is E. coli. Which is worse.

'What about the staff, Nina? E. coli hits people as hard as it hits horses.' It's another ubiquitous one although you'd grow it from a faecal culture rather than from your skin. Most of the time it's fairly harmless too. But if you get the right strain, it kills people with no effort at all. Even before you've beefed up its resistance. I've read reports of E. coli deaths. I don't particularly want to be one of them.

'Not this one, it doesn't.' She levered a lobe of lung to the gap in the ribs and drew the knife down one side. Bubbles of blood-pink foam gathered on the cut surface.

'Terminal pulmonary oedema,' she said. I wrote it down.

She pushed her knife into the foam. Amusement flickered darkly through the professional shell. 'It's species specific, Kellen. If it wasn't, we'd know about it by now.'

Curiously, that doesn't make me feel any better.

She turned round, a small blob of blancmange-lung balanced on the blade of her knife. 'Left cranial lobe,' she said. Swirls of colour and small, red-lined bubbles spun through the formalin as it settled on the base of the specimen jar. I wrote the label and sat the jar in the row with the others. She was still looking at me when I turned back to the horse.

'Kellen, listen to me. We've been living with this for

six months now. We've run every test we know how to
run. It affects horses and only horses. And only horses
that have been in theatre which means there has to be
some kind of haematogenous spread. We didn't quaran-
tine the first two because we didn't know what we'd got
and there was still no spread to any of the other animals
in the ward. We had three sheep, a goat and a half-dead
Charolais calf in the ward the week it first hit and it
didn't touch any of them. It didn't even get the horses in
the next box.'

'But you made Steff shower twice before you let her
in theatre with the mare. She was washing her hair with
Hibiscrub when I was in the changing rooms.'

'I know. And you and I are going to shower before
we go and see your mare and foal. For exactly the same
reason. I'm not about to take any chances. But you have
to believe me, we've been through the mill with this one.
If nothing else, we have sixty-three final-year students to
take care of. Public Health would've shut us down by
now if there was the slightest risk of zoonosis.'

She turned back to the horse and lifted a lobe of
liver. Whatever it told her triggered another thought.
There was a kind of flat ache in her eyes when she
looked up. A memory of the week just gone. 'Your
mare's been under the knife in theatre and she may get it
yet,' she said. 'You knew the risk when you brought her
in. But you and I and the foal are all safe. I promise you
that.'

'It's OK,' I said. 'I believe you.' And I did.

We finished soon after that. Fragments of liver,
spleen, pancreas, left and right kidneys and five anatomi-
cally distinct sections of gut joined the lung and heart in
jars in the sample rack. The spinal cord and the brain,
being more difficult to get at, were left to the real professionals. We washed him, inside and out, with the power

hose and then slid the hoist and the bulk of his body slowly along the paired ceiling tracks into the vast floor-to-ceiling freezer that takes up the whole of the far end of the room. During term time, the place is a repository for everything that dies—endless fodder for student teaching. On the first Saturday after the end of term, it was well-nigh empty although I still counted the bodies of four different species stacked up against the side wall like so much firewood, awaiting Monday morning's pathology round with the eternal patience of the dead.

It took a while to get him where she wanted and to label the tubs of organs. There was frost forming on his eyelids by the time we were ready. Mine felt much the same. Scrub suits, even two of them, are not a match for a freezer set to minus fifteen. Nina, who had the forethought to wear overalls, looked at the white ends to my fingers and grimaced.

'You can have a hot shower,' she said, 'and a coffee. Then you can either talk to your new arrival or go home to bed. Your choice.'

'I'll think about it when my brain's defrosted.'

'OK.' She held the door while I walked past her into the frosted air of the dawn. 'You can have the first shower.'

The door sealed shut behind us with the solid finality of a tomb.

The staff common room is on the first floor of the old block, lodged between the library and the Dean's office. It was designed in the days when the university still had money to spare and believed in pandering to the greater dignity of academia. The walls are panelled, the chairs are large and well padded and the carpets have, miraculously, survived several decades of veterinary footwear

relatively intact. The crowning glory is a wide bay window with glorious leaded lights that must once have
granted the professors and dons of the Faculty an unim-
peded view of the vast acreage of Garscube Estate. Now
that the various planning deals have rendered the acreage rather less vast, it simply offers a better-than-average
view over the eight-foot-high, wire-topped wall on to the
manic piece of dual carriageway that links Anniesland to
Bearsden, and beyond that, into the rabbit warren of a
housing estate that is the focal point for most of the local
drugs trade. For all that, it is still a useful vantage point
from which to watch the rest of the hospital.

I was huddled on the floor in front of the night storage
heater trying to keep warm when the first of the blue
flashing lights blared past. The second, viewed from the
window, proved to be a fire engine, as did the third. The
officers' tender screamed past just as Nina came back in.
She was damp and scrubbed and her hair was wet again
and she looked very much the same as she had done the
last time I saw her step out of a shower. The spark of life
that held her through the night had snuffed out the moment we closed the door to the freezer room and what
replaced it was more exhausted than any human being
has any right to be and still stay standing.

'You need a coffee,' I said. The thought of the acrid
muck from the machine made my throat cringe but the
principle was sound.

'No. If I drink any more coffee I'll go into orbit.' She
took a bottle from the fridge, green with a tartan label
and a daft cartoon of a Highland cow. 'I've got this.
Twice the magnesium and half the nitrates of the stuff
that comes out of the tap. Probably has a wider range of

oestrogens, too, but they don't bother to put that on the label.' She held out the bottle. 'Want some?'

You're joking. 'I'll live without.' Last time I drank plain water I was in a bed with a gunshot wound in my shoulder and two medics, two police officers and an organic chemist all trying to dictate the good of my health. I haven't drunk it out of choice ever since.

'Thought not.' She drank, straight from the bottle and then slid quietly down the side of the radiator to sit at my feet with her knees pulled up to her chin and her head on her arms. A wave of lemongrass and ginger washed past me, caught on the up-current of the radiator. Pleasantly peaceful.

'You can sleep at the cottage if you don't want to drive back.' Her voice came, muffled, through layers of green cotton scrub suit.

'Mmm. Thank you.'

A police car burned past in a hurry to be wherever the fire engines had been going. I craned my head round the corner in time to see it indicate right across the dual carriageway and then vanish from sight. A haze of blue smoke hung over the river, right at the edge of my field of view.

Squeezing in between the heater and the window gave me a wider angle of view. I followed the trail of the smoke back and down towards the valley. A flicker of blue showed through the trees, mapping the path of the panda car. I drew a sketch map in my head, trying to work out where the horse ward lay in relation to the library. The blue light stopped somewhere behind a bank of rhododendron near the river, about five hundred yards from the ward. The smoke turned from blue to grey. Black fragments floated clear on the breeze.

'Nina?'

'Mmm?'

'Nina. I think . . .'

She came slowly to her feet, as if the act of standing required a lot of forward planning. 'What are you . . . ?'

I felt the warmth of her behind me, felt her see the smoke, felt the nightmare ignite.

'I think it's the cottage,' I said.

She was out of the room before I finished the sentence.

■■■■■

'I never lock the door.'

Nina sat beside me on the stone trough by the garden wall. Her gaze flickered back and forth across the smouldering hulk of her home. Whatever she was watching wasn't in any reality I recognised. Her pupils were wide. Very wide and very dark and she made no effort at all to hide them. She shook all over in a steady, fine tremor.

'Never,' she said. 'Any time, any day. Unless I go away for longer than a weekend. I never lock the back door.'

She delivered it slowly, one syllable at a time, the way you might lecture the first-year students when they're right on the verge of failing exams and need the basics spelled out in black and white.

Or the way you might speak when the nightmares are all spilling over into reality and your hold on language is slipping.

You would have to have known her a long time to tell the difference.

Neither of the officers of the law towering over us had known Nina for any length of time. They had, in fact, made no effort at all to move beyond the basic facts of her gender and marital status. Single woman. Mid-thirties. Lives alone. What else could you possibly need to know?

The younger of the two, the one with the modified East End accent, slipped off his jacket and slid it on to Nina's shoulders. She continued to shake, but less visibly.

He crouched down at the side of the trough, his hands folded loosely across his chest. Soft, pen-pusher's hands with bitten nails. 'That's not very safe, miss,' he said. East End Glaswegian sounds very odd if you try to make it easy on the ear. Like a duck with blocked sinuses. 'There's lads across the road there you wouldn't want in your home at any time of the day or night.' He favoured her with a twinkle from a pair of baby-blue eyes. The knowing, streetwise twinkle he saves for the girls in the typing pool, the ones who were still young enough to be impressed by a hard East Ender in uniform. 'What about the window?' he asked. 'I suppose you didn't close the window either?'

She shook her head. 'I left the cottage at two-thirty this morning to attend to a case.' She said it in the same steady monotone. 'I did not close the window.' Beside me, her nails fractured on the edge of the trough.

Baby-Blue made a note and then tapped the tip of his pen to his lips, thinking it through. 'And there's nothing missing inside?' His jacket hung warmly around Nina's shoulders.

'Not that I can see.'

'But a lot of stuff damaged,' he twinkled again, more gently, 'which is a pity, you see, because this is going to cost the insurance people a lot of money.' His hand shifted on to her knee. 'It really would have been a good idea to lock the doors when you left, Dr Crawford.'

Oh, please.

'I hardly think the state of her doors is your problem,' I said.

He stared at me blankly. I don't think he had even
noticed I was there. The smile hung on his face. His
colleague coughed discreetly and took a step backwards,
distancing himself from the field of conflict. Directly behind him, the back door to the cottage stood open. In
the background, the crews of three fire engines directed
their hoses on the window at the back where her office
had been. Twenty years of back copies of the *Veterinary
Record* clearly burn better than five-hundred-year-old
oak.

I turned back to Blue. The smile hadn't changed but
his hand was no longer on her knee.

'Arson,' I said, 'is a crime. Leaving one's back door
unlocked is a mode of free speech. Only one of these is
your problem.'

His face changed shape. Synapses fired at the back of
his eyes. He lifted his jacket, with care, from Nina's
shoulders.

'Falsifying an insurance claim is also a crime,' he said
softly, and left.

The fire chief was a balding man in his late forties with a
wife and three kids and two decades' experience of hos-
ing people's homes. He knew the fine line between con-
descension and pathos and he trod it with care. He stood
over us and did his best not to abuse the advantage of
height.

'Can I ask a few questions?' he asked.

Nina nodded. Her gaze followed shadows from another dimension that moved from the doorway to the
top window and back again.

He lifted a bucket from the side of the compost heap, knocked the worst of the mud off, turned it over and sat down in front of us. I developed an uncommon interest in the lads jogging in and out of Nina's kitchen and willed myself invisible. He pulled out a notebook, small and black with a corrugated elastic band holding it shut and a gold-nibbed pen tied to the binding.

A very careful man.

'It's very mild for April, Dr Crawford,' he said. 'Do you usually sleep with the electric heater full on?'

Nina stared at him, her mind elsewhere. 'Killer,' she said.

'I'm sorry?' Twenty years of fire work doesn't necessarily prepare you for someone else's hell.

'Killer. My cat. He was on the bed when I left.' She sounded remarkably lucid.

'The window was open,' he said. And then: 'I'll get one of the lads to check.'

She nodded again and I followed her gaze to the bedroom window. Shattered remnants of glass clung to the frame in a square-edged shark's maw. From that distance, there was no sign of cat hair. Or of blood.

The fireman tried again. 'The heater was on,' he said, 'all three bars. It seems odd for the time of year.'

'I never use the heater.'

He closed the notebook and looped the elastic carefully over the end. A signal brought one of his lads at a trot. 'The heater,' he said. The lad nodded. You don't need a wide vocabulary in a fire.

They brought the heater. A simple, three-bar, 2 kW electric heater, melted into a Dali watch with springs for the hands and a misshapen rhomboid for the case. The flex had fractured where the heat and the electric current met and fused; internal and external fire. A lethal combination.

'The heater,' said the chief. 'It was beside your bed. The duvet caught in the coils. The fire spread through the gable loft to the office across the landing where a large amount of stationery and other paper sustained the heat. A down draught spread the flames to the living room. We caught it before the damage spread any further.'

Which means that the kitchen and the bathroom are intact. Except for the back door, of course, which won't keep out the lads from across the road now, with or without a lock.

If this was the farm, I would be in pieces. Some things I could cope with. The loss of my home is not one of them.

Nina spent a while admiring the Dali heater before she looked up. 'I keep it in the shed,' she said equably. 'It was there when I left here earlier this morning.'

He studied her for a while, chewing the edge of his thumb. Then he made a single-line note in the small black book and stood up to leave.

Nina dropped her face to her hands as he stood and for a moment he and I were alone in the garden together.

'We'll come back later,' he said. 'When the shock's had time to settle.'

He smiled. He could have been amused. He could have been furious. He could simply have been tired. You would have had to have known him a lot longer than five minutes to tell the difference. A very professional man.

'Thank you,' I said.

We shook hands. He had a line of sharp-edged calluses along the palm, the after-scars of a lifetime spent axing doors and directing fire hoses. Pushing pens came late in life for this one. He laid his other hand on my shoulder. Heavy but not unduly hard.

'Winding up the officer-on-scene doesn't help,' he said.

Probably not. It's a hard habit to break. 'Should I apologise?'

He smiled, a little sadly and shook his head. His eyes held something that might well have been reproof. 'I think it may be a mite too late for that.'

6

The residents' Lodge is on the top floor at the far corner of the building, almost directly above the small animal ward but two floors up. It has the feeling of a hurried conversion, as if, having created the position of underling, the hierarchy suddenly realised that the appointees might conceivably require somewhere to sleep between nightshifts and someone with rudimentary carpentry skills was sent upstairs to spend the afternoon knocking together a string of spare broom cupboards to make something inhabitable. Which they did. After a fashion. Two broom-cupboard bedrooms sit on either side of a broom-cupboard living room that doubles as kitchen-diner and emergency dog-kennel. The toilets and showers are at the far end of the corridor, presumably because that was the only other spare storeroom available at the time of conversion.

The middle room still shows its heritage. The floors

are unsanded wood covered haphazardly with a scattering of rugs and Vet-Beds. The walls are plaster-board partitions painted in industry-standard magnolia. Marks on the boarding show where generations of residents have plastered posters in an attempt to instil a sense of personality. If you walked into this one, you would know that one of the two occupants collects past advertising hoardings from the Citizens' Theatre while the other has a taste for Stubbs' sketches of equine anatomy. Either one of them could have invested in the 21-inch television that dwarfs the rest of the furnishings.

It is the windows alone that make this place inhabitable. The room is set, diamond-wise, into the corner of the building and has windows on two adjacent sides. The right-hand one overlooks and is overlooked by, the Parasitology building. It has permanent screens up as a deterrent to prying eyes. But the one on the left has a clear view out over the cattle byres, across the lambing pens and on beyond that to the screen of trees that marks the edge of the estate. Looking out of here, you could believe yourself in any one of a dozen rural castles and not right on the edge of Scotland's largest city. It's probably the only thing that has stopped any of the residents of the last twenty years from calling in the university authorities and demanding relocation.

I stood with my shoulder wedged in the corner hugging a mug of fresh coffee to my chest and watched a gang of week-old lambs wage war for rulership of a pile of hay bales stacked at the corner of the lambing pen. Two feet behind me, Steff Foster juggled a pair of pans above the single, reddened ring of a bed-sit cooker. Flavoured steam filtered across the room. If I thought about it, I could put a name to the thyme and the coriander and the overtaste of hot butter. The rest blended to something more subtle with a warm, mid-Asian tang.

There was a rustle of movement and one of the pans hissed steam in the sink that stood between the cooker and the door. The second followed it. Steff walked past me with two plates and a handful of cutlery. Omelettes. Very nice-looking omelettes at that. I'm not overly keen on eggs these days but I think by then I would have eaten rat-bait and been happy with it. If I bothered, I could probably have counted the hours since I last slept. I couldn't begin to count how long since I last ate anything you could call a decent meal.

Steff laid the plates on either side of a low table that sat in front of the television. She pulled a couple of cushions from a pile in the corner and tossed them on to the floor, sinking down cross-legged on to the one further from the windows.

'Breakfast?' she offered. And then, because I didn't move: 'I'm sorry, we don't have any chairs.'

I noticed. If you added chairs to this room, there would be no room for the people. It's hardly a problem. 'What about Nina?' I asked. 'We could wait a while longer.'

She paused, her fork halfway to her mouth. 'My mother brought me up not to waste food,' she said succinctly. 'You might be able to make omelettes that keep for days at a time. Mine don't.'

'You think she'll take that long?'

'I don't know.' She shrugged. 'You probably know her better than I do, but I'd say she'll keep going till nightfall or until she finds him. Whichever comes first.'

Which was more or less what I was thinking. 'Then we ought to go down and help.'

'I wouldn't recommend it.' She looked up at me then, and smiled. A dry smile with something close to the quirked edge of her superior. 'There's one clear rule of healthy living around here: don't get between a cat and its mother. Not that cat anyway.'

It's astonishing the number of people who don't get on with that cat. 'I don't think he's ever actually killed anyone.'

'Not that she's letting on. But on the other hand, if he's snuck off into the woods, he won't come out for anyone but her. Going down to help won't earn you any favours.'

Probably not. If I was less tired, I would have worked that out on my own. I sat down on the spare cushion and picked up a fork. Steff leaned over and fired a remote control at the television. 'I videoed *ER*,' she said. 'Essential viewing.' And that, effectively, rendered us both silent.

I got rid of the television the day after Caroline left. Three years of freedom from the box does odd things to your appreciation of modern culture. I watched for a while and then, when my knees and my mind couldn't take any more, I stood up and finished the rest of the omelette by the window watching while the livestock down in the paddocks made up their own ad-lib soap. We followed up with blueberry crumble. And then coffee. The video ended and whined through its rewind. Three different lambs had held the fort by the time we finished. There was still no sign of Nina.

'She'll crack if she keeps going like this.' I said it quietly, to the lambs, to the sky, to myself.

'Some of us have been thinking that for the past six months,' said Steff Foster from the floor. 'She hasn't yet.'

'She needs sleep,' I said. 'And she has nowhere to go.'

'She needs to get rid of the jinx more than that,' said her resident. 'And she needs to find something to live for outside of work before she drives herself into the ground. Or someone.'

'She had Matthew,' I said. 'It didn't help.'

'She didn't have Matthew. He had her. There's a difference.'

Isn't there just.

Steff sat on the floor. The windows cast overlapping shadows on her face although I doubt if proper light would have made her any easier to read. For someone who came into the picture almost halfway through a four-year relationship, Stephanie Foster had a particularly astute sense of its dynamics.

'Did Nina tell you that?' I asked.

'No. She didn't have to. It was obvious.' And then: 'She didn't tell me why she tried to kill herslf, either. You wouldn't like to fill me in, I suppose?'

I wouldn't. 'If Nina wants you to know, she'll tell you.'

'OK. Let me try this.' She leaned over and pulled the video from the slot. Her face slid deeper into shadow. 'She was less than two years out of college and she was working in a two-man practice with a rising caseload where the boss has a reputation for taking two months off every summer. I would guess she had a bunch of horses die while she was on her own and she decided she was responsible. Is that close?'

Frighteningly so. 'You can't ask me that, Steff. You'd have to ask Nina.'

'I did.'

'What did she do?'

'She walked out of theatre.'

'Then I'd say you have as much of an answer as you're ever going to get.'

'Maybe. But if I'm right, Kellen, then we aren't too far

off a repeat prescription. I don't think she'll blow it a second time.'

And that, too, was frighteningly close. She smiled thinly, and leaned over to tug at the door. Two flights down, a light tread sounded on the stairs. Steff turned back to me, her face clear now, in the light, her grey eyes fixed hard on mine. The jewellery seemed oddly still. 'Think about it, Kellen,' she said. 'She can only take this kind of pressure for so long. Something has to give in the end. I think we'd all rather it wasn't her.'

'Right.'

I'm sure we would. But I have no idea at all what I am supposed to do about it.

The footsteps reached the top landing, heading for the Lodge. Steff stood in one fluid movement, and reached forward to open the door. 'She's found him,' she said.

'No she hasn't.' Nina stood framed in the doorway, her face a study in ash and mud, her clothes beyond reasonable repair. Light fell into the dark wells of her eyes and never returned. In one hand, she carried an empty green, plastic bottle. The other hand was simply empty. She carried no cat.

'I don't think I can . . .' She stepped forward and sank, suddenly, at the knees. We moved, both of us, and caught her as she fell. Laid her out on the floor by the table.

'What now?' asked Steff.

She needs sleep. And she has nowhere to go.

'If I can get enough coffee on board to manage the lorry,' I said, 'I can take her back to the farm.'

'No. You're no more fit than she is.' She pulled open a door on the far side of the room. Beyond it, a double bed took up the entire floor space of the converted

broom-cupboard bedroom. 'Jason's away at Congress.'
She pulled at a crumpled duvet and spread it out across
the bed. 'Matt paged me just before you got here. We've
got a cocker with a spinal disc coming in right about
now. We'll do a myelogram at the very least. If it goes to
theatre, I'll be out of here for most of the afternoon so
there's a room free for each of you if you don't want to
share. We can sort something more permanent this evening.'

'Fine.'

We laid Nina on Jason's bed, washed the ash off with
damp kitchen towels and changed her into a T-shirt of
Steff's. Steff's pager sent her messages of dogs in need
and she left us. I was just about awake enough to take
my shoes off before I fell, fully clothed, on to her bed.

————

'No . . . You have to listen . . . I didn't mean . . .
Please . . .'

'Nina. Nina. It's me. Kellen. I'm here. It's all right.'

'I can't . . . Kellen . . . you can't . . . please don't . . .
no . . . GET AWAY!'

'Shhh. Don't shout. I'm here. You're safe. Whatever it is,
you're safe. I promise.'

'No . . . Kellen. I didn't . . . Jesus Christ can you not
just leave me alone . . . please . . . please . . . leave
me . . .'

Her eyes are open. Wide, wide open. Totally black. In
broad daylight, with a light on by the bed, still they are black.

Her fingers are twisting the sheets. Knotting them. Tearing them. Using them as a shield. From the light. From me.
From whatever it is that is eating her soul.

We'll have to replace the sheets. Jason's sheets.

God alone knows when these sheets were last
washed . . .

'Nina, please listen. You . . .'

'Get AWAY!'

'Kellen? What's up?'

I should have taken her back to the farm. I should have had another coffee and braved the lorry. I should have had the sense to take a taxi. I should have borrowed her car. Anything to get her away from the hospital. Absolutely anything to stop her falling into the pit right in the middle of a working day with people three floors down. People she works with, who have never seen the inside of Hades. People who never need to know.

'Kellen? Are you all right?'

'I'm fine.'

Hell extends another tentacle. Beckons from somewhere a foot in front of her eyes. Grasps tight in a loving, fertile, crushing embrace.

'NO!'

The sheet tears. A single straight line down the centre.

She is off the bed and by the window. Anything could happen.

I had no idea it was this bad.

'Kellen, what's happening in there?'

'Steff? I think I might need help. She's trying to break out of the window . . .'

I have had less than three hours' sleep. It is over four days since she last had an unbroken night. One of us has to stay sane.

I'm just not sure I can do it on this little sleep.

'Jesus. How long does this go on?'

'I don't know, Steff. Just hold her. Please? Can you? Just hold her and don't let her go.'

■■■■■■

'Kellen?'

'Mmm?'

'What time is it?'

How the hell should I know? 'Eight o'clock.'

'It can't be eight o'clock, it's dark.'

'So my watch is lying.' I don't care.

'Can I look?'

'Mmm.'

A hand takes my wrist and stretches it out from under the pillow. A light switches on. Bright. I don't need
that. I need dark. And more sleep.

'You were right. It's eight o'clock. We've slept right
through.'

Marvellous. 'Go back to sleep.'

The light dies. Dark, blessed dark, returns. There is
rain muttering on the windows. Not enough to stop me
sleeping. The sheets smell of sweat. Age-old sweat. And
lemongrass. Very peaceful.

I need a drink but I can't be bothered to get up. I
could dream of drinking. Drinking rain, big drops of
rain. Big enough to swim in . . .

'Kellen?'

'Mmm?'

'I think I'm bleeding.'

'*What?*'

My hand found the light. Neither of us needed that.
Nina lay beside me in one of Steff's T-shirts, three sizes
too large. It came halfway down her thighs. Almost decent. Decent enough. There were marks on her palms
where her nails had dug deep and a long cut on her right
forearm that looked as if she had tried to gouge out the
scar with a blunt penknife. In reality she used the broken
glass from the tumbler that was sitting on the windowledge by the bed but the effect was much the same. I
thought Steff had glued it with wound glue. Clearly, it
didn't work. We should have dressed it at the time. I
can't remember why we didn't.

'Here. Let me look.' There wasn't as much blood as it looked on first sight. Thin beads weeping in places where the glue wasn't holding. A trail of red commas on the sheet.

A loose-weave bandage and a VetWrap sat on the bedside table, courtesy of Steff. Between us we made a reasonable bandage.

'We'll have to change these sheets,' she said.

'We'll have to change them anyway.' I showed her the rent in the sheet.

She bit her lip and looked at the tear. At the bandage on her forearm. At the bruises on her other arm where Steff had held her still, to stop her throwing herself out of the window. Steff, who walks on eggshells because she has a grip that could fracture bone and knows it.

'I'm sorry,' she said.

I should hope so. 'How often, Nina? How often is it like this?' I was angry. More than I had reason to be. But I was also a lot more worried than I had ever been about her state of mind.

'Not often. Not until now.'

'What do you mean?'

'This is the second time in two days. I was out of it when you came to the cottage the other night. That's why I came home.'

'Jesus Christ, Nina . . .'

'Don't, Kellen. I said I was sorry.'

'Why didn't you tell me?'

'Do I have to tell you everything?'

There's no answer to that. I just lay on the bed and stared up at the ceiling and wondered what else there was that I didn't know. And why.

I turned over, eventually, when the anger had passed and lay on one side so that I could see her properly. 'I'm supposed to be here to help, Nina.' I said it quietly, because it was late and it was dark and the walls are plasterboard with a broken layer of posters. 'I'm not going to tell you to give up work.'

'I know.' She lay still, facing me across the pillow, the sheet tucked under her armpit. Her hair, dry now of sweat, sprung across the pillow in bronze knots. Her eyes were walnut brown with pupils that spun down to pinheads in the dim light of the bedside lamp. 'But you're on your own there and if I tell you all of it, I might not be able to keep pretending to everyone else that I'm all right.'

'Someone has to know what's going on.'

'Maybe.' She shrugged, a half-centimetre lift of a shoulder into the pillow. We waited, both of us, while she thought that one through.

'There isn't much you don't already know,' she said eventually. 'I've been getting flashbacks, that's all. Classic ketamine flashbacks.'

I really believed we had beaten this.

'Why, Nina? Why has it come back now?'

'I don't know.' She rolled over and propped her chin on one hand so I could see her better. 'Stress, I guess. Lack of sleep. I wonder sometimes if it's hypoglycaemia. It's always worse when I haven't eaten.'

Which is most of the time, these days.

'How long has this been going on? Weeks? Months?'

'Six months.' She thought back. 'Maybe closer to eight by now. Since September, anyway. It only comes on after a long day in theatre. I see things. I hear things. Things that attack, usually . . . things that tell me it's all my fault . . . standard ketamine paranoia. If I get to bed, I have the dreams—you know about the dreams— but I've never passed out before. Never. Not since I was in hospital. Since before I met you.' She turned her wrist over, examining the fingermarks that ran up the length of her tendons. 'They had Velcro ties there. To hold me to the bed.'

'That was because you were injecting air into your drip lines. You weren't trying to throw yourself out of the window.'

'I think I probably would have done if I'd had the chance. There are bits I don't remember when they said I was pretty violent. But I knew what I was doing with the air.'

Christ.

Nina was the first of my suicides and I did some serious research before I ever agreed to take her on. I read her case notes from cover to cover, all sixty-odd pages of hospital handwriting. Then I took the junior psychology registrar out for six pints in the Man and pumped him for all the relevant details, the ones they hadn't committed to paper, so that, afterwards, I thought I had some kind of idea what I was working with.

The case notes were brutal and to the point. Nina Crawford tried three times to kill herself. On the first attempt, she ruined her arm. On the third, she nearly drained herself of blood. But it was the second time, the one in between, that was the most desperate and by far the most frightening. On the day after her admission to hospital, the day after they cut all her hair off for the scan, the young Nina Crawford sat up in her bed and bled a 50 centimetre column of air into the drip line feeding her left cephalic vein. She was watching it slowly edge its way through the catheter when a staff nurse came to see what it was that was holding her attention for so long. Then they panicked, shifted her to ICU for the rest of the night and had round-the-clock shifts waiting for an arrest that never happened.

The case discussion at ward rounds the next morning was alive with debate as to whether she had got a big enough volume of air into the line to create a fatal pulmonary embolism. The physicians went into a huddle in the corner, wrote formulas on the backs of envelopes and decided that, if the whole lot had gone in, she would probably have succeeded in killing herself. The psychologists fought over the authorship rights to the case study. The pathologists would have killed for the chance to examine the body.

According to the registrar, the general consensus was that if she had succeeded, it was probably one of the most painful ways to die imaginable and that she must have known that.

'I thought you were out of it when you tried with the air?' I said. I spent all of the past seven and a half years believing that she was still high on the morphine and ketamine from the original death-wish cocktail. I wanted quite badly to continue to believe that.

'No.' She shook her head, her eyes on the smaller scar on the back of her hand where the hospital drip line had gone in.

Christ.

'Kellen?' She put a hand on my shoulder. Lightly, on the scar. Her touch was warm and dry and firm and nothing at all like the scratching, screaming demon of earlier.

'What?'

'That was seven years ago. I was different. I am different. I don't want to die now, Kellen. Absolutely. Whatever it is that I hear in the dreams, whatever I see, when I'm out of the dream, I want to live. You have to believe that. Of all people, you have to believe in me.'

'I do.' I wouldn't be here otherwise. Of all people, I need to believe that.

'Nina . . .' I folded the pillow tighter under my

head, '. . . if I ask you a question, a therapy kind of question, will you give me an honest answer?'

'I'll try.'

'When you were dreaming, completely dreaming, you looked at me as if I was trying to kill you. Was I?'

She thought about it. Closed her eyes and drifted back to the border-lands. The planes of her face changed the way they change in the consulting room. Her fingers on my shoulder tightened. We don't touch in the consulting room. We don't share a bed in the consulting room. Things are different there.

Her eyes moved behind closed lids. Like REM sleep but faster, less rhythmic.

'Nina? What are you seeing?'

She flinched.

'There are horses. Again. Still. These ones are big. Bigger than Branding Iron. With teeth like mink. And they're hunting in packs. Like dogs.'

'Hunting you?'

'Yes.' Her head was jammed back against the pillow, her neck rigid. Her closed eyes scanned a slow semi-circle. Watching.

The paranoia of ketamine. Vivid and real.

'Am I here?'

'Yes. It's your pack. You're the hunter. You're driving them on and you . . . shit . . . I'm sorry, I can't stay . . .'

She opened her eyes, snapped back to the present. Sweat ran along the line of her collar bone. Tremors ran in waves down her body, shivering the fine cotton of Steff Foster's T-shirt.

'It was you, Kellen. You as you are now. Everything else is weird. Surreal. Distorted. Blown up out of all proportion. But you were . . . just you.'

Hell.

'Why, Nina?'

'Because I killed Rain.'

'You didn't kill Rain. You haven't killed Rain. She's still alive.'

'In the dream, I killed her. I didn't mean to, but she was dead and it was my fault. You knew that.' She looked past me at something out in the night darkness beyond my head. 'You and the horses.'

Her arm lay across the pillow beside my head. I took her hand and held it in much the same way the fire chief had held mine outside the cottage. So that she would know that I meant what I said.

'Nina. The mare might die. We both know that. And if she does, it won't be your fault. I brought her here. I asked you to cut. It was my choice and my risk. If she dies, there is no one to blame but me.'

'I know.'

I have heard her sound more convinced.

■■■■

We dozed then, I think. I did, anyway. When I woke again, her eyes were resting on the scar at my shoulder and the fingers of her free hand traced the twisted tissue. A long-sided triangle, like a butterfly wing that stretches from below my ear down over the top of my collar bone and back up to the top of my arm. The product of a gunshot wound with overlying secondary infection.

'I didn't know you had your own scar,' she said.

Some things I don't advertise. 'It's more recent than yours.'

'But you don't show it. You told me I should show mine.'

'No. I simply suggested you didn't need to plan your entire wardrobe around covering them up. This is different. I'd have to be half naked to show mine.'

'True.' Her smile strayed into a small frown, the way it does when she's gone somewhere else. Her hand stayed where it was. 'I thought there were rules,' she said, pensively, 'about sleeping with clients.'

There are. Absolutely. The boundary between acceptable, constructive support and unacceptable abuse of trust is well defined. I know exactly where it is. With Nina, I have always known. A distinct, luminous line, hovering somewhere in the middle distance. Not ever quite close enough to matter.

Right now, I could reach out and touch it.

'You were hallucinating,' I said, 'and dangerous. I wasn't about to leave you alone. If it's going to be a problem, I can move next door till the morning.' There's no bed and no bedding but I expect we can find something.

'I don't think it'll be a problem.' Her hand moved then. Moved in a circle that had nothing to do with the scar. Lit up incandescent fires in its wake. Fired panic beyond anything I have ever known.

The line became a circle. A ring. Snapped into place around the bed.

I caught her hand and pushed it back to the pillow. Rolled over to see her eyes and found a dry, knowing laughter.

The fires caught light and burned of their own accord.

'Nina, no. I can't. We can't. You know that.'

'And if I wasn't a client any more?'

'But you are.'

'I don't think so. We can't keep crossing the lines like this, Kells. One minute I'm the client and you're the professional, the next, it's the other way round. We can't keep going like this. It's too confusing. Neither of us is handling it. We have to stop. Now.'

She rolled over, her wrist still held by my hand. Her knee pushed between mine, slid upwards.

I stopped breathing.

'Nina. No.'

I let go and turned over. She moved in behind me. Her teeth grazed the top of my shoulder, by the scar. Bit harder. I was not wearing one of Steff Foster's T-shirts. I wasn't wearing anything at all. Big mistake. I felt the length of her body press against mine, her hand snaked forward, reaching, exploring.

'No.' I pulled away. Swung my legs off the bed and sat up.

All I could hear was her breathing. Steadier than mine.

There was a glass of water on the windowledge by the bed. I drank all of it, without pausing for breath.

Her eyes followed me. Dancing, burnished walnut, intense and intent.

'I'm not playing games, Kellen.'

'Neither am I.'

'So then why not?'

Because you are straight and I am not.

Because whether you like it or not, you are still a client and always will be and for all of my life I have despised therapists who abused their position with their clients.

Because we are in the residents' quarters in the middle of your place of work with, for all we know, your resident next door and your ex-fiancé downstairs and if Matt comes in and finds us like this, whatever you see in your nightmares will be nothing compared to what happens next.

Because if I say just one of these, we will have crossed the line beyond all chance of ever returning and I'm not going to do that.

'We just can't,' I said.

Her arms wrapped round my waist, her chin on my shoulder, resting on the scar. Her breath sang in my ear.

'Kellen,' she said. 'It's two o'clock in the morning. There is no one here but Steff and she's asleep. I have just taken myself off your client register. I will not, ever, I promise you, come to you again for therapeutic advice. All you have to do now is close your eyes, lie back and try, just once in your life, to let go and enjoy what's happening.'

'I can't.'

'You can, Kells. Really. You can.'

And because I was tired, because I was half-asleep, because I was stupid and I wasn't thinking, because it was three years since Janine left and Nina's hands were lighting up fires I hadn't felt since Bridget—and because she was there, I did.

The world filled with lemongrass and ginger.

It wasn't peaceful at all.

I'm not used to waking up beside a lover and feeling as if the world has caved in.

I'm not used to treading through breakfast as if I was treading on landmines, waiting for the fabric of reality to shatter around me.

I'm not used to censoring every wash of feeling before it lights fuses I can't contain.

Steff made breakfast of pancakes with lemon juice and maple syrup and fresh-ground coffee. Said it was a tradition for Sunday morning breakfast in the residents' Lodge.

I stood by the window staring out at empty fields and I tasted sawdust and river water.

Steff passed me a tray with a second pancake. 'You

two look wrecked,' she said, as if she noticed these
things on a regular basis. 'You need to go back to bed.'

I don't think so.

It's Sunday morning and I have to go into work tomorrow and find out if I can, with any integrity, continue my career. There is only one person in the world I
talk to about this and she's climbing mountains in Colo-
rado. I don't think I know what to do on my own.

'No. Thanks. I'll have another coffee and then I need
to go home and sort out the rides. We're down one on
the yard staff and Sandy's got the day off. I have to get
back.'

'Sandy Logan?' Nina poured me the rest of the coffee.
Her eyes said things I didn't want to hear. 'He called
your mobile while you were in the shower. He said to
tell you that Kate's back and not to worry about the
rides. He wants to come and visit Rain and the new foal.
He said he'd bring your car and take the lorry back to
the farm for you. I told him you weren't up to driving it
yet.'

And a sixty-three-year-old chronic arthritic is? You're
too kind.

'Thanks.' I concentrated on the coffee, ignored everything else.

The surgeon and her resident looked at each other
across the table, sharing wry amusement. For all I know,
sharing everything else as well.

'Is she always this much fun in the mornings?' asked
the resident.

'Only after she's had eighteen hours' sleep,' replied
the surgeon.

I poured the remains of my coffee down the sink and
left while I still had some idea of what I was doing.

7

My car is probably as much of a challenge to drive as the lorry, although once you've got used to starting in second and keeping your foot on the gas to fool the electric choke into staying alive, it's probably a touch easier to handle on the open road. Sandy Logan drives it with roughly the same degree of enthusiasm as he writes his letters and with every bit as much care.

I was with Rain and her colt, sitting on the grass just inside the gate to the recovery paddock at the side of the wards, feeding Polo mints to the mare, getting to know the foal, trying to get some kind of grip on reality, when he turned into the gateway at the top of the drive, rattled with joint-jarring care over the cattle grid and rolled down into the yard.

My mare circled around me, keeping herself between her foal and the source of dangerous noises until she saw a friendly face emerge and whickered a greeting. The foal followed her lead, snickered something small and throaty and, with the naïve innocence of the infant, trotted over to the paddock rails to say hello.

The old man eased his stiff joints in through the rails and crouched down, the way he always does with foals. He took off his cap and laid it on the grass for the new one to explore. They love his cap, horses. MacDonald believes that he soaks it nightly in herbal mixtures made to recipes inherited from Romany ancestors and there's every chance he's right. Personally, I would say that thirty years of farriery have probably impregnated it with a far more fascinating array of smells than any gypsy grandmother could concoct. Neither of us has yet found it necessary to ask the gnome himself.

The colt was smart, smarter than average. He worked out where the cap came from and left it lying on the grass. Instead, he applied himself to exploring the shining dome of skin with its surrounding rim of coarse cotton-wool hair. If he'd had teeth, he would have bitten anything he could get his jaws round, just for a taste, but he was a good day away from breaking his first milk teeth and so he gnawed with his gums, smearing milky saliva across the bald surface of the gnome's head in random exploration.

I've never seen a human purr before. Sandy Logan purred. Or at least, he let his eyes rest on the colt's chest, tipped his head back against the railings and rumbled something uncommonly feline from the depths of his chest. After a while, he sat up and started moving his hands, very gently running the knotted-hawthorn fingers over the soft chestnut skin, getting the colt used to the alien sensation of the human touch and then, slowly, probing deeper, feeling the muscle and then the bone underneath.

It's the bone that makes a foal what it is. The skin

alters colour often as they age; from chestnut to grey, from dun to roan, from black to white. Muscles and fat come and go with exercise and feeding. The hoofs, when they come from the womb, are soft and have long feathered fronds of silky horn round the edges, protecting the mare from the sharp-edged weapons they form in later life. All these things change. But the bone of the day-old foal tells you what the horse will be if you have the hands and the eyes to read it.

Sandy has both. And a lifetime's experience to go with it.

He explored the full length of the colt, from head to croup, from withers to feet, from the shining white socks to the newmoon star and at the end of it, when he had let the lad amble off to suck from his mother, he sat back beside me against the railings and his eyes shone.

'He's a cracker, so he is.'

He is. Bright and sharp-edged. New from the other side of beyond with the wonder of it still shining on his skin. But the other one carried the magic and she is gone.

'I'm sorry about the filly.' In a night of uncommon guilt, that weighs almost as much as the rest.

'Aye, I can see.' He shuffled round so that he could read my face. If I knew him less well, I would have got up and talked to the mare. I didn't. His eyes read whatever was written on my face. I don't want to know.

'You shouldn't take it to heart, lass,' he said, and if I was kind on us both I could believe he was talking only about the foal. 'It happens. And we've got a cracker of a colt. He'll make a grand wee horse a year or three from now. He'll be a jumper, no doubt about it.'

'But you wanted a filly. For the breeding. We've no use for a gelding.' We don't want jumping horses either. Or at least, it's the first I've heard about it if we do.

'No, no.' He looked shocked at the thought. If I hadn't seen him hold three of his own colts while Ruaridh Innes knocked them over for the knife, I might think he wasn't one for letting a horse lose its testicles. But he's got more sense than that.

'We'll no' be gelding this one. He's too good for that. We've got our very own stallion here, lass. You couldn't ask for more.'

'I can't handle a stallion, Sandy.' There are times when even the mares walk right through me. I've seen stallions and the men who handle them and I admire both unequivocally. I don't pretend that I could ever handle horses that well.

'I know you can't.' He has a nice line in tact. 'I'll handle him for you. And Duncan will help. He's aye been wanting a son of The Lad to carry on the line. I'll not say anything but he'll be wanting to buy this one, you watch. We'll maybe let him have half-shares.' He came slowly out of the haze of his dreams. 'If that's fine with you, of course,' he said.

'Of course.' I wouldn't argue with Sandy Logan's breeding programme for worlds. 'So long as I'm not expected to act as temporary stallion-man when you're both off at some show somewhere.'

'It's a deal.' He spat on his hand and held it out. In three years, I've not cured him of the habit. I've just got more used to it by now. We shook on the deal. He held on longer than I was expecting, as if he could read more of me from the touch of a hand than he could from the lines on my face. 'You need sleep, lass,' he said, finally. 'Suppose we take these horses home and get you to bed?'

I hadn't thought of taking the patients home but, on reflection, the idea had a great deal to recommend it.

The clinicians involved were less enthusiastic. At

least, one of them was, the one that it seemed safest to talk to.

'You can't take her off-site, Kellen. She's less than forty-eight hours away from a midline laparotomy. There's no way she can travel. Absolutely not.'

There are times when I can believe everything everyone says about Stephanie Foster and her lack of human relationship skills. She stood in the doorway to the pharmacy with her arms folded, making full use of her extra four inches and she was not giving any ground.

Personally, I think that just because something isn't in the rule book, doesn't mean you can't at least consider it.

'It's a Sunday,' I said. 'The roads are clear. We'll take it slowly. And she'll have round-the-clock cover at home if we need it. If she shows signs of infection, we'll bring her straight back in, but I would have thought she was a lot safer out of here.'

'They need treatments, Kellen. Both of them. Intravenous antibiotics twice daily for the mare. Intra-musculars for the foal until we check out if his colostrum hit the spot.'

So?

'I'm a medic, Steff. I did my time in paediatrics. If they let me jag babies, I can cope with a mare and foal. Just tell me what and where and when and I'll call you if I have problems.'

'Nina won't let you,' she said flatly.

'So does Nina have to know?'

'What?' She's big and she's very, very blonde and she does know what her height does to people. She sank down to sit on crossed legs. Very slowly. Very gracefully. She put one elbow on her knee and her chin on her hand and she looked at me hard. Then she laughed.

'You guys need to talk,' she said.

No. Not now.

'Maybe later,' I said. 'Just now I have Sandy waiting to load up the lorry. He's been here long enough. He's supposed to be away today. I don't want to waste any more of his time than we have to.'

'Oh, right,' she nodded gravely. 'And he really believes that sitting out there making love to your colt is a total waste of time.' She stood up but she leaned back against the wall so that her eyes were more or less level with mine. 'Sandy's not the only one with better things to do,' she said. 'I haven't been out of here for the best part of three weeks. The boss just said I could go out for the day and I'm not about to have her ground me just because I've let you run off with her star patient. If you want to take your horse, you'll have to ask her yourself. If you're in that much of a hurry, she's in the small animal ward doing morning rounds with Matt and the students. If you want to wait, I guess she'll be up in the residents' Lodge for a coffee in about half an hour.' She blinked. A kind of bilateral wink. Her nasal jewellery flashed. Her smile was nothing but friendly. 'I'll be gone by then,' she said, 'so you can talk to her in peace. I really do think you need to do that.'

On the whole, if I have to see her today, I think I'd rather do it in public.

I was halfway down the corridor when Steff's voice caught me up. 'If you want the ward, it's down at the end on the right,' she called. 'If you want the Lodge, the stairs are on the left. The keys are behind the fire extinguisher across the landing.'

I turned right at the end of the corridor.

███

She was in the ward. I knew she was in the ward before I ever went to talk to Steff Foster. I could have found her,

I think, anywhere in the hospital, from the time I walked out of the Lodge after coffee. At times like this, I have skin like radar. It aches, as if the top surface cells have been stripped off and the ones underneath seek her out in the way that a compass seeks north.

She was standing to one side of the group. The tidy professional with the freshly laundered white coat and the stethoscope. The surgeon, running a clinical eye over the radiographs of a colleague's case: the 'before and after' shots of a German shepherd with a smashed-up body and a lot of metal-work holding it all together. The morning-after lover with the glow that sets everyone else alight even if they don't know why. Nina Crawford. The woman who sets the world on fire. Because she can.

The ward is newly built and has doors that glide without noise. Still, she knew when I slid it open two inches and stepped inside. Matt Hendon knew too, from the change in her. And then the students from the change in him. Dominic grinned as if we shared a secret. The rest looked blank. But they looked all the same. And then Nina cleared her throat and they all turned their heads, if not their minds, back to the bank of X-ray viewers in front of them. A ginger-haired lad in a creased white coat who thought he had just been let off the hook went back to explaining the individual pieces of scaffolding bridging the gaps in the iliac crest. He needed an hour or two in the library with a good book on the anatomy of the canine pelvis and some basic revision of orthopaedic surgery. I slid open a second door and walked through to the kennels area to visit the in-patients.

The shepherd was big and long-coated and it lay in one of the larger kennels near the front looking as if someone with a particularly savage sense of humour had mauled it with a razor. A wide swathe of its abdominal

wall and most of its hind quarters were clipped so close
you could see the clipper-marks on the skin. Two hairless tracks ran down its jugulars and a third ran up the
right foreleg. The left foreleg stuck out sideways, encased
in a synthetic resin cast. If you were feeling charitable,
you could say that it looked like a lion. If you were more
inclined to honesty, you would say that it looked like a
bad parody of a miniature poodle. It's difficult to take a
dog seriously when it's got a haircut like a stuffed toy
and one leg in a cast. If I was the owner of a new-
registration Four Trak, I'm not sure I'd be thrilled with
the X-rays if the surgeon who produced them wasn't
about to glue all the hair back on to my big, bold guard
dog.

I knelt down on the tiles of the floor and the dog
stared out at me through the bars of its kennel like a
drunk on a Sunday morning. I didn't know dogs could
look hung-over but this one managed it. All drooping
eyelids and red conjunctiva and that for-God's-sake-
don't-breathe-so-loud pain in his eyes. A sign above his
head said: 'Care. Kennel guards.' I pushed my hand
through the bars anyway and, when he didn't make an
immediate move to eat me, I dipped my fingers in the
water bowl and drizzled fresh water into the corner of
his mouth. He swallowed it and twitched an eyebrow for
more.

We were halfway to an empty water bowl and closer
than that to a reasonable understanding of life when
Matt came in and stood beside me. The dog focused on
him, swimmingly. I dipped my hand back in the water.
It seemed a safer option than speech.

'He's a nice dog when he's up to his eyes in morphine,' said Nina's ex-financé carefully. 'On a good day,
he'd have your hand off.'

'I thought he might.' Morphine has its uses. I tipped

more water into the waiting maw. The dog swallowed as if its throat hurt. 'Will he do?'

'I think so.' He stood up and lifted the case notes from a rack above the kennel and crouched down beside me. They spend a lot of time crouching, vets. The same way doctors spend a lot of time standing at bedsides.

Matt Hendon can crouch and read and talk and ask oblique questions, all at the same time. 'We spent most of yesterday piling blood into him,' he said, 'while you and Herself were busy sleeping off the effects of the Saturday from hell.' His eyes were on the notes. His tone never faltered. Either he's a very good actor or the man knows less than the resident knows. There's always hope.

He ran his fingers down the most recent page. The one with the overnight clinical record on it. He stopped at a haematology printout. 'His PCV's not as good as I'd like it but he's probably got just about enough oxygen going to his brain to keep him alive.'

His pen is the twin of the fire chief's except that Matt Hendon has his name inscribed on his. He unclipped it from his top pocket and began to write something lengthy on a fresh page. 'If we're lucky, we've cooked his brain long enough to make our overnight change in behaviour more permanent.' He smiled at the dog as if the extra warmth might tip it over the edge into liking people. 'It might not be the morphine after all.'

'It might be my winning personality.'

I open my mouth, sometimes, without thinking.

'It might.' He stopped writing and looked me straight in the eye. He doesn't do that often, Matt. Not since she handed his ring back.

With some people I can be fairly sure of what they can read in the lines of my face. Matt Hendon is one of them. He saw only what I was ready for him to see and he broke the contact before I did.

'Did she get hurt last night?' he asked, eventually.

'You'd have to ask Nina that.' Professional confidentiality. The only shield I've got. Transparent.

'Right.' He snorted, mocking himself, or mocking me, or both. 'That would do me a lot of good.' He closed the notes, stood up and put them back on the shelf. He leant back against the kennel opposite and folded his arms. 'Shall I tell you what I see, Kellen?'

If you must.

'Go on.'

'I see a woman in a white coat who hasn't worn one since the day she finished her PhD,' he said. 'A woman who is keeping both hands in her pockets.'

'Is she?' I would have had to stand up to look through the glass in the door to know if he was right. I would have had to look at her. Just at the moment, I'd rather not.

'She is. She did. Except when she was putting the last of the radiographs up. Then she forgot.' He let frustration show through the rest. 'Steff doesn't do bandages like that and it wasn't me. It couldn't have been her, you can't wind anything like that on your own arm.'

He waited for me to say what he wanted to hear. I said nothing.

'And she has bruises,' he said, 'as if someone has been holding her. Hard.'

Silence can bruise if you let it hang heavy enough.

The shepherd had no interest in the water.

Matt Hendon watched me through green-grey eyes and it was more than lack of sleep that drew the lines on his face.

Two nights ago, this man tried to save my foal. Difficult to believe we are in the same world.

I stood up to walk down the ward, found a cocker spaniel further down the line of kennels that had a neat line of blanket stitch down the middle of its spine.

'Lumbar disc,' said his voice behind me. 'We did a hemilaminectomy on it yesterday.'

'Will it walk again?'

'I expect so.' He took hold of my shoulder and turned me to face him. He's never even shaken my hand before this. 'Kellen. She can't go on like this.'

True.

'I'm not her keeper, Matt.'

'She tried to cut the scar out, once,' he said, and the words came only with effort. 'With a scalpel. Did she tell you?'

'No.'

There was a time when I thought there wasn't anything she hadn't told me.

He watched through the door as she pointed out details of pelvic anatomy to the ginger-haired student. Watched her do his job so that he could come and talk to me. 'It was the holiday on Skye,' he said. 'The second one. I got some Vicryl from the local small-animal practice and stitched it up.' He shrugged. A good piece of surgery. 'Nobody else ever counts the suture scars,' he said. Except her. And him. 'So nobody knew.'

Including me.

They had two holidays on Skye. On the first one, he gave her a ring. On the second, she gave him it back. They each drove home alone after that one. I believed I had heard every moment of that fortnight in endless, repeating detail. But there are things she forgets.

'Was she seeing things when she did it?'

The X-ray viewers were visible from where we both stood. The ginger-haired student picked up a shoulder-bag from the floor and left. Heading for the library. The

other students dispersed. Nina began taking down radiographs. With her right hand. The cuff of her shirt
stayed close to the base of her thumb.

'She was having nightmares,' he said, his eyes on the
back of her head. 'Vicious, savage, self-destructive nightmares. I suppose you could say she was seeing things.'

She put the X-rays in an envelope and turned. Saw
us both through the glass of the door. Smiled. You could
transform a hundred personalities with that.

'She's cracking up, Kellen,' said the man who
thought he had reason to know. 'She won't listen to me.
She won't even listen to Steff any more.' He turned, just
before the door opened and he said, with the honesty of
total desperation, 'All she has left is you. You can't let her
down.'

Two hours later, Sandy Logan and I took Rain and her
colt home with us. It took most of that time to load them
up on to the lorry. Sandy won't have a box-shy horse in
the yard and he was hardly about to make his new stallion's first introduction to transport anything other than
a truly inspiring occasion. In the time it took him to get
everything exactly as he wanted it, Matt and Steff between them managed to find me a spare treatment box
and fill it with everything I could possibly need for
emergency care of the mare and foal. Steff made up a bag
of heparinised saline and showed me, in case I had
somehow forgotten, how to flush an intravenous catheter
and keep it sterile for the next time. Matt gathered together an array of syringes from 1 ml to 20 ml sizes, and
needles for all occasions. He signed out all the necessary
bottles of antibiotics and antiinflammatories and wrote
on each the dose, volume and times of injection for
mother and son. As a parting shot, he produced a record

chart with the names of each horse (Rain and Son of Rain) and filled in the times of the next four injections with boxes for me to tick when they were done. Down at the bottom he wrote three numbers. The first was the emergency number for the Lodge, which meant, effectively, a hot line to Steff. The second was Nina's mobile number, because she had asked and I had promised. The third was the number of his own mobile phone.

'If something goes wrong,' he said, 'call me. I won't be far.'

It was the only comment he ever made on the whole crazy deal.

8

With a particularly poor sense of timing, the horses and I hit the yard right at the height of Sunday lunchtime chaos.

Two separate rides were scheduled to set off at one thirty; the first took a party of Canadians out over the ben to circle the loch and back. The second was a random assortment of Sunday riders going out by the lower route, following the shoulder of the ben round beyond the village and coming out in a patch of native Caledonian forest that sits on the outskirts of Galbraith's farm. Three-hour treks, both of them.

I drove the lorry down the lane just as both strings were mounting up, ready to file out of the yard. Sandy was in there ahead of me, tightening girths, checking stirrups, finding hard hats and sticks of appropriate size for horse and rider from the collection in the barn. My car sat just outside the gate, neatly sandwiched between a yellow hire car and Kate Swan's rusting blue Beetle. Last time I saw Kate, the lass had her left ankle in a fibreglass cast and was doing her best to persuade Sandy that you don't need to be able to walk to muck out stables and lead rides. I was under the impression that Sandy had won that particular battle. I leaned out of the cab in time to see her mount Balder at the head of the second ride. Kate saw me and waved and then spun him in a circle, showing a length of leg encased in a riding boot and no cast. I waved back and she sidled him sideways across the yard to see me. She's very proud of that manoeuvre. When Caroline left, the horse would barely go in a straight line without complaining about it. Since Kate came, he has won two local three-day events and he sweats up with anticipation as soon as he hears her car in the yard.

'Hi.' She stretched across from the saddle and leant an arm on the cab window. 'Heard we got a real cracker of a foal from Rain.'

'So I gather,' I said drily. 'How's the leg?'

'Mended.' Said with the conviction of one who has never seen a radiograph of an eight-week-old lateral malleolar fracture. 'Doctor said I could ride.'

Doctor must have been on something colourful at the time.

'Have you got it strapped up?' I asked.

'Sure.'

Sure. I looked at her boot, hanging close to the stirrup leather. If there was strapping in there, it was extraordinarily thin.

The first string left the yard a bare five minutes late. Someone else took control of Kate's ride, got them lined up into some kind of order and heading out past the duckpond towards the moor. The girl looked up anxiously and Balder stepped sideways towards the gate. I eased the lorry into gear and followed her forwards. 'I was going to put these two in the Hawthorn field,' I said. 'Can you manage not to bring the ride past that way when you come home? I'd rather not have fifteen foreigners feeding them plastic bags unless we absolutely have to.'

'No problem.' She smiled, the kind of relief-ridden smile of the newly released. As if there was any way I might have had the power to stop her riding. We reached the gate together. She leant down from the horse and pushed it open for me to drive the lorry through.

'If you need someone to keep an eye on the pair of them later on,' she said, 'I've got nothing planned for after the ride.'

I stuck up a thumb to let her know I had heard and got an answering wave as she took Balder back at a neat hand canter to catch up with the ride just as it reached the far gate leading out of the farm on to the moorland beyond.

I was twenty-one once. I just didn't have quite the same sense of freedom.

The yard slipped back into peace. I backed the lorry past the house and up through the orchard to the gate at the foot of the Hawthorn paddock. Sandy followed me up and waited as I stopped, ready to hop in through the jockey door and check his new charges.

'Travel all right?'

'Travelled fine.' I moved round to the back to unhook the catches. The dog arrived, called by my voice, and sniffed around as I lowered the ramp on to the grass by the gate. She caught foal-scent and backed off to a safe distance. She gets on well with Rain these days but she's tried herding foals once before and found that maiden mares are less tolerant than they might once have been to the ministrations of a horse-herding collie.

Twenty-four hours and a wash of reproductive hormones
do odd things to your sense of perspective.

Sandy came slowly forward with the mare and foal in
hand. They paused, all three of them, at the top of the
ramp to survey the new domain. An old man with
cramped, arthritic fingers; a soft dun mare with dark
eyes and an eel stripe down her back; a shining chestnut
foal with three white socks and a new moon bright on
his forehead. The colt, with the inborn star's sense of
timing, snuffed the air and whinnied. The same kind of
call he made in theatre the night his sister died. A greeting. And defiance.

A magpie, caught by the spark of bright metal on the
mare's headcollar, hopped on to the roof of the box and
cawed its own welcome. The foal rolled his eyes, showing pink at the edges of the white but he didn't retreat
and after a moment, when the bird didn't move, he took
a step forward, inquisitive and stretched out his neck to
explore the world.

Sandy Logan stood holding the foal slip with the
world alive in his eyes and for the first time in nearly
thirty-six hours I felt the weight of the filly's death lift
from the dark holes in my heart.

If all the rest were to lift as lightly, the world would
be a happy place.

I stepped forward and shoved open the gate to let
them into the paddock. Sandy walked them carefully
down the ridged wood of the ramp and out into the
field, turning them round to face me before he unclipped
the lead rope from the mare and let go of the foal slip.
They both stood for a moment, sniffing the damp April
air, reading the stories through it of the bracken from the
side of the ben and the heather from across the moor and
the sharp, wet smell of sphagnum moss from the bog on
the far side of the hill. Then, with perfect horse-on-horse

communication, they spun round together and trotted up the hill towards the stand of hawthorns at the top that gives the field its name.

Sandy stepped carefully round the soft mud in the gateway and pulled the gate shut. We leant on it together, sharing the short space of peace; the weak April sun and the new buds of the hawthorn, the call of the blackbirds and the harsh answering cackle of the magpie, the sight of the mare and her foal, exploring the first new grass of the springtime under the trees at the top of the hill. The foal shied at the waving shadows of the hawthorn, testing his feet, winding up to a full-blown buck. Beside me, Sandy sucked in a breath, a rare kind of smile lighting his face.

'He'll make you proud of him, that one.'

'If he lives.'

Darkness shadowed the edge of his smile. 'D'you think he'll not?'

'I don't know, Sandy. He's well enough now and Steff checked him over this morning. I don't think he's going to give out on us tonight. But if the mare goes down with whatever the others have gone with, I wouldn't hold out much hope for the foal.'

'But that's why we brought her home.'

'I suppose it is.' And the rest is too complicated to think about now. I turned my back to the field and sat down in the drying grass at the base of the hawthorn hedge. 'It's all we can do. Get her out of the site of infection. That and watch her for signs of it starting. I want a round-the-clock watch for at least the next week. Hourly checks overnight. More if it looks rough. Do you think we can do it?'

'For Rain?' He didn't sit down, his knees wouldn't wear it, but he turned and leant back on the fence so his head was only just above mine. I felt the touch of his hand on my head. 'For Rain and her wee man, Kellen, we can do anything. There's Kate and there's Alec Saunders and wee Jack, who works with Duncan. All three of them are sane and able for a good night up. Between them and you and me, we can see to it that there's one of us here while she needs it.'

'I'll take tonight,' I said. 'We can sort out the rest of the nights after tomorrow. I'll need someone here by the time I have to leave for work.'

'No problem. I'll be here by seven anyway. You talk to Kate when she comes back from the ride. See if she can do some of tonight for you. I'll go off and find wee Jack now. I'll see Alec in the morning when he comes in for the ten o'clock ride. Does that sound OK?'

Very. 'It sounds wonderful, Sandy. But I thought you were going out this afternoon?'

'Aye, well.' He was hoarse, then. Shy, like a child bringing a gift. 'I was going to see a man about a mare. Nothing big. I called him and put it off till next weekend.' His hand fell lightly on my shoulder. Squeezed once through all the tension to the bone. 'I'll be off now. You try and get some sleep when Kate comes back.'

'Thanks, Sandy.'

I watched him walk his bow-legged walk down the path through the orchard to the yard. There's something very pleasant about reliable people. Sandy Logan is so very reliable.

I spent the next couple of hours in the yard. Not for any special reason but that there was no one else there. It's a rare thing to have the place to myself at a weekend in the trekking season and I badly needed some space and time on my own to think. Or not to think. Whichever came easier.

There's a cupboard on the wall in the tack room that we use for storing wormers and the basic drugs that Ruaridh leaves us for the horses. Twenty minutes' work on the clutter inside it made room for the drugs and treatment sheets I'd brought from the vet school. I arranged the various bottles in order along the shelf and then spent a frustrating half-hour hunting down a padlock in the garage; a remnant of the brief period when every gate and doorway on the farm was double locked and rigged with intruder alarms. I don't have enormous faith in padlocks as a way of stopping folk getting at what they want but they're good enough to stop wandering members of the public from opening cupboards and borrowing bottles of penicillin because they want a souvenir of the Campsies and they like the colours on the label. The locals wouldn't do it but the tourists have an odd idea of what's included in the package when they come in to hire a horse for the afternoon. It's one of the more tedious spin-offs of being part of a service industry.

There's an odd kind of refuge in anger. A wilful escape into righteous resentment at the unreasoned and unreasonable and the general unfairness of life. When I came down from the Hawthorn paddock, I was feeling a kind of dead resignation that bordered on peace. By the time I had finished sorting the tack-room cupboard, I was seething. Pissed off to the back teeth with tourists who lift things that aren't theirs. With the Sunday hang-around kids who leave the tack room looking like the fag end of a rave. With Kate, who hadn't bothered to bed down the foaling box when she knew I was coming in with a mare and foal. With Sandy. With Rain. With the foal. With the weather. With the fork I was using to make up the bed in the foaling box. With the bales of

straw that fell off the barrow. With the faulty handle on
the water bucket and whoever it was that should have
fixed it. With the bolt on the door that wouldn't slide
shut when it was all bedded down and I wanted to leave
the box. With the dog who buggered off early and left
me to finish tying up hay-nets all on my own. With
the ducks wandering mindlessly across the yard.
With the bit of angled iron I use to pull off my boots
outside the back door which always, without fail, scrapes
a layer of skin off the inside of my ankle and leaves me
swearing for weeks. With whatever disorganised son of a
motherless camel left the back door open and let all the
heat out of the kitchen. With the unwelcome, unwanted,
unasked-for poacher's assistant of an off-duty police officer who was standing there in my kitchen, leaning back
against my Rayburn, nursing a mug of my coffee with
one hand and teasing the red kittens with the other; who
was dribbling a crumpled ball of Post-it paper across and
across the breakfast bar between their legs as if Sunday
afternoons were made for staying in and drinking coffee
and playing with cats and seducing my dog into a warm
chair by the fire and not bothering even to come out to
the barn and say hello.

Some folk have absolutely no sense of timing.

I screwed my jacket into a bundle and threw it at the
dog. Stewart MacDonald. 'What the fucking hell are you
doing here?'

'Just passing.' He nodded agreeably. 'Coffee?' He was
pouring it anyway.

'Need you ask?'

He looked at me sideways and carried on pouring.
'Sandy's well pleased with your colt,' he observed peacefully. 'He and Duncan are up there at the forge planning
the next three generations.' Duncan is MacDonald's
brother. The man who owns the chestnut three-quarter

bred that is father to Rain's colt. The local farrier who is
child-by-default to Sandy Logan. As I am, possibly, to
MacDonald.

'If I hear right, he'll be covering every mare in the
village before he's turned five.' He spooned sugar into
one of the mugs.

Oh, really?

'Interesting, isn't it, how men find they need to proj-
ect all of their sexual inadequacies on to a horse?'

'Is that right?' He handed me the coffee and took the
kittens to play out of harm's way by the fire, leaving me
to the heat and space in front of the Rayburn.

The coffee was black, too weak and not nearly sweet
enough. I threw in some more sugar and fought my way
past two New Zealand rugs into the pantry for some
milk. He was waiting for me when I came back, sitting in
his chair by the fire, the kittens laid out along either
knee, their heads hanging over the edge into space. The
dog still had my chair, a special concession to the prevailing temper. He doesn't believe in dogs on the furniture, MacDonald. Neither did Bridget. I only ever saw
Tan share a bed with her once and that was when she
was dead. His successor, without Bridget to sort her out,
has learned softer habits. As far as I'm concerned, there's
more than enough room for both of us on any of the
chairs in the house. And there's something very pleasantly uncomplicated about sharing one's bed with a dog.

I stirred the milk into the coffee, watched it form
thick curdled clumps on the top and flung the whole lot
down the sink. I didn't want coffee anyway. I wanted tea.
And something to eat and a chair by the fire and some
kind of space to sort myself out. You wouldn't think it
was too much to ask.

I clicked on the kettle and made myself a fresh mug
of tea. With two sugars. And no milk.

'She's in heat,' said MacDonald, completely out of the blue, 'did you know?'

'What?'

'Your pup,' he said carefully, 'she's in season.'

'My pup? You mean my three-and-a-half-year-old bitch? *Our* three-and-a-half-year-old bitch?'

There's no pretending ownership over this one, she's a two-man dog. She always has been. Except possibly before he brought her here. Then she would have been his alone. 'I thought you and Ruaridh had decided she wasn't ever coming on heat?'

'Aye, well,' he shrugged a loose shrug, 'looks like we were wrong.'

'Congratulations.'

And doesn't that just make the weekend perfect? A bleeding bitch on the furniture for the next three weeks.

Marvellous. I must have broken a mirror and nobody thought to tell me.

MacDonald was looking over at me, smiling a kind of shy, paternal smile; the kind you save for your youngest daughter's first wedding. 'I was thinking,' he said, circumspectly, 'that maybe we could think about having pups. Duncan's got a friend with a good coursing greyhound at stud. The lass is a grand hunter and she'd make a rare dam for a lurcher . . .'

I think I have had just about enough of this.

'Stewart, I think it's time you left. I can't handle any more. I don't want any more horses. I don't want any more dogs. I didn't particularly want any more cats but they turn up on the sodding doorstep without bothering to ask. Life is too bloody complicated. We have a brand-new day-old foal out there that might not live to see the end of the week and Sandy Logan has already planned its sex life for the next decade. I don't need you wandering in here with your testosterone out of control, waving the nearest penile substitute you can lay your hands on just because there's a bitch might be up to standing for a dog. I'm not having any more. There's too much going on that we can't handle already. Too much that's out of control. It's not on. OK? The answer's no.' I paused for breath and a mouthful of tea. 'And I really do think you should go.'

I looked out across the room. MacDonald was sitting in his chair, the kittens still on his knee and he was watching me with a kind of curious intensity. Balanced somewhere between horrified fascination and morbid concern, the way you would watch your sister, the trapeze artist, try out a new act on the first night without a safety net.

I'm not keen on heights. Particularly not without a rope to break the fall.

The black hole that had been hovering just over my shoulder for the whole of the day finally closed in somewhere around my solar plexus. The floor dropped out from under me and, underneath that, there was nothing at all. I stepped off the edge and began the long, long fall to nowhere.

I put my mug down, very, very carefully on the counter and I stuck my hands in my pockets. I chewed a line of skin off the inside of my lip. I breathed and counted down from fifty, in odd numbers. I came round to the front face of the breakfast bar and I sat down with care on the cold, quarry tiles of the floor with my knees up to my chin and my hands locked round my legs. It was only then that I realised that I was shaking all over.

MacDonald leant over the edge of his chair carefully, so as not to displace the kittens, and he patted me on one knee. 'Do you want to talk about it?' he asked.

I don't discuss my relationships with MacDonald, I never have.

He has seen whatever he has seen and he has never yet made any comment. He spent long enough watching Janine while she changed her mind on a daily basis and then packed up and left the farm to go back to Rae. He spent another three months after that watching me make a total idiot of myself with one of his junior colleagues and he said nothing at all when she and Caroline moved together to a brand-new flat on the south side. He just turned up three days later with Sandy Logan and the pair of them helped me put my life back together.

MacDonald knows more about what goes on here than almost anybody else I know.

But we don't talk about it. Ever.

There really isn't any point.

I stood up and went over to sit on the bench by the window and started opening the mail that had accumulated in the two days since I was last at the farm.

'Tell me about the dog,' I said. 'The greyhound.'

There was quiet for a while. I felt his eyes on me and said nothing.

'Aye, well,' he leaned back in the chair and stroked the side of his nose, the way he does when he's working his way round to something else, 'there's no rush. She'll not be ready to stand for a week yet, at least. I'll maybe get a picture of him and a copy of his pedigree and drop it in sometime.'

'Fair enough.' I slid the paperknife through the envelopes and tried not to think of tearing sheets. 'Are you staying for lunch?' At four o'clock in the afternoon.

He had the decency not to look at his watch. 'No, no,' he said. 'I'll be going in a minute. I just called in to see how you were.'

'I'm fine.'

'So I see.' He still had a sleeping kitten draped across each knee. He stood up, lifted them off, and laid them

down on the hearth rug, curled round each other in a
tangle of red tabby limbs. 'And how's your friend?' he
asked. 'The one with the burned-out cottage?'

I forget, sometimes, that he has the Strathclyde police at his fingertips. You would think that on a Sunday,
the grapevine would twitch a tad slower than that.

I ran my eye down the first of the bills and then
shoved it on to a paper spike on the counter top. A spike
heavy with other, unpaid bills. I have to be pretty desperate for something to do before I start writing cheques.
This afternoon, I could pay every bill we've got.

I looked up and realised he was still expecting an
answer.

'She's fine,' I said.

'Is that right?' He crossed the room and crouched
down in front of me, in much the same way Matt Hendon crouched down by his man-eating German shepherd. He took the letter knife from my one hand and the
half-cut envelope from the other and he laid them both
down on the bench beside me. He waited until I raised
my head to look at him and then his eyes were level with
mine.

He has five different shades of grey in those eyes.
And a small, spherical patch of black caught down in the
outer corner of the left one that shivers sometimes, when
he's laughing, or trying not to laugh. Just at that moment, it hung absolutely still. A fly caught in ice.

'And do you think she'll still be feeling fine when she
finds the insurance aren't paying for her home?' he asked
softly.

Oh shit.

I need to eat.

There was cheese in the fridge and relatively new
bread in the bin. The chutney in the cupboard had a thin
veil of blue on the top but the layers underneath seemed

relatively healthy. The combination wasn't particularly appetising but it did something towards lifting my blood glucose to the point where I could think straight.

I made another two rounds of the same and took it to share with MacDonald.

'Why?' I asked as I sat down. 'Why wouldn't they pay for Nina's cottage?'

He inspected his sandwich and then took it round to the Rayburn, placed it neatly on the toasting grid and closed the lid.

'Because they're tight-fisted bastards and they aren't in the business of being ripped off,' he said. 'They'll maybe pay if it's negligence and they'll pay if it's arson. So long as it was someone else that lit the fire. The one time they won't pay is if she did it herself in which case she won't get a penny.'

'She didn't do it herself. The duvet caught on a heater. The fire chief said so.'

'He did. But the heater was standing right close up to the bed which seems a mite odd in the middle of April. If it was an accident, it was hellish convenient and, reading between the lines of your lady friend, she doesn't sound to me like the kind of person to make that kind of accident.'

My lady friend. Bloody hell. Stop fishing. 'She's a client, Stewart.'

'Is that right?' He knew that. You could hear it in the sound of his voice. 'So then would you care to pass comment about her mental health?'

Dear God. I don't believe this.

'No, I would not. That's confidential information, *Inspector* MacDonald. And even if it wasn't, it's none of your sodding business. I thought you weren't planning to stay?'

'Maybe not.' He leant forward on the breakfast

counter, his weight on his elbows, watching me. His
stare became uncomfortably fixed. 'I didn't come here to
fight with you, Kellen.' He has a way of rounding his
vowels when he's stressed. Just then they were very
round. 'It's not my case. Garscube's not on my patch,
you know that. I just thought maybe you could do with
someone on the other side who might have a different
view on things. If it doesn't matter that much, then, no, I
won't stay.'

He chewed the edge of one fingernail, watching still.

Behind him, hot chutney mixed with molten cheese
on the Rayburn. The smell of it spread out across the
room, warm and wet and savoury-sweet.

He's careful with his words, MacDonald. It pays to
listen.

'What kind of a different view?' I asked. 'Different
from what?'

'Different from the one currently taken by my colleagues.'

'Go on.'

'They think she did it herself, Kellen,' he said simply.
'And they're not stepping out of their way to prove otherwise.' His voice took on a different edge. 'Not after
what you said to them this morning.'

Oh bloody hell. I really am losing my grip.

I pushed the heels of my hands to my eyes and kept
pushing till the stars turned red. Then I let go and
watched them flare back down through the spectrum to
black. When I could see again, he was still standing
there, on the other side of the breakfast bar, watching
me.

'How did you know it was me?' I asked.

'The entire department knows what was said.' He
shrugged. 'It just took me a wee while to work out who

might have said it. Don't worry,' he crinkled a bit of a
smile, 'they didn't think to take your name and nobody
else knows you well enough to work it out for themselves.'

Thank you so very much.

I stared into the heart of the fire and watched further
fragments of reality crumble around me. This time yesterday I had a friend I valued, a client I cared for and a
career that looked as if it might be going somewhere.
And Nina Crawford had a home. And an outside chance
of holding herself together.

MacDonald lifted the lid of the Rayburn and recovered one perfectly toasted cheese sandwich. A halo of
toasted cheese hung around him as he came back to sit
by the fire. He laid the plate on his knee and cut the
thing into squares with a kitchen knife.

'What can we do?' I asked.

'I don't know.' He popped the first square in his
mouth and chewed on it, ruminating, like a sheep, 'So as
far as my colleagues are concerned, there's no question
but that the lassie did it herself.' He paused for a second
mouthful. 'The only question is whether she did it with
malice aforethought, so to speak, or whether she just
had a wee bit of a brainstorm and didn't know what she
was doing.' He stopped for a second bite. Bubbles of
warm chutney dribbled down the edge of one finger. He
licked it off with catlike precision. 'I thought maybe you
might be able to cast a bit of a light on things,' he said.

A red kitten clawed at the leg of his moleskins. He
drew out a long string of cheese, blew on it to cool it
down and rolled it into a small, kitten-bite-sized ball.
This is one of the other ways we differ, MacDonald and
I. I might let the dog on the bed, but I don't feed animals
from the table. I think if you asked him, he would say he

didn't either but the cats have him just where they want him.

Clearly, I'm not a cat.

I picked up the sibling kitten and sat in the other chair with the dog warming my back. She sighed in her sleep and laid her nose in the crook of my arm. If she's really in season, I'll need to start covering the furniture.

'Nina Crawford's been a client for close to eight years,' I said, so he knew, then, as much about us as he needed to know. 'She's brilliant. She's driven. She's one of the best surgeons around. She's also very, very unstable and she knows it. The two things in her life that stop her falling apart are her cat and her cottage. She's just lost both of them and she's right on the edge of a breakdown. There's no money in the world would be worth that kind of heartache.'

'Aye, well, there's more in the world than money, right enough.' The kitten clawed its way up his leg and waited by his plate for the next offering. He rolled another ball and made it follow his hand back down to the floor. 'And is she "unstable" enough, would you say, to do it to make some kind of statement?'

Oh God.

I was out of it when you came to the cottage the other night. That's why I came home . . .

'No,' I shook my head slowly, 'she's never been that "unstable".'

I am such a bad, bad liar.

'That's what I thought.' My kitten joined his for a toasted cheese-fest on the floor. He pulled a handkerchief from a hidden pocket in the moleskins and wiped both hands free of grease. 'But, under the circumstances, I think she might need something a wee bit more concrete than that if she's to stay clear of trouble.'

With MacDonald, it's what he doesn't say that is usually the most important. At that moment, he was putting a lot of effort into not saying all kinds of things.

I collected the plates and took them over to the sink. There's a small leaded window set in the wall above that sink at just about eye height. From there, you can see out over the duck pond to the foot of the ben and beyond. I peered out, looking for riders and tried not to listen to any of the things he wasn't saying.

I don't like being rail-roaded.

I don't like being made to feel responsible.

I don't, at this moment, want to become any more involved in the life of Dr Nina Crawford, equine surgeon, friend and client. Ex-client.

It's not my fault if her home got burned down. However it happened.

There was a weekend's accumulation of plates and pans waiting in the sink. More than enough. I washed and he waited and eventually he got the message.

He stood up and collected his jacket from the back of the chair.

I felt the draught as he opened the door and turned, the last of the plates dripping in my hand.

He was standing peacefully in the porchway, looking out across the moor to where the first of the returning riders was just coming into view.

'Gary Mitchell runs a racing kennels out on the Dumbarton road,' he said. 'He's got an ex-Waterloo Cup winner standing at stud if you want to go and have a look. Nice black dog. Name's Jupiter's Joy. If you tell him I sent you, he'll know who you are.'

'Thanks.'

He pulled on his jacket. 'I'll may be drop in and see the wee colt in the morning.'

'Fine. Sandy'll be here after seven.'

'Right.' He stepped out of the door and then stepped

back again, nodding towards the dog. 'You'll be wanting
to keep her on a lead for a wee while now,' he said,
'Unless you want her covered by every penile substitute
that happens past.'

He whistled quietly to himself as he left.

9

A half-hearted sunset lit up the western side of Bearsden as I turned in through the lower entrance to Garscube Estate and followed the tyre marks of three fire engines and a police car along the dirt track that leads to the out-buildings of the university farm and from there along a smaller track, little used before the weekend's excitement, that leads through a five-bar gate and up the slope to Nina's cottage. As far as I know, there hasn't been anything bigger than a pedal cycle along that lane since the day she moved in. When the furniture lorry left on the evening of the move, she shut the gate and never went near it again. Her car is parked permanently in the vet school car park and visitors get used to the five-minute walk down through the trees and out by the path that runs along the side of the river. The only reason I know the lower route is that I was one of the three people helping her to shift the furniture on the day she moved in.

The cottage stood in darkness, shaded by the massed rhododendrons and the overhanging birch. I stood for a moment, feeling oddly dishonest, as if the mere fact of being there in darkness was a confession of liability.

It was quiet. Country quiet. Not what you'd expect on the edge of the city. The river splashed gently somewhere out of sight. I expect the toads were calling if I had any idea what they sounded like. If there was anything else alive, the noise of the car had warned it to silence. Somewhere, if I thought about it hard enough, there was traffic on the switchback.

In front of me, the cottage was a chaos of burnt wood and water. The smell of soaked fire lay like a blanket across the clearing and a layer of wood ash made shadows even where the dusk light was falling. I found my torch in the back of the car; too small and with batteries that were long overdue for a change. Every time I use that torch, I swear that I'll buy a new one. It still lies somewhere under the driver's seat.

The dog followed me out of the car, sneezing on the updraughts of ash that swirled around us as we jumped over the stone of the wall and across the uncut lawn to the back door. In the dark, it looked more desolate than it had in the daylight with the bustling activity of the fire team around it. Desolate. Derelict. Wasted. Someone had tied the back door shut with baler twine because they'd taken the lock for forensics, 'Just in case'. A pane of plywood blocked the upstairs window like a shop front after a ram-raid.

I held the torch in my teeth and tried to undo the knot in the twine. When that failed, I picked up a piece of glass from the grass under the window and cut the knot out altogether, leaving two bare ends of twine hanging free so that I could tie them again on the way out.

Inside, the kitchen was a wasteland. A dozen pairs of booted feet had left indelible marks in black on the sanded oak of the floor. The rugs in the living room were beyond repair. The stairs looked as if someone had fallen at least once, on the way up or the way down and used the banisters as a crash barrier on the way to the floor. The bedroom, predictably, was a cave. A windowless, airless, smog-filled pit. And dark. So very, very dark. A dark that sucked. Took the torchlight and swallowed it whole and gave out sounds in its place. Soft. Hidden. Painful. The final keenings of heat-tortured wood. The whispers of falling plaster. The guttered groans of timbers shifting suddenly in the roof space. This place has stood for nearly three hundred years. Generations have lived here and died here and the cottage has never changed. It doesn't like the intrusion of fire. It hates the intrusion of men afterwards. The air held something close to loathing about it.

Fine fingers of fear traced their way up my spine and squeezed tight in my throat. The dog flattened her ears to her skull and pushed carefully past me on the way downstairs. She's not often wrong.

I shook my head, once, to clear the air and then stepped over a fallen lintel and into the room. The place that was her bedroom before the catharsis of the fire. The torchlight played games with the shadows as I swung it around, changing sizes and textures and adding odd dimensions to the looming outlines of things that used to be furniture. Some things were far beyond the shadow-play. Like the bed. The bed was, quite simply, not there. She sleeps on a futon. She used to sleep on a futon. They are not resistant to fire. I could see the space where it had been and no doubt if I were a trained fire officer

with the benefit of daylight, I could tell you which bits of
blackened fibre had been the duvet. I could probably
have told which bits of the mess were the wall as well.
She kept the bed hard up against the wall and the wall
was cow-dung plaster. Horse dung perhaps. Whatever
they used to make walls in the days when building mate-
rials were largely organic and came from the land. Either
way, it wasn't any more fireproof than the bed. There
was no longer a wall where there had been a wall. Instead, a gaping hole stretched from the floor up to the
ply-boarded window and led through into the loft space.
I angled the torch beam inside. Five years of lecture
notes and a decade's worth of conference proceedings sat
in charred, sodden bundles. There are easier ways of
letting go of your past.

She didn't do this as a way to let go of the past. Nina
Crawford could throw these things in a skip tomorrow
and not notice they were gone.

I would like to believe she didn't do it at all.

I came here looking for something and I am not
finding it.

I know Nina Crawford. In every way possible, I know
her. I know the structure of her days and the unformed
terrors of her nights. I know the intangible promises of
her childhood and the tangled realities of her adult life. I
know the shape of her scars and the taste of her tears
and the ragged edge of her voice in extremis. If I had
never been in her bedroom, still I could map out the
places of things. Somewhere in all of this, there is a
footprint. Something to say if someone, anyone, else was
here in the space between a midnight phone call and a
fire at dawn.

All I have to do is find it.

I stood in the centre of the room, switched off the torch and worked out in the space around me where everything ought to be. The bed with the hard mattress for her back and the pillow heading eastwards because if it's facing any other way then the nightmares are worse. The phone, within hand's reach of the head of the futon so she can lift it without waking up. The watercolour of Sgurr nan Gillean on the wall to the left of the window. The curtained alcove on the far side of the room where she hangs her clothes. The pine-backed mirror on its stand in one corner. The chair for the one-eyed killer cat because even she wouldn't dare let it on to the bed while she slept. The chair further back against the wall where she hangs her clothes after work. The lamp.

I clicked on the torch again. The thread of the beam wove around the room. Bed, phone, picture, chair, mirror, chair, clothes. All of them there in shadow. Scorched black on paler black.

Nothing missing.

No footprint.

There has to be something or else why am I here?

A second circuit. Everything in place. Except that the chair for the cat is back against the wall and the small curved reading lamp is sitting on it.

There is no reason for the lamp to be over there. You couldn't plug it in. There's only one socket in Nina Crawford's bedroom and that's at the head of her bed. Put in by the university electricians at her instruction so that she could have a light at night. For reading. For reading papers and journals and letters of referral and writing notes for lectures in the morning. She couldn't sleep if she didn't read something before she slept. And she never switched off the light without checking that the cat was on his chair by the bed. Some folk have security blankets. Nina Crawford has her cat.

The beginnings of a footprint.

The torch dimmed as I fixed it on the chair, the batteries pulled in the last few scattered electrons and threw them, one at a time, at the dark. A dampened match would have given more light. I stepped carefully over fractured floorboards to the wall and found, mostly by feel, that the lamp was, indeed, too far from the bed to read by. Almost half the length of the room away. And not plugged into the wall. In the final few seconds of torchlight, the pins of the plug glowed back smoke-encrusted brass, a final shimmer of warmth in the cold and the baleful dark.

And so the light was moved before the fire. And the chair with it. Nina wouldn't do that by accident.

But there's nothing here to say she didn't do it deliberately.

I stood in the gloom and listened to the whispers of the broken room. Here, in this place, I could begin to have nightmares too. If I stayed here long enough, I could begin to build pictures of anything. Here, I could think the unthinkable and believe that it happened.

A displaced lamp is not a footprint. Not enough to say if Nina Crawford simply lost it after four nights without sleep or whether she had, after all, found a new way of fighting the nightmares. Fire is a very cleansing thing. I can't imagine it ever being a good way to go but then I wouldn't inject air into my antebrachial veins, either. Or try to cut out my scar with a scalpel blade.

I thought I knew her.

I don't really know her at all.

She could have been trying to die. She could simply have been too tired to think. Or she could have been trying to rid herself of the encumbrance of the cottage. As a prelude to something else more permanent.

And if I can't tell, how in heaven's name is anybody else supposed to know the difference?

I felt my way out of the room and down the stairs. The dog was waiting for me in the kitchen doorway, her pale coat blackened to normal collie colouring by the smoke and the falling ash. She shoved her nose against my wrist as I stopped to tie the baler twine, a cool canine reminder that we had outstayed our welcome.

We'd outstayed it before I ever stepped in through the door.

The sun was long gone and the car was waiting in darkness beside the woodshed. A thin layer of cloud hid whatever moonlight there might have been. White light filtered through the trees from the streetlamps on the switchback and mixed with the harsh sodium orange from Bearsden. Enough to see by, more or less. I made a final circuit of the garden, looking for something more concrete than a shifted lamp. Something to take the whispering nightmares and make them somehow less damning.

I was grubbing around in the glass beneath Nina's bedroom window, trying to work out if it was broken before, during or after the fire, when the dog whined. Not her hunting whine, but something almost as urgent. I hopped over the wall and found her by the woodshed with her nose jammed through a six-inch gap in the base of the door. She whined again as I got there. The woodshed snarled back. They started up a dialogue; dog and shed. The dog stood, almost on point, wheedling promises through half-closed lips, her face jammed midway to her eyes in the jagged space near the hinge where the

wood had rotted away. The shed hissed something vi-
ciously uncompromising that ended in a spit and a slash
and a yowl of pain from the dog. She jerked suddenly
backwards. Beads of blood welled like dark warts along
the side of her nose. She sat down on her haunches with
her nose a safe distance from the wood and she whined
again.

Very telling. There aren't many cats who, given the
relative security of a closed shed door, would find it
necessary to attack a dog. I put my head down near the
gap and risked a look in. A muscled shaped moved
somewhere in the gloom.

'Don't go far, Killer,' I said. 'Help is at hand.'

I don't smoke and I don't sit in my car any longer
than I have to, but I carry a cigarette lighter in the glove
compartment because, on the whole, it's a more useful
source of light than my torch and I carry a travelling rug
in the back seat of the car to protect the upholstery in
case I ever have passengers who object to dog hairs on
their clothing. I dug the lighter out from under the mass
of old service contracts, dragged the rug off the back seat
and then let the dog into the car, ignoring, for the time
being, the combined effect of fur, fire-smoke and blood
on the furnishings.

The woodshed door was damp and swollen and the
hinges were rusted almost solid but it gave way to a
couple of kicks and a hard shove with a shoulder. The
cat lay sideways at the hinges, pushed that way when I
opened the door. A wreck of a cat in black and almost-
black with a single black-in-green eye that glared hatred
at me in the gloom.

'Killer, old pal. Good to see you, too. Are you hurt?'

The cat hissed something evil in feline and slunk,
lame-legged to the corner. His left foreleg gave way as he

turned to face me, twisting out from the elbow at a painfully improbable angle.

The wavering flame of the lighter showed a hairless
burn across his back just behind the ribs and a gleaming
white spike where there should not have been white,
poking through the skin just below his left elbow.
Second-degree burns and a compound radial fracture. At
the very least. The cat spat blood at my hand. His teeth
shone red. Add mandibular fracture to the list.

I crouched down with the lighter held up high for a
better look. 'Hell, Killer, you need to see someone about
that, old son.'

He whispered low-throated threats and pushed himself hard back against the rough wood of the wall.

I advanced on him slowly, the rug held forward like
a shield. The cat spat three-fold curses and slashed at my
face.

'Go on, Killer. You love me really.'

I held the lighter just out of his reach, a flickering
decoy, and, when he lunged up to destroy it, I dropped
the rug on him from above and behind and grabbed
through it, in one single movement, for his scruff. The
cat screamed the war-scream of the damned and twisted
round, fighting through four layers of woollen plaid for
the fingers of my left hand. Or my arm. Or my heart. Or
anything else he could reach with any one of four sets of
claws and his gin-trap teeth. I held on, held him out at
arm's length and prayed to the memory of my grandmother for strength in her rug.

The battle was brief, very vocal and quite bloody.

The rug won.

I carried the bundle back to the car and laid it on the
front seat. We had a minor battle of wills and established
the fact that he could have his head out to breathe as
long as he didn't try to kill me in the process. The dog

was less than impressed. The cat hissed poison every
time I moved, but he didn't fight.

The problem with acting on impulse is that you have to
deal with the consequences. I sat in my car in front of
Nina Crawford's cottage with a homicidal cat bundled
on the front seat, a dog on the verge of mutiny in the
back and a major crisis of conscience.

I prodded the bundle experimentally.

'OK, Killer, what now?'

The thing writhed and swore ten types of vengeance,
none of them helpful.

I pressed my forehead on the steering wheel and
stared in darkness at the obvious. 'You need your
mother, cat.' Which was a pity, really, because I had no
intention at all of talking to his mother before I had
myself a lot more sorted out.

When you are backed in a corner, there are always
other ways out.

I toyed, briefly, with the idea of walking quietly up
the path and leaving him wrapped in his rug in the
pharmacy. Or in the doorway to the small animal ward.
Or somewhere else warm and relatively sheltered that
gets regular human traffic throughout the night.

Nice idea. Difficult to justify in reality.

I considered, quite seriously, walking into the local
police station and handing him in as a stray. 'Found him
on the switchback, officer. Must have been hit by a car.'
A car with a flame thrower as a bolt-on accessory, but we
won't mention that.

Or I could simply lay him out on the dual carriageway and leave him to go the way of all urban fe-
lines. There are those of my acquaintance who would
believe I had done the rest of the world a favour. Almost

all of them. Everyone except for Nina Crawford, who has just lost her home and is already too close to the edge.

Whatever else is going on, I owe her more than that.

Less than five minutes later, I turned in over the cattle grid and rolled down the hill towards the hospital.

I surprise myself sometimes with my own innate sense of responsibility.

10

She was in the anteroom of the small animal ward, kneeling on the floor by the examination table, doing her best to pass a stomach tube down a struggling wolfhound with only Dominic-the-student to hold it down. Viewed from the doorway, the wolfhound was winning.

The door clicked shut behind me. Dominic and the dog both looked over to check whose side I was joining. Nina kept her eyes on the stomach tube. She hit target and a flood of canine vomit siphoned out into the bucket at her feet.

'Welcome back,' she said. 'You should've kept your pager switched off after all.'

'I dropped my pager in the loch eleven years ago,' I said.

She didn't turn around. She clamped the end of the stomach tube and drew it slowly out. The wolfhound, freed from restraint, shook its head and tried to stick its tongue down her ears. Fronds of dog-spit spun round its muzzle and on to the shoulders of her white coat. She moved the bucket carefully from under the trampling feet and nodded to the student.

'OK, Dom. He can go back to bed. No food, no water. TPRs every fifteen minutes till he's stable. See if you can get the drip to run. I'll be along in a minute.'

Only when the dog had dragged the student out through the swing doors to the kennel area did she turn round. Even then, she didn't stand up.

'Kellen . . .' She looked me in the eye and I had no idea at all what she was feeling. 'Why are you here?'

The bundle in my arms moved spasmodically. The cat yarled at the sound of her voice.

Nina Crawford stood up faster than I have ever seen her move and suddenly it was very easy indeed to see what she was feeling.

I stepped forward and laid him with care on the table. 'He was in the woodshed,' I said. 'Fractures to the left foreleg and the mandible. Second-degree burns along his back. And,' because something else was wrong as I laid him down and I hadn't stopped to think about it before, 'he's not breathing as well as he was.'

'Jesus Christ Almighty.' She reached in her hand and drew him out from the cocoon of the blanket. The cat growled engine noises deep in his chest, the kind of noise Rottweilers make before they take out your throat. This cat's idea of a greeting. He licked her hand and his tongue left a bright trail of blood. He lay on the table while she felt the raw ends of his radial fracture and he panted. Purred and panted simultaneously.

I've never seen a cat pant before.

'He wasn't breathing like that when I picked him up,' I said.

She said nothing. She pulled a stethoscope from her pocket and laid it across his chest and listened. Left side. Right side. Chest. Abdomen. She tapped across his rib cage. Down over the heart and back. The noise came back solid, like tapping on wood. The cat opened his mouth wider and mewled. His gums and the back of his palate showed pale violet through the red-stained mesh of his teeth.

'Nina. I think we need oxygen.'

Oxygen. A drip. And an X-ray.

In that order.

Fast.

There's something deceptively simple about an X-ray. Everything sketched out in two dimensional black and white. No blood or guts to get in the way. Just infinite shades of grey frozen in a shaved fraction of a second.

I sat on the floor in the dark in the small radiology room next to the main ward. The cat lay beside me in a basket with an oxygen pipe coiled near his nose. A paediatric drip set ran some kind of plasma substitute in small drips into the long vein on his one good foreleg. The other leg lay splinted at his side, the bone ends hidden beneath two layers of loose-weave bandage. He wasn't purring any more. He wasn't panting. He was simply trying to stay alive.

A digital clock on the wall advertised the latest brand of X-ray screens in glow-in-the-dark colours. The time glowed less brightly. It clicked just past eight o'clock. I promised Kate I would be home by half seven.

Three radiographs hung on the viewer, shades of black on grey on bright-light white. Two showed his fracture; the nice clean edges of the break, the sharp spike of bone poking white through the almost-black of his skin. And the second, smaller fragment near the carpus that made it a bastard to fix. But bones heal. Bones, in a way, hold the same kind of black and white simplicity as a radiograph. They are either broken, or they aren't. They either fit together, or they don't. Orthopaedic surgery is high-tech carpentry and if the worst comes to the worst, you simply take off the leg. The world is full of three-legged cats. Some of them even manage to kill.

But they don't manage to kill if they have their liver lodged somewhere up near their heart. Or their small intestine crowding in where their lungs ought to be. Then they go blue and they pant and if you don't do something very fast to pull their guts out of the chest back to where they belong in the abdomen and close up the gaping hole in the diaphragm, then they die.

I sat on the floor watching Killer Crawford fighting for one dark blue breath after another and thought about what I could do if he stopped.

'I can't find her. I've tried three different people and they don't even know if she's in town.'

'So then page her again.'

'There's no point. I found her pager. It's in the Lodge.'

Nina Crawford stood in the doorway. The hard light from the viewer pulled out fresh shadows from under her eyes. She held out the offending bit of electronics as if it were evidence. As if, at this stage, I might think she was making it up.

'So then try Matt.'

'I can't, Kellen.' She came into the room and knelt by the basket. 'Matt's not . . .' The cat mewled again. A breathless noise, made without air. She lifted the lid of the basket and put her hand to his head. And then she said simply, 'Matt wouldn't come.'

'He'd come. He still loves you more than he hates your cat.'

'Not any more.' She leant across me to change the rate of the drip and the flat planes of her face showed far more than her voice. It always gives her away, her face. If it matters enough.

I felt again the same kind of fear that I felt with Stewart MacDonald sitting on the floor of my kitchen. The sudden vertiginous plunge into panic.

'He knows,' I said. It wasn't a question.

If Matt Hendon knows then by tomorrow the whole world could know.

We don't need this. We really, really don't need this.

She nodded, still counting the drips. 'He knew this morning. As soon as we met in the ward.' She looked up and there were so many layers of pain in her eyes it was difficult to see what came first. 'We slept together for four years, Kellen,' she said. 'You couldn't expect him not to.'

I didn't.

I didn't expect anything at all.

And the only thing I can do to make things better is get in the car and go home.

She picked up the basket. I picked up the oxygen cylinder and followed her, a foot behind, as she led the way back through to the ward.

'How is he?' I asked as we put the basket down. 'How's Matt?'

'He's coping. What else? But he isn't happy.'

He always copes. And he is never happy. Not since the holiday in Skye has he been happy. But he has coped. The question was always how he would cope if there was ever anyone else. And whether that was in any way her problem.

We never did sort out an answer.

We lifted the cat out and laid him on a padded bed on the table. He let me hold him and he didn't notice it was me.

'Well then, if he's coping,' I said, 'call him. That's a ruptured diaphragm in there, Nina. You need another surgeon.'

'No . . .' She paused for a moment to calculate the dose of antibiotics going into the line. 'I can do it alone. All I need is someone to watch the anaesthetic.'

'So the man's an anaesthetist. Get him in.'

'No.' She took some scissors from a drawer and started clipping matted hair away from the burn on the cat's back. 'I can't do that to him. Anyway, he's not in Glasgow. He's going up to his parents tonight. He was going tomorrow morning anyway. When we . . .' They don't fight. She's never acknowledged so much as raised voices between them. '. . . when he left, I told him I'd cover clinics for him this evening so he could set off early. I'm not calling him back.'

'Well then, call in whoever else is on duty.'

'There isn't anyone else on duty, Kellen. It's Congress week. They're all in Birmingham getting pissed and putting lines on their CVs. There were three of us left to cover clinics. Me, Steff and Matt . . .'

'And Dominic.'

'Quite. Us three and Dominic. I sent Aiden and Lucy home this morning. On any normal Sunday that would be enough. With the equine side shut, it should have been more than enough. Matt and I could have handled anything between us.'

Or not. As the case may be.

A water bowl overturned somewhere down in the

kennels. The muffled woof of an enthusiastic wolfhound rode roughshod over the faint appeals of a frustrated student.

'Well then, get Dominic,' I said. 'He's three months off finals. He can't be that bad.'

She said nothing.

I stood up. Pulled my car keys from my pockets. 'I can't stay, Nina,' I said. 'Kate's still with the foal. I have to go home.'

She lifted a set of clippers from a hook on the wall above the sink and turned them on. They whined, high-pitched, like a hive of wasps. The cat sank back in the basket and hissed. She turned them off. The silence burned. Like acid. 'If it was the dog,' she said slowly, 'or Rain, or the foal, would you leave me here alone with Dominic and go home?'

There's no answer to that. None I can reasonably give.

I shoved my keys back into my pocket and looked around for the nearest phone.

'Show me how to get an outside line,' I said. 'I'll have to call Kate and tell her I'm going to be late home.'

■■■■■

Sleep comes very gently to a cat with no lung space. A sighing transition from gasping air-hunger to the rhythmic puffs of the oxygen bag with only the barest of stops while the tube goes down the trachea. The monitors don't like it. They have alarms set to scream when the arterial oxygen levels are this bad. They scream without remission unless you silence them with the flick switch at the back. Then they blink in silent, pulsing resentment. Electronic malevolence with 'I-told-you-so' ready scripted for the post-mortem printout.

If you ventilate carefully by hand, squeeze over and

over on the small latex bag, push oxygen down into overcrowded lung space, then the monitors stop blinking. Then they sit in technological anticipation of the moment when you forget to breathe. Waiting to record the moment when you forget to squeeze the bag. Waiting to scream.

I squeezed the bag, gently, the way I'd been shown. I watched the monitor silently register in-breaths and out-breaths, flickering up the kind of numbers that haven't made sense since third-year Physiology. Not even then.

Sweat trickled in slow trails down my nose. Greasy sweat, not the healthy sweat of a run, or even the washed sweat of fear. The nasty, sticky sweat that comes from a breath half held for too long. From the dead tension hanging heavy in the air. From the baking glare of the operating lights.

I watched Nina Crawford lay the green cotton drapes in a rectangle across her cat. Watched her lift a scalpel, a swab, a pair of rat-toothed forceps. I saw her run her thumb experimentally along the line of the cut and I tasted something hot and acid in the back of my throat.

'Nina. I don't think I can do this.'

She looked up slowly. All I could see, between the hat and the mask, were her eyes, miles away eyes, already halfway to his diaphragm.

'Kellen, you can do better than Dominic, believe me.'

I doubt it.

'Nina. It's ten years since I did anything more than feel a pulse. I've never given an anaesthetic in my life.'

'It's OK. You're not giving it. I am. You're just a spare pair of hands, that's all. You don't need to know what you're doing. You just have to have the sense to do what you're told, when you're told. That's all I need. You can do it.'

'If he dies, you'll never forgive me.'

She smiled, the quirked, half-smile that shows even under the theatre mask. 'Now you know how I feel about Rain.'

I knew that already. I didn't need this to drive it home.

She looked once at the figures on the monitors and the oxygen regulator. At the spiked waves of the ECG. And she said; 'He's fine, Kellen. Seriously. He could tick over for hours like he is now. The hard part was knocking him out. That's when they go. If they live through induction then the rest is plain sailing.'

'You didn't tell me.' I thought it was so peaceful.

I saw her shrug beneath the theatre gown. Somewhere, underneath the mask, she was laughing, caught between the tension and the absurdity of it.

'I thought it was better if only one of us was panicking,' she said quietly. 'Now can I get on with the surgery? Please?'

Sleep comes very gently to a cat with no lung space.

Life on the other side of surgery is less gentle.

It was half-past ten at night when we lifted the half-shaved mass of black and white and bruised tissue and wrapped him in a prewarmed blanket and carried him out of the theatre.

Night life hummed through the ward. The sleepy mutterings of the well and the unwell and the occasional keening cry from the genuinely sick. In a human hospital there would be night nurses and porters, interns and junior SHOs all running backwards and forwards trying to cover three times the ward space of their senior consultants in half the time. In here, there was Dominic, cocooned in a white coat and sleeping bag on an air bed in the far end of the kennels area. We walked past him quietly. He sighed and turned over in his sleep. The wolfhound grinned and flicked spirals of dog-spit at us as we passed.

I sat on a high stool with the sleeping cat on my knees, ventilating still, the way I'd been taught, while Nina set up an ex-human neonatal incubator with an oxygen in-flow line and a humidifier and an ambient temperature only slightly less than the Saharan heat of the theatre. We laid him on his good side, injured leg uppermost and ran lines in through the ports in the clear plastic of the incubator hood. The fluid line. An ECG. A digital thermometer. Only three lines. By all reasonable standards of ICU, he should be coming out alive.

'Will he do?' It was my first coherent sentence in over two hours. My throat was dry, like old parchment. I would have killed, cheerfully, for a coffee.

'I don't know.' She pulled up another stool alongside mine. 'I suppose there's only one way to find out.' She disconnected the oxygen line from his tube and suddenly I was ventilating fresh air. I stopped. My fingers ached, robbed of a reason for moving.

'Now all we have to do is wait for his CO_2 to rise and see if it kicks him into breathing. If he does nothing in the next minute, you can have your job back.'

We waited ninety seconds. I counted them out as the clock ticked round. Quietly. Not out loud. For something to do. When I looked at Nina, she was doing the same. Except she was counting his heartbeats. Just in case they weren't there.

It was odd to see him begin to breathe on his own. As if he might, perhaps, have forgotten how. It was odder still to watch him come slowly back to wakefulness. To see him feel the pain, dull at first and then sharper as the stitches gripped in his diaphragm, in the skin of his abdomen, over the steel of the plate in his leg. He only has one eye. But that's the first time I have seen it look at me, and know who I was, and still feel anything other than murder. He opened his mouth and only pain came out.

I never thought I would feel pity. Not for this cat.

'Is there nothing we can give him?'

'We can give him morphine. Now that he's breathing.' She cracked open a vial, drew up a tiny fraction of fluid and fed it in through the drip.

In time, the cat breathed more slowly. His eye lost its grip. Wavered. Watched other things in other places. Things that crept up the walls and across the ceiling. Things that joined him in the incubator. The cat purred.

'He's hallucinating.'

'He probably is.' She should know.

We sat together in silence. The monitors all stayed in rhythm. The cat kept breathing. I thought of other things. Remembered the desert in the back of my throat. Remembered the black hole in my solar plexus. Not entirely unlike a ruptured diaphragm but you can't see it on X-ray. I remembered work. Tomorrow is Monday and I have to be at work by nine. Seven hours from now, I have to get out of bed. Just now, I could sleep for ever.

'I don't suppose you have any coffee?'

'Nope. We have water. If you want coffee, you have to go to the Lodge and get it. I'm staying here with the cat.' Nina crossed the room to the fridge and produced another green plastic bottle with yet another daft, kilt-wearing cow on the front. You're not supposed to keep human food in clinical fridges. Even I know that. She drank the water. I thought seriously about visiting the Lodge. Found I couldn't be bothered to move. Nina held out the bottle. 'Caffeine's a diuretic,' she said. 'You're dehydrated. Everyone dehydrates in theatre. It's the lights. You won't get better without some water. And you'll never sleep if you have coffee now.'

Watch me.

The cat purred at something big and friendly that walked across the roof of his incubator. He rolled over on to his back to watch it. The line of stitches ran neatly along the midline of his abdomen. Around it, a curved arc of bruised tissue stood out starkly against the almost-white and almost-black patches of shaved skin.

I leaned over and looked at it more closely. A footprint.

'Nina, he's been kicked.'

She joined me by the incubator. Took a long drink of water. Placed the bottle with care on the floor at her feet. 'Yes, I know,' she said.

What?

'I don't understand.'

'It's obvious,' she said evenly. 'If you were really unlucky you might fracture your radius falling from a first-floor window. Or even if you jumped badly off the bed. But you only get a ruptured diaphragm from a high velocity impact. Road traffic cases come in with their diaphragms gone. And the ones that get kicked by horses. Not the falls.'

'I found him in the woodshed.' Even for a cat, the nearest horse is ten minutes' walk away and it's dead. 'He wasn't kicked by a horse.'

She nodded slow agreement. 'He hasn't been hit by a car, either. The bruising would be different.'

'Why didn't you say something earlier?'

'Why should I?' She shrugged. 'It's not your business.'

Her eyes were on the fluid pump. She did some

mental arithmetic and altered the drip rate. Kept her face in the shadows. Shifting, teasing shadows.

'What do you mean?' I asked.

'I mean it wasn't you that kicked him. I know you better than that. Even if I don't, you would hardly kick his guts out and then bring him in to me for surgery.'

'Thanks.'

'You're welcome. Anyway, this is old bruising. And there were fibrin tags forming all round the diaphragm. The lesion's well over twenty-four hours old. This happened the same time the fire started at the cottage. Close enough. You were in the PM room with me then. It can't have been you.'

'But you still could have told me.'

I spent half an hour in the Calcutta hole of her bedroom looking for a footprint when all I needed to do was go to the woodshed and drag out the cat.

And I came so close to missing it.

'Kellen . . .' She bit the edge of one hard-pared nail, kept her eyes on the cat. '. . . I've been trying to talk to you all day and got nowhere. I've had more conversation from Dominic and he spends most of his time asleep. Do you think I would have asked you to stay and help me cut if I wasn't desperate?'

'I don't know.' I didn't think about it like that.

She took a long, long drink from the bottle. We watched the cat. I thought about footprints and whether it was possible to match foot size to feline bruises, even after thirty-six hours. I thought about coffee and how long it wasn't till I had to get up in the morning and how long it would take to go up to the Lodge and boil a kettle. I still didn't do anything about it. There's a curious apathy that takes over in a clinical unit late at night. A deep-seated reflex from some hidden layer of under-conscious that knows it's going to be a long night and there's no point in planning anything as normal as sleep. Or coffee. I breathed in lemongrass and breathed out yearning and tried not to remember anything at all about the night before.

Nina simply sat and drank water.

'Well,' she said finally, 'are we going to talk about it?'

'Talk about what?'

'The thing we're not talking about. Last night.'

'I don't know that there's very much to say.'

Or alternatively, there are a hundred things I could say and all of them push boundaries we have crossed once already.

'Do you want me to apologise?'

'For what? Taking advantage of me when I was low on sleep and high on stress? I hardly think so.'

'That's unnecessary, Kellen.'

'I'm sorry.'

'I know. That's obvious.'

'I'm sorry.'

'Could we not just pretend it didn't happen? Transient bilateral amnesia? Go back to where we were?'

If only.

'Is that what you want?'

'I don't think what I want comes into it, really, do you?'

I don't know. I don't want to think about what you want. Or what I want. It isn't safe.

'It should do.'

'I know. That's not what I asked.'

'I know.'

Silence. A wary, pivotal silence. A silence where the one who makes the first move loses. A silence where the only safe thing left to do is to wait.

We waited. I thought about going home. Watched the drips fall through the fluid chamber with the regularity of a water torture. Listened to the clicks of the fluid pump. Tried to make sense of the pattern on the ECG.

The cat purred and watched fantasy television flicker past the walls of the incubator.

Nina sighed, a long, hissing sigh, through clenched teeth.

'Kellen, if I said that the incubator walls were burning, what would you say?'

Hair pricked upright on the back of my neck.

I really can't take another night like last night.

Neither can she.

'Where's the cat?' I asked.

'He's gone. Vanished. The fire started in the red marks on his abdomen. Burned him up. All that's left is his skull. It has teeth like a snake. But it talks like Matt. It thinks . . . it thinks the world would be a better place if I joined the cat.'

'And what do you think?'

'Just at this moment, Kellen, I couldn't care less.' She sat beside me, less than two feet away. Her voice was flat. Deliberately empty. Her fingers dug into the soft vinyl of the stool. Her eyes were fixed on the cat. I reached out, held her chin. The closest I've touched her in twenty-four hours. Turned her face to mine. Her pupils were wide. And black.

She turned her head back, suddenly. Violently. Not quite in control. 'Don't, Kellen.' She let go of the chair and took my hand from her face. 'You don't look good without the skin on your face.' Her voice lost its flatness. Gathered the first jagged edges of panic.

'What's happening, Nina?'

She shrugged. 'The same as always happens. It always starts like this. Normal things start to go just a little bit abnormal. I can cope for a while. Until it gets out of hand.'

'Is it out of hand now?'

'Not quite. I can still hold a sane conversation.' She smiled the ghost of a smile; strained, self-mocking. 'If this isn't sane, Kellen, I don't want to know.'

'How long?' I asked. 'How long has it been running this time?'

'Since we gave him the morphine. Could have been earlier. It has to be really bad to get in the way when I'm cutting.'

The cat's drip ran out. The fluid pump bleeped and flashed red. She focused hard on the drip set, a drunk with a mission. A vein pulsed at her temple. 'Can you change that drip?' she said. 'I'm not sure I want to touch what it looks like.'

'It might bite?'

'At the very least.' She grimaced. Spoke slowly through whitening lips. 'Use Hartmann's. Warm it up in the microwave first.'

I found the right bottle in the cupboard above her head, gave it three minutes on high, changed the drip. She watched me the way I would watch an unstable schizophrenic, waiting for the flip.

'Cut down to half the drip rate,' she said when I'd finished. 'He didn't lose too much blood in theatre.' Her voice came from a long tunnel, each word enunciated with care to reach the far end of sanity.

I took hold of her hand. She took it back again. Carefully. As if both of us were fragile.

I wonder sometimes if it's hypoglycaemia. It's always worse when I haven't eaten.

'Nina . . . have you had anything to eat today?'

'We had pancakes this morning.' She smiled. Just for a moment, she looked normal. How could I forget?

'Is that it?'

Frustration made her more lucid. 'It's a Sunday, Kellen. Where am I supposed to get something to eat? I'm not about to go down to the cottage to see if there's anything left in the freezer.'

'Is there food in the Lodge?'

'I expect so. There usually is.'

'If I go and find some, will you still be here when I get back?'

'I'll do my best.'

Somehow, this is less than encouraging.

I ran for the Lodge. Found the key, exactly where Steff said it would be; behind the fire extinguisher opposite the door. The remains of the filling from the omelettes was in the fridge. There was fresh bread on a shelf below it and cheese below that. And the jug with the remains of the morning's coffee. And, thanks be to Jason, two one-litre cartons of orange juice with 'JGG, PAWS OFF' written across in indelible ink. I took them both.

██████████

She was still there when I got back. Sitting tight on the stool staring at the floor as if it was the only safe place left in the room. I tore the lid of the first carton open and held it where she could see it. 'Here. Fructose. Get going. It's safe, I promise.'

She drank. She didn't like it, but she drank.

'How are you doing?' Dumb question, but you have to ask.

'I'm still here,' she said and the tunnel was halfway to the Antipodes.

'It'll take a good ten minutes to hit your brain.'

'I know. It always does. I'm not going anywhere.'

'I know.' You don't have to. Everywhere is coming
at you.

I sat by her chair and talked her through drinking
half the carton. She watched the floor turn to sea water.
Conger eels with Matt's face and my voice gibbered at
her about infidelity and commitment. She kept drinking.
I stuck the remains of the morning's coffee in the microwave in the corner. The one with 'ICU only. Absolutely
not for human use' printed across it in green. I made her
drink coffee. The conger eels became mealworms and
then maggots and they writhed their way up the legs of
her chair. The coffee was red and it tasted of blood. It
tasted of old, bitter coffee to me. In the incubator, the cat
came slowly up to the surface of pain. It stopped watching things run along the plastic of the walls. Watched me
and its mother instead. It made one trial flex of its ruined
left leg and it howled.

'Your cat needs more morphine,' I said.

Talking was hard. 'In the vial on the side . . . 0.4
ml . . . Needles are in the box on the shelf under the
syringes.' She whispered it. Not to wake the maggots.

The vial was there. It holds one ml of morphine. I
drew up all that was left—0.6 ml. If she's self-injecting
with morphine, she didn't get it from here.

I loaded the dope into the cat, watched him float
slowly back into dream space. When I turned round to
look at his mother, I found her looking back at me. Her
eyes were not black.

'Nina, what can you see?'

'I can see you.' She smiled. A slow, quirked smile. It
carries the world in it, that smile.

'Who am I?'

'Do you really want me to answer that?'

No. Not now.

'Who are you?' I asked.

'Don't ask difficult questions at this time of night, Kellen Stewart.'

She couldn't talk like that when she was seeing things.

'You're back.'

'I think so.' She stretched, a long, joint-cracking cat-stretch. Stuck out the end of one shoeless foot and pushed it gently somewhere up near my ribs. 'That's twice in two days you've stopped me going over the edge, Dr Stewart.' Her toes played over the skin of my side. 'It's becoming something of a habit.'

I wrapped my hand round her foot. 'Maybe if you didn't keep playing in the danger zone, Dr Crawford, you wouldn't fall over so often.'

And maybe she's not the only one.

Memory followed in the afterwash of relief. I could have lived without that, just then.

She took her foot away from my ribs. Cocked her head on one side. 'You're worried about work, aren't you?'

'Fairly.'

'Is it so very unacceptable?'

'Yes.'

Her eyes were thoughtful in the gloom, walnut patched with flickering amber reflections from the ECG. She fiddled with the drip rate. For something to do. Her voice was soft when she spoke. 'I asked you, Kellen, not the other way around. Doesn't that make a difference?

'No.'

'So then don't tell them. You may not be able to forget, but you don't have to make a song and dance about it. I won't.'

Yes, you will. I have been through this too often in the last day and a half. It doesn't get any better with each revision.

'Nina . . .' I turned round so that I could see her face, so that she could see mine, '. . . you need professional help. I'm not sure I shouldn't be referring you to psychiatrist as we speak. At the very least, you need a lot of time with a therapist. Whoever it is, it can't be me. Not now. And the first time you go, maybe the second if you want to spin it out, you need to tell them about last night. You have to. There's no point otherwise. And then . . .' I shrugged. It didn't seem necessary, then, to spell it all out. 'On the whole, I'd rather jump before I'm pushed, that's all.'

'You're going to resign?'

'Yes.'

'Because of me?'

'There were two of us, Nina. I could have gone home.'

She moved her head. Amber patches wavered across the bridge of her nose. Somewhere down the ward, a dog yelped in its sleep. She reached out a hand. Her fingers curled around mine. 'I'm sorry,' she said. 'I didn't realise.'

'I know.'

'When will you do it? Tomorrow?'

'Maybe. More likely Tuesday. I need to think what I'm going to say.'

'And then what?'

'I don't know.' I haven't thought that far ahead.

'So could we . . . what the hell . . . ?'

She turned. Her hand fell out of mine. The door to the ward hissed softly shut.

Stephanie Foster stood on the far side of the room. Out of breath, damp from a run. Or from a shower. Or both.

'Sorry to break up the party,' she said. 'Beth said you'd been looking for me. Urgently.'

I made coffee in the Lodge. Brought it down to the ward
and found Nina explaining the details of surgery and
post-operative care. The cat slept, curled in the corner of
the incubator, twitching a brow at the occasional passing
mouse in the dream. The monitors blinked life-signs in
luminescent colours. Nothing out of the ordinary. Nothing to say that the cat wasn't going to see out the night.

Steff leaned back against the wall, filling in the
noughts and crosses and technical numbers on an intensive care chart. The planes on her face had changed since
the morning. Lost a tension I didn't know they had. Her
hair stood vertical and freshly damp. She smelled faintly
of shower gel and sweat. As if she had worked out and
then showered and then worked out again. When she
smiled, it reached up to her eyes and beyond.

Nina Crawford sat on her tall stool beside the incubator and the need to sleep hung from her shoulders like
a shroud.

Steff finished her chart. Her eyes met mine over the
head of her boss. 'I could take him up to the Lodge if
you want,' she offered. 'I can rig up an oxygen source
and keep him in a basket by the bed. That way you two
can go home and get some sleep.'

Nina reached forward and toyed with the fluid
pump. Changed the rate and then changed it back again.

She needs sleep. And she has nowhere to go.

'Can she use Jason's room?' I asked.

Steff shook her head. 'Jay's driving back from Congress tonight. He just phoned from Carlisle. He'll be
back by three.'

There was silence. Steff looked at me. Said nothing.
Very pointedly said nothing. Nina put an extra dose of
antibiotics in the drip.

I pulled my keys from my pocket. Thought of Kate and wondered if the spare room was still free. 'OK.' I looked at the clock. Just after two. 'I have to be up in something less than six hours from now. Let's get you home.'

11

The barn smelt of horse abdomens. Of old hay and hot urine. Of horse-breath and new-born foal. The horses slept. Peaceful, standing sleep, heads over the door, one leg crooked at the stifle, changing legs once in a while to shift the weight. The foal slept lying down, tight-curled like a cat, flicking his tail in time to the dream. Rain stood over him, eyelids drooping, her nose brushing the straw. A pile of fresh dung steamed in the corner. Small, firm balls of dung. Just as they should be. I opened the door to let Nina into the box to check it. All the others started with loose dung. After a day like to-day, we're not leaving anything to chance. She checked over the mare. A hand on a pulse, a fast look under the eyelids, a finger pressed to the gums. A rectal thermometer. The colt balked at the strange touch. He stood up and shuddered, once, to shake off the straw and the hand and then skitted sideways, white-eyed, until she had him in the corner. She crossed her ankles and sat down in the straw at his feet. He stood over her, flicking his ears like a deer. She reached up a hand and he let her touch his muzzle, stroke the side of his face, feel along the edge of his jaw to the pulse. She shifted back against the wall and he pushed past her, pushed his way up under his mother and sucked. Milk dribbled white down his jugular furrow.

Nina stood up slowly and left the box.

'They're fine.' A whisper, because the horses slept. 'All safe so far.'

'Do we need to watch them through the night?'

She looked at her watch. Two thirty. 'No. There's no need.' She shook her head. 'I'll check them at four, if you want to take a look in at six.'

Very tempting. I would give a lot, right now, for a night's unbroken sleep. I don't suppose I'm the only one. 'No. It was me who brought her home. I'll do four. You do six. We'll need to be up by then anyway.'

'If you like.'

I led the way back across the yard. Frosted gravel crunched underfoot. A late moon hung yellow over the hill. Kate's Beetle sat just outside the gate in the place it had been since morning. Frost sprayed leaf-vein patterns round a crack in the windscreen.

Inside, Kate slept under a blanket in the big chair beside a fire that was banked to last all night. My alarm clock ticked softly on the mantelpiece, set to ring on the hour. I turned it off. We woke her. At least, we brought her close enough to the surface to walk upstairs to the spare room with a hot-water bottle and an extra blanket. She was asleep again before we closed the door.

We stood outside on the landing, whispering again just because it was late. 'Looks like the spare room isn't free after all.'

'Looks like. I could sleep in the barn if you want. It's warm enough. I'm sure the horses are very accommodating.'

'I'm sure they are. But the bed's big enough for two. So long as it's clear that we're going to sleep. That's all. Nothing else.'

'Kellen.' Weak, silent laughter. Bubbling close to the edge. 'I couldn't . . . really, honestly, I couldn't. Even if you wanted to. Just show me the bedroom and show me the bed. If we stand here talking about it much longer, I'll pass out at your feet.'

'Oh. OK. Sorry.' I forget she's never been here before. She fits in. Like one of the cats. 'Bedroom's down here. At the top of the stairs. Bathroom's next to Kate's room.' I opened the linen chest on the landing. 'I'll get you a towel.'

'Forget the towel. You'll have to live with me filthy.' She put her hand on my shoulder. Lightly. Without fire. 'Do you think I could borrow a toothbrush?'

She slept without the nightmares. I know because I watched her. Watched her slide down through the shell of total exhaustion into dreamless unconsciousness and then, later, after I'd been out to check Rain at four, I watched her roll on to one side and saw her eyes flicker into the sleep of dreams. Pleasant dreams. Dreams to smile for. No blood. No talking skulls. No whispered incitements to death. I dozed, half-awake, unused to the foreign feeling of a woman beside me in the bed again, listening to the alarm clock tick through to five and then on again towards six. The first time, I switched it off before it rang. The second time, I didn't set it at all. I lay watching the squat outline grow sharper against the rising grey light from the window. It's not often I see the dawn after the end of March. Twice in three days is at least once too many. I got up at five thirty.

The ponies have Monday mornings off. Which means everyone else has Mondays off too. Except me. On Mondays, I get up early and come home as early as I can. On wet Mondays, I feed the herd in the morning before work and spend the best part of the evening mucking out. If it's anything other than pissing wet, I rug them all up and turn them out before work and then all I have to do when I get home is feed them, skip out and brush off the mud.

The reeds on the duck pond were bending gently towards the barn, pushed by a wind coming down from the top of the ben. In April, the wind comes from anywhere and everywhere and it usually brings rain with it. I stuck my head outside the back door and looked out past the Hawthorn paddock towards the mountain. The grey rock at the top stood out sharply against the almost-blue of the sky. No rain between me and the crags. In April, that counts as a fair enough day by anyone's standards. I lifted the two New Zealand rugs from outside the pantry and dragged them off to the barn.

They're a resilient lot, our ponies. They cope remarkably well with being thrown out half an hour earlier than usual into fields where the grass is still stiff with early morning frost and there's ice still crackling at the edges of the river. I left the doors to the barn standing open and walked down the line fitting rugs, checking feet, feeling legs. They ambled out, one at a time, as I finished and they let Tîr herd them, in ones and twos, down the slope behind the barn, round the back of the beech wood and in through the open gate of the far paddock. If I could teach the dog to bolt the gate behind the

last one, we'd have a fully automated turning-out system. As it is, I get to amble down the same path, following the swinging rump of the grey garron gelding that we
bought to replace Midnight when she retired. He's not
the brightest of ponies but he's solid and safe and he can
carry an overweight businessman on a full day over the
ben and still find the energy for a quick canter on the
home run which says a lot for three centuries of Highland breeding.

I closed the gate over behind him and waited for the
dog to slide through under the low rail of the fence
before turning to face the wind and the long slow climb
back up to the farm. It's not a bad way to start the week.

Nina was in the barn with Rain and her foal when I
got back. She was wearing my work clothes, the ones I
left in the basket by the wardrobe, waiting for some
spare time to do the ironing. My spare fleece looked
good on her. She has the knack of wearing things well.
Even my unironed work clothes.

I leaned on the door and watched her sweet-talk the
foal into letting her take his temperature. There's a fine
line between necessary handling and abuse of a youngster. If the youngster's going to be your star stallion, it's a
good idea to persuade him that people are friendly before he weighs more than five of them put together. She
took it gently, with professional care. He stood quietly
enough.

She looked up and saw me watching. 'I raided your
wardrobe, do you mind?'

'Of course not. Take what you need.'

'I did.' She let herself out of the box. Rain followed
her to the door and banged hard against it with her foot.
The noise of it rang down the barn. A staccato rhythm of
horse-frustration. She hates being separated from the rest
of the herd. I lifted the headcollar and foal slip from the

hook outside the box. Nina stood with her hands in the pockets of my jeans. A thin vertical line bisected her forehead. The human equivalent of a horse banging on wood.

'You should have woken me, Kellen. I said I'd do the six o'clock check.'

'I know. But it's not six o'clock yet.'

She looked at me, long and pensive. 'Did you sleep?'

'Enough.' Enough to run on coffee for the kind of day I have planned. 'I don't have to go in to work and save lives.' Which is one of the many reasons I am truly glad that I'm not a surgeon.

'Nor do I. I just have to go in and explain why we've got another dead horse in the PM room.'

'Leave that to the pathologists.'

I let myself into the box and sat down in the straw as she had done and spoke promises to the foal. Promises of new grass and open spaces and the strange stories told by the wind. All that was his if he would let me put on the foal slip. He snored at me through flared nostrils and backed away behind his mother. I stood up and slipped the head collar on to the mare instead and then tried again with her son. Second time round he listened to the promises, let me slide the fine leather over his nose and fasten the buckle at his cheek.

I handed the mare's lead-rope to Nina. 'Are they OK to turn out?'

'As far as I can tell.' She stood back to let me out of the box. 'Have you done the morning treatments?'

'Not yet.' I lifted a tack box full of syringes and needles and Matt Hendon's supply of the necessary drugs. 'I thought you could do it. Since you're here.' And that way I don't have to stick needles in a foal that might grow up to hate me if I do.

'Really? I thought you wanted to bring them home

because you didn't trust us to keep them healthy?' It was difficult to tell if she was being serious.

She made up a vial of Crystapen, drew the resulting solution into a syringe, fitted a needle and passed it to me with exaggerated care. 'It isn't me that needs the practice, Dr Stewart.' She dribbled spirit on to a swab and held that out, too. 'You do it. I'll watch. And don't forget to flush with hepsaline afterwards. You don't want to be calling someone out here at eight o'clock because the line's clotted up.'

Too true. By five past eight tonight I fully intend to be fast asleep. I don't want to spend any more time than I absolutely have to playing doctors and nurses with the ponies.

Nina held the mare and watched me inject three times into the catheter; drugs, more drugs and the heparinised saline to keep the line clear. Just what the doctor ordered. It's hardly complicated stuff.

Nina took the empties and stashed them in a clear section of the tack box. 'Did they get their eight o'clock shots last night?' she asked.

'I don't expect they did.' I hadn't thought of that. 'I didn't ask Kate to do it. I wasn't expecting to be home that late. Does it matter?'

'I doubt it. This is insurance. If you're lucky they won't need it.' She caught the foal. 'If you're unlucky, it probably won't make any difference.' She kept her face straight. Teased with her eyes. 'It's all fairly academic, really.'

'Thanks.' I just love academic medicine. 'Did anyone ever tell you that sixty per cent of the people in hospital are there because some cretin with a degree prescribed unnecessary medication?'

She shrugged loosely. 'See it as a safety measure. We don't want you getting complacent too early.'

'I don't want the foal getting needle-shy, either.'

'Then do it gently. It won't do him any harm.'

She held the foal and reminded him of the stories that run on the wind. I fitted the finest needle I could get on to the syringe. The colt nibbled the wilder ends of her hair and chose not to notice the stabbing itch of steel in his rump.

'Good.' She flicked up a thumb. 'I'll check his bloods when I get into work. If his globulin's high enough, you won't need to give him any more after this.'

'That would make Sandy's day.' Mine too. We brought in a needle-shy mare once. She stayed less than a week. A needle-shy stallion defies imagination.

We turned the mare and foal out and walked back together from the Hawthorn paddock. Walked through the orchard where the late frost had caught all of the early buds. Across gravel that was softening in the first touch of the sun. Past the duck pond where half a dozen mallard drakes were contemplating gang-rape on the two available ducks. Through the back porch where a tortoiseshell queen was teaching the red kittens a hundred and one ways to murder a dead mouse. Back into the kitchen where the kettle had long since boiled dry and the room was fog-thick with steam.

Nina sat on a stool at the breakfast bar and left me to sort out the mess. 'You haven't considered going electric, I suppose?'

I pulled out a packet of J-cloths and mopped condensation from the surface of the breakfast bar. 'I'll go electric when you get double glazing.'

We remembered, both of us at the same time. Ugly, awkward and painful.

'I'm sorry,' I said.

'Don't. It's not your fault.'

'Not yours either.'

'No.' She shook her head, slowly. 'But there was a while, before last night, when I was wondering, if I really could have been that crazy.'

'But you wouldn't have kicked Killer.'

'No.'

I checked the base of the kettle for holes and, finding none, filled it with cold water and put it back on the heat. She watched me do it, biting her lip, pensive.

'Why did you go to the cottage, Kellen?' she asked.

'To see what was there.' I dug an enamelled pot from the cupboard under the sink. 'Porridge?'

'Mmm.'

I can cook porridge. It's one of the few things I do well. I can do it, even, with someone watching every move from the other side of the counter. It just requires a little bit more concentration. The trick is to catch it, just on the edge of the boil, and hold it there until it starts to stick on the spoon.

It was just about there when she spoke again.

'So what did you find?'

'Nothing.' If you leave it too long it burns. I lifted the pot off the heat. 'Just the cat.'

'Did you go inside?'

'Not for long.' It was burnt. Just at the edges where the enamel was thin. I used a ladle to spoon out the unburned surface layers. 'Here,' I slid a bowl across the counter. 'Should stop you going hypo 'till lunchtime at least. There's salt in the mill.'

She opened three drawers and found herself a spoon. Ground salt absently over the bowl. Watched me eat with eyes that were not about to let go. 'Why, Kellen?'

You can only push these things so far.

'Because I was wondering, too, if you really could have been that crazy.'

'And what if I wasn't just being crazy? Were you wondering that too?'

I made crystal circles with the salt. Stirred them in.

'Anything's possible.'

She sat still and watched me eat. The kettle boiled. The smell of coffee brightened the air. I drank. She watched and didn't drink.

'Do you really think if I was going to try again, that I would use fire?'

'I didn't think you'd try to cut out your scar, but you did.'

'I was hallucinating, Kellen, I didn't know what I was doing.' She wasn't hurt. She wasn't angry. Something in between both and more than either.

'And did you know what you were doing on Skye?'

'What?'

'On Skye. The holiday with Matt. When you tried to cut out your scar with a scalpel blade, did you know what you were doing then?'

She stared at me. Lost focus and found it again. Asked questions and answered them before they ever reached her lips. When she spoke, it came slowly. 'I cut my arm on a window, Kellen. I fell. I wasn't hallucinating at all.'

'You "fell" through a window?'

She looked past me, over my shoulder, to where the window looks out to the ducks. Looked through a different window to different mountains. She took a long time to answer. 'It was an accident,' she said finally. 'He was angry. He didn't mean it.'

'Matt?'

'Mmm.'

'And did he ask you not to tell me?'

'No. It was me that was in therapy, Kellen. Not him.
You didn't need to know.'

Really.

'So why did he tell me you did it yourself?'

'I don't know, Kellen . . .' She reached out across
the counter and laid her hand over mine. Smiled, dry
and ironic. Her forte. 'Maybe he wants you to think I'm
unstable.'

Maybe he does.

I took back my hand.

Maybe he's right.

A car crunched to a halt in the yard. Something small
and underpowered. The dog nosed her way out of the
back door. Size twelve Doc Martens padded across the
gravel.

Nina crooked her head to look out of the window.
'Company?'

Naturally. Some folk have no sense of timing. The
back door opened. I stood up to make the introductions.

'Stewart, meet Dr Nina Crawford of the University of
Glasgow Veterinary Teaching Hospital.' MacDonald
stood in the doorway, a red kitten balanced on either
palm and he nodded to Nina as if he'd known her all his
life. 'Nina, this is Inspector Stewart MacDonald of Strathclyde Central Constabulary.' And then, because she was
looking at him as if he might spontaneously throw his
jacket around her shoulders: 'Garscube isn't on his
patch.'

MacDonald handed her a kitten by way of greeting,
took off his hat and then settled himself on the bench by
the window. Even sitting and without the hat, he looked
oddly formal. He always looks that way when he's in
uniform. Which is, no doubt, what it's for.

Cats have a limited sense of formality. Kittens have none at all. The remaining red kitten scaled the vertical slope of his arm and set up a belay at his shoulder. He lifted it off and dropped it back to his knee. It dug in its claws and then set off up a different route, using his buttons as footholds. 'I spoke to Gavin Long before he came off shift this morning,' he said. '*Sergeant* Gavin Long.'

Ah. Hence the uniform.

Is this wise?

'And?' I asked.

'And I gather there's a claim been lodged. An investigator will be out to look at the cottage some time in the next day or two.'

Nina laid her kitten on the counter. It fell on its side and sank milk teeth like sharpened needles into the ball of her thumb. She spun it round on its back and played games with its tail. Her eyes were on me.

I'm really not sure this is wise.

'I went down to the cottage last night,' I said. 'I found Nina's cat in the woodshed. He had a ruptured diaphragm. From a kick, a human kick. Nina thinks it happened around the time the fire started.'

'Is that right?'

The tortoiseshell queen walked the tightrope along the back of the bench and settled herself on the windowledge by his shoulder. She pushed her chin against his arm. MacDonald tickled her absently along the line of her back. He watched Nina play with the kitten. Looked to me for permission.

I don't think it's up to me to set the boundaries in this.

I shrugged. When he did nothing more, I nodded.

He pulled a piece of baler twine from his jacket pocket and showed the kittens how to tie a bowline and then make the loop dance across the floor. Both of them joined the new game. 'Was the cat in the cottage when you left it on Saturday morning?' He asked it circumspectly, as normal Monday morning conversation, the kind you would have in the bread shop while they slice the morning loaf.

Nina doesn't buy bread in the mornings. She cuts horses and runs drips into cats. And she spends half her life asking circumspect questions of students. The kind that determine careers. 'He was asleep on a chair,' she said evenly. 'Beside the bed.'

'You're sure he was still there when you left to see to Dr Stewart's horse?'

'I'm sure. He woke up when the phone rang. I told him where I was going.' Like you do. Like she does, anyway. 'And I left the window open. Like I always do. So he can go out if he wants to.'

MacDonald nodded as if this was entirely normal behaviour in Greater Glasgow. He looked at Nina. 'Can anyone else verify the injuries to the cat,' he asked. 'A second opinion, so to speak.'

'We have the X-rays,' she said. 'You could time it fairly well from that. And I can get dated hard-copy printouts from the ICU monitors.'

The X-rays may be definitive but the monitor printouts won't be. It could have been any cat.

'You could get the hospital photographer to take pictures of the lesions as soon as you get in,' I said. 'Get him to record the date and time on the prints. Then we can get a third party to estimate the time of injury from the bruising.' You can do it in people. I don't see any reason at all why we can't get it done in a cat.

Nina thought about it. She found a pen in a pile on the breakfast counter and wrote a note to herself on the back of her hand. 'I'll have it all ready for the investigator, shall I?' she said. Threads of neat acid wound their way through her voice. 'Do I take it they want to know if I set fire to my own cottage?'

MacDonald has faced worse threats than acid. 'That would be the way of it.' He nodded agreeably. 'I'm sure they'll back off once you can prove that you didn't. In the meantime, they'll most likely come in and see you at work sometime in the next day or two. If it's after hours I'll tell them you're going to be here, shall I?'

He has his own way of ripping the floor out from under you. He watched Nina. She said nothing, just leant forward on the breakfast counter and studied something important on the duck pond. Neither of them looked at me.

Sometimes it's easier to make decisions without thinking.

I nodded slowly. 'For tonight, anyway,' I said. 'I expect we'll both be home by six.'

12

On Mondays, Wednesdays and Fridays, University of Glasgow Counselling Service runs a drop-in clinic from its office on the second floor of an anonymous sandstone terrace hidden in a back street just behind the Queen Margaret Union. On the first, third, and if there is one, fifth Mondays of the month, those who drop in, see me.

On the first Monday in April, two weeks into the Easter break, undergraduates and staff were both fairly thin on the ground and those who dropped in were mostly highly cerebrated post-graduates crumbling under the pressure of impending thesis deadlines.

If I have to work for a full day after a night with no sleep, this is the kind of day I would choose. A day divided neatly into fifty-minute slices, each spent listening to the mind-scrambling intricacies of particle physics or high temperature ceramics, trying to garner a sense of perspective from which the world will not necessarily fall apart if the Introductions and Reference Lists are not finished by Friday. It's the regular pattern for Mondays out of term-time. It's enlivening. It's refreshing. It's a very pleasant contrast to the real world. More importantly, on this particular Monday morning, not one single person, not even Juliette, the post-gothic biker who acts as receptionist, ever got around to asking me what I'd done with my weekend. There are days when that kind of freedom matters more than most.

There were seven 'clients' in all. A pair of MAs and a post-doc in the morning and a triad of PhDs in the afternoon. And then, at the end, Barnaby Thompson; a man who has more degrees than the other six put together and considerably less chance of using them.

I wasn't expecting Barnaby. I never do. I was sitting in my office just after five, watching the last of the post-grads book a follow-up appointment and planning a route home that would take in the supermarket and miss the worst of the traffic. I was thinking through an easy dinner and evening treatments for Rain and the foal and a quiet evening putting my life back together. On my desk, lay a printed list of possible psychiatric referrals for Nina, together with a letter addressed to my immediate superior with news of my impending resignation. Both of them waiting for a new day. I wanted a decent meal and a drink and time to think before I did anything else I couldn't undo. And sleep. Most of all, I wanted sleep.

Barnaby was waiting outside on the doorstep. He could have knocked. He could have hit the buzzer downstairs and announced his arrival. He could, having made his way into the building, simply have turned the handle and walked into the lobby. Instead, he folded himself, concertina-style into the doorway and waited for Anne-Marie Wallace, a postgraduate botanist of fairly robust constitution, to trip over him on her way out of the door.

He was drunk, clearly. He was also, just as clearly, flying on injectable pharmaceuticals. He was clothed only in his dressing gown and underpants and he was badly in need of a bath. There were old, clotted bandages wrapped loosely round his wrists. There are often bandages on Barnaby's wrists. So far, the razor cuts have been shallow and they have followed tracks from the base of his thumb across to the base of his little finger. Scaphoid to pisiform, right across the digital flexor tendons. Colourful but not fatal. Two of Dr Thompson's degrees are in medical science and he knows the track of his radial artery as well as I do. On the day he cuts up and down, not across, I will know that he really means to die. In the meantime, it would be nice if he still had the use of his fingers in the morning.

I stood in the doorway to my office and watched him terrorise a perfectly sane academic simply by existing. Anne-Marie inhaled deeply, which was a mistake, stepped over his knees and ran heavy-footed down the stairs. Barnaby waved her good-bye. Juliette packed her bag and collected her leather jacket and helmet from the rack. She said nothing but she said it with vehemence. Barnaby is not, strictly speaking, entitled to treatment at the clinic. He is currently neither a student nor a member of staff although he has, in his time, been both. Barnaby comes straight from the raw end of the real world and he offends the very foundations of the ivory tower. Even Juliette. Particularly Juliette. She is very particular as to what rules she breaks. Speed limits, for instance, are made to be broken. And the rules regarding recreational pharmaceuticals. Up to a point. If you can eat it, drink it or smoke it, it's in. But needles are out. Failing to wash is out. Wearing unwashed underclothes in public is out. Barnaby does all three simultaneously and worse besides, and he's so far out he's untraceable.

Except that it's difficult to ignore something in quite that much pain. I walked over and stood by the open door. 'Come on, Barnaby.' I held out a hand so that he had to make some effort to stand up. 'It's warmer inside.' He grasped my wrist and pulled himself upright. He weighs less than I do. And stands at least six inches taller. Or, he would if he chose not to stoop. Juliette walked round him and out on to the landing. She made the mistake of looking back. Years of genteel conditioning are so much harder to hide than the colour of your hair. I checked my watch, pointedly. She's not supposed to leave before half past five. Thirteen minutes to go.

'Could you call the farm and tell them I'll be late home, please?' She got as far as the third step down before she stopped. I dropped a business card on the desk, the one with Nina's extension number on it. 'And could you call this number and leave a message for Dr Crawford telling her that I've been delayed and I'll call her as soon as I can leave?' I smiled. The kind of smile that got her back up the stairs faster than she'd gone down. 'Thanks,' I said. 'You can go after that.'

It was seventeen minutes past five when Barnaby Thompson followed me into my office. It was almost the same time after seven when he left. He wasn't what you would call sober by then, but he seemed relatively straight. He had clean bandages on his wrists and he promised me he wasn't going to play with the razor blades ever again. He promised me also that he was going to go out in the morning and sign on the dole, but I found that one harder to believe. In Barnaby's case, unemployment would be preferable to some of the things he is doing to make ends meet. Particularly when they create a lifestyle that pushes the ends quite so terrifyingly far apart. I followed him out on to the landing and he promised me he was going to go home and have a bath. Of all that he offered, it seemed the most likely.

Juliette, predictably, had left. In her place, a message light flashed on the answering machine. Three message lights. Nobody calls for me at the UCC. All my messages go up to the main clinic at Sauciehall Street. I set the alarm and followed Barnaby down the stairs, planning a route up to Garscube that made the most of the time and the relative lack of traffic. I dug in my bag for my mobile and flicked through the address-list for Nina's number. Her office number. I thought about removing her home number altogether and decided it was too early for that kind of pessimism. The number rang and wasn't answered. I started hunting through the memory for the university switchboard. I listened to the first ring and hung up. Turned round. Took the stairs three at a time on the way back up. Nobody leaves messages at the UCC after six o'clock, period. It's all routed through the university switchboard to a call-answering service. Unless it's personal and they know who's on duty. Then they forward it through.

████████

Three messages, timed at half-hour intervals between half five and half six. All from Sandy.

'Kellen? Are you there? It's Sandy. Rain's no' well. I'll give her the evening jags and call you back.'

'Kellen? She's not right. I'm calling the hospital.'

'Kellen? We're taking her into the vet school. If you get this, meet us at the ward. I'll try your mobile when we get there.'

I broke every limit there is between Hillhead and

Garscube. The tail lights of the lorry lit the way ahead of
me as I turned in over the cattle grid. I followed them
slowly down the hill and round the corner to the ward.

He was right. She wasn't well. They stood at the top of
the ramp together, all three of them. A soft dun mare
with the sweat running dark down her withers and the
first folds of a frown crinkling the skin above her eyes. A
dull, chestnut colt, all tucked up like a whippet from
lack of milk with a smear of mud masking the new moon
of his star. A wee gnome of a man holding the lead ropes
with cramped, arthritic fingers, his head shining bald in
the hard glare of the light, his eyes all red at the edges
from the pain of it.

They were not well, any of them. But of the three,
the mare was the worst.

Steff was there, waiting at the doors to the horse
ward, dressed in theatre greens with a white coat pulled
over the top. Her surgical mask hung loosely round her
neck. Spots of blood ran across it, wet trackways of surgery not long past. She didn't say much, just nodded to
me and grunted to Sandy and as if they'd done all the
talking they needed to do on the phone. Like: 'She's not
well.' And: 'Get her in.'

Together, they walked Rain off the lorry, down the
unloading ramp and into the stocks on the left just inside the door. She walked in as if she already knew the
way. Or as if she didn't care. As soon as they stopped,
the foal nudged up against her. Pushed his nose round
the steel upright of the stocks and shoved urgently at her
udder.

'She's drying up,' said Sandy. 'There's not enough
milk. We'll have to feed the wee lad.' His voice had odd

inflections. Foreign, somehow, to the ear. Pinched in, like the lines around his eyes.

I was wrong. In the brighter light of the ward, Sandy Logan was worse than the mare.

███████

Steff was in overdrive. She had a pulse rate, a respiratory rate and a capillary refill time all noted down on the chart before we'd closed the stocks. She drew blood and took nasal swabs into bacterial and viral transport media. She picked up a phone, let it ring and dropped it again without comment. A stocky lad with oil-dark hair and the beginnings of a beard appeared in a different door-way, panting from the run. Another one in theatre greens. Without a white coat. 'This is Jason,' she said. 'He'll help while we're waiting for Nina.'

Jason ran the bloods and swabs to the lab. Steff rolled up her sleeve, rolled on a glove and performed one of the fastest rectal examinations I've ever seen. She oiled a stomach tube and slid it, with fluid care, up one nostril and down into the stomach, blowing into the end and watching the side of the neck for the air bulge to make sure it didn't slip straight down the trachea and into the lungs. She blew again and sniffed at the gas that refluxed back. Made a face and jerked away from the smell. Stuck the end of the tube into a bucket of water and watched a chain of gas bubbles roll up to the sur-face. No fluid. No gastric contents. Just gas. She kinked over the end of the tube and drew it out again with just as much care. She said nothing to anyone, but the glint at her nose flashed semaphore signals of things held so tight that I thought she would crack.

Jason ran back, breathing whistles through lungs not meant for running. Between them, they clipped and cleaned a small patch on her belly alongside the line of her stitches. They stuck a needle up into her abdomen and held a blood tube underneath for the drips of perito-neal fluid. Few and far apart. But clear. Which was good. Peritoneal fluid should be clear.

The phone rang. Jason took it and wrote numbers on a chart. Showed them to Steff. Then to me. They meant nothing. I looked carefully at Steff, not wanting to inter-rupt.

'PCV's up. Plasma proteins are up. Urea's up. White cells are through the floor,' she said shortly. 'Huge left shift.' And then, because I didn't make the right noises, 'She's septicaemic. And she's dehydrating. She hasn't twisted a gut. Her uterus feels fine. There's no haemor-rhage in there from the surgery. There are no bacilli on the smear but I don't think that counts for anything right now. We can wait till tomorrow for the results of the endotoxin assay or we can assume she's starting what all the others had and treat her with everything we've got.' She unhooked the front gate to the stocks. 'I wasn't plan-ning to wait,' she said.

We let Rain out of the stocks. Sandy walked her with the foal up the barn to the box at the far end. The one with 'ICU' etched on the copper plaque on the door. The one that housed Branding Iron before he died. The in-side had been steam-cleaned. It smelled of Dettol and other, less fragrant, disinfectants. I am prepared to be-lieve you could have taken a swab to the floor and it would have come up sterile. We waited outside while Steff and Jason wheeled bales of straw down from the hay-store. I found a pitchfork and made up the bed. It was good straw; bright and fresh from the barn with no dust. You could smell the fields and the east wind and the August sunlight as I forked it out. Rain noticed it when she hadn't noticed anything else. She breathed in deeply and snored out gently. I piled it high up against

the walls, just like her bed at home. Sandy stood outside the box and held them while the foal tried to drink
from the mare for the third time in as many minutes.

'We'll have to teach him how to suck from a bottle,'
he said, 'for now. Till her milk comes back.' He waited
for someone to correct him. Nobody did. There seemed
no point.

'We'll have to move him to one of the calf pens,' said
Steff. 'I don't think we can risk cross-infection.'

I didn't look at Sandy. I just heard him breathe. A
long, sore breath in. 'Leave him with Rain for now,' I
said. 'Until we've got the bed sorted out and found him a
bottle.' And then, because it had been a long day after all
and I hadn't been thinking: 'Where's Nina? She was going to call me with blood results. To see if the wee one
could come off the antibiotics.'

There was silence in all of the furious movement.
Jason bit his pen and then wrote something new on the
chart. He hasn't got Steff's presence of mind. Steff was
halfway out of the box to collect the clippers from outside. She turned in the doorway, her hand on the foal.

'His globulins are fine,' she said and she knew she
wasn't answering the question I had asked, 'but we'll
have to keep him on the pen-strep for now. Switching
from natural feeding to the bottle does crap things to
their immune system. It's not worth bringing him off the
antibiotics now.'

I let it go. Time enough later. I held Rain while Steff
and Jason took a pair of clippers each and shaved hair
from both sides of her neck. They slid catheters into the
jugulars. Two catheters; one left, one right. So now she
has three. One from the surgery—which is the one that I
used in the morning—and two from now. Branding Iron
had four. They wore gloves while they put them in and
when they were finished they turned them inside out

and knotted them before they dropped them into the yellow clinical waste bag. The air smelled suddenly of blood.

The foal began to grizzle for his mother. He tugged against the foal slip. Flashed white around the eyes and flicked a hind foot at Sandy. We let the mare go, let the foal into the box and shut the door. Just in that moment, you could look over the door and believe it would all be all right. The smell of the straw and the mare and the foal were more than the smell of the disinfectant and the hibitane they had poured on her neck. Just in that moment.

Steff gave Sandy directions to the feed room and sent him off to mix milk for the foal and a hot mash for the mare. Jason got a list half a page long and ran off to get the fluids and antibiotics and intravenous feeding solutions. And a flask of coffee for an overnight watch.

I stayed with Steff. We let ourselves back into the box. To be with Rain and her foal. The foal tried to suck. The mare flicked her tail and lifted a leg in threat and then she gave up the protest and stared, dull-eyed at the straw while her foal butted hopelessly at her belly. I could have wept.

I sat down in the straw. Steff pushed her hands deep in her pockets, leant back on the door, kept her eyes on the far end of the barn for signs of someone, anyone, returning.

'So where is she?' I asked.

She didn't ask who I meant.

'I don't know.' She chewed skin from her lip. 'I haven't seen her since just after Sandy rang.'

'What happened?'

'We were operating. One of Matt's cases. A retriever for a triple pelvic osteotomy. To correct a—' She stopped, shook her head, the way the foal shook off hands. 'I'm sorry. It doesn't matter what it does. It's a big, long, complicated orthopaedic op. And it took us about an hour longer than it should have done. I sent her out about ten minutes after Sandy rang.'

'You did what?' You can't do that. Residents don't order their surgeons out of theatre. Never.

Steff stared straight at the mare. The muscles ran tight along the line of her jaw. Inside the pockets of her overalls, her hands curled tight into fists. She shrugged. 'I requested that she leave,' she said.

'Why, Steff?'

'Because I had to. She wasn't part of the game. She wasn't exactly up to scratch before the phone call. She was a complete mess afterwards. We weren't going to get it done with her in there.'

'And she went? Because you told her to?'

'Hardly.' The foal gave up on the mare. Tried Steff as the next most likely mother substitute, mouthing across her hands for milk. She cupped her hands for his searching lips. 'We . . . had words. I said it was her or me. That if she wanted to stay and cut, I would scrub out and go do something more useful.' She looked at me, then. There was fire eating out round her eyes. 'She knew that if I went, she couldn't finish it on her own. She wasn't that far gone.'

'So where is she now?'

'I don't know. She said she'd be waiting in the ward for when Sandy arrived. I came straight over from theatre. I thought she'd be here.'

'Have you tried her office?'

'Twice. When you got here and just before Jason arrived. And I told the switchboard to page her at five-minute intervals and then to page me if she showed up.' She held her pager up to the light. Dead to the world. 'I don't know where she's gone, Kellen. But wherever she is, I can't find her.'

Time goes very fluid in a crisis. The air turns to treacle so that nothing can move. Inertia sucks. I stood up. It took an age to make it to vertical. The door to the box took hours to open. 'So why are we here, Steff?' My voice came from too far away to make sense. 'Why are we not out finding her?'

'Because the last thing she said as she walked out of theatre was that she was relying on me to sort out your mare.'

'Oh Christ.' I was running down the barn by then. Like you run in dreams. Not going anywhere. Just running. Running too slowly. Running down the barn. Away from the stocks and the feed room and the hay-barn. Down towards the theatres and the offices and the changing rooms. And the pharmacy.

Steff was at my shoulder. Long, loping strides. Like a tiger. The door at the end stopped us. Time hung in the vacuum while Steff fumbled for the keys, unlocked it, heaved it open. I was panting. Hyperventilating. Worse than Jason. Panic does that to you, if you let it push you that far. I breathed in, deep and slow. Caught the last edge of sanity before it all unravelled completely. Breathed deeper and slower. Brought the nightmare into focus. 'Was she hallucinating?' I asked. 'Was Nina seeing things before she walked out of theatre?'

'Kellen, she couldn't tell the difference between the needle holders and the scissors by the time she left.'

We ran, both of us, for the far building.

13

I have a new nightmare. It is this:

It is dark. Dark like the inside of her bedroom. I have no torch. I can't find the light switch. All I can see is the dark. But I know she is here. In the pharmacy. Because I have radar for skin and it says she is here. And because this is where she always knew she would be. In the nightmares. When the gravity got too much.

She is here. All I have to do is find her.

I hunt. I feel. Reach out. Call her name. The darkness speaks silence. Her silence. She has lived with this dark for so long she can call it a friend. She knows I will come. Sometime, I will come. She doesn't want to be found. Not yet. And so she has made a bargain with the darkness, her ally, to keep me away. I need to find the light. I feel my way back to the door. Bump into shelves. Trip over packing boxes. Knock bottles off shelves to smash on the floor. Liquid mixes with glass to make glue. A trap for unwary feet. Strange, noxious gasses mix and rise in the air. I can't breathe.

The light switch is here. Where it should be. By the door. And so now, in the nightmare, there is light. Nasty, flickering, off-yellow fluorescent light. And the ceiling is blue. Blue like the sky over Skye.

She is there. In the corner. Where she said she would be. Half sitting against the fridge. The tangled mass of her hair shows henna-red against the white of the door. Her skin is yellow. Pentobarbitone yellow. A trick of the light. A bright yellow drip bag floats upwards from the vein in her arm like a fat, bloated balloon. There's enough pentobarbitone in there to kill a horse. Several horses. I can tell by the colour, even from here. Even from halfway across the room. But I can't see if she's breathing. From here I can't see if she's breathing.

'STEFF . . . *Stephanie. In the pharmacy. She's in here.*' In the nightmare, I can scream if I want to. Wake the dead if I need to. And I can run. Now, I can run.

The drips run in a steady stream. Lethal, yellow, poison. Between one drip and the next, I grab the drip set. Shut it off. Remember, just in time, not to pull the catheter from her arm. She got it in. It might still save her life. Last time, after she blew the vein, it took the ambulance team three tries to find another one. Three tries take time. We don't have any time.

We may have no time at all.

I find her wrist. Find no pulse. Try her throat. Give up. Try her heart.

Please. Have a heart beat. Please.

She has a heartbeat. If I put my ear to her sternum and hold my own breath I can hear it. Regular, rhythmic, drumming. Slow, slow drumming. Pentobarbitone slow. But there could be other things with it. Who knows what she might choose to mix in her cocktail this time? It was morphine and ketamine before. Neither of them quite enough to be fatal. She's learnt more pharmacology since then.

But now she isn't breathing. Dear God, I don't think she is breathing.

ABC. The first lines of the crash. Airway. Breathing. Circulation. I was trained to do this once. Except we always did it on dummies, plastic models who didn't matter. And once on Lee. For the practice. Thirteen years ago.

Tilt the head back. Hold the nose. Make a seal, mouth to mouth. Deep breath in and then exhale everything you've got. Watch her chest rise and fall. And again. And again. And again. Watch lips that were blue turn to lilac. Feel for the heart. The slow, even canter of the drumbeat. Still drumming. Keep drumming. Please, whoever is listening, don't let her heart stop now.

And Steff is here. Steff who runs like a tiger. Steff who is weeping, fast tears of frustration and anger and other things, less easily read. 'She can't do this . . . Fuck it . . . Kellen, she can't do this.'

'She's done it. Call an ambulance. Get me some oxygen. And some adrenaline. Get the crash cart. Anything. Just get me something to keep her alive.'

There's a phone on the wall. They say the ambulance is on its way. In Greater Glasgow, that could be anything up to three hours from now. Make them understand it's urgent. They say that they do. If they get here too late, I will kill them. All of them. One at a time. Slowly.

Breathe. Just keep breathing. Head back. Fingers on the nose. Mouth-to-mouth seal and keep breathing.

Steff is back. Throwing the crash cart ahead of her like a demon shopper. No grace in her movements now. But she has brought me the crash kit from the ward. With oxygen and face masks and adrenaline. We don't need the adrenaline. Not yet. We just need oxygen to keep her lungs full. To keep her heart moving and to keep her brain alive.

Just breathe. Just keep breathing.

The mask's the wrong shape. Built for a cat. Or a dog. Something with a nose that sticks out like a cornet. The seal doesn't fit round her mouth or her nose. Oxygen blows out round the edges.

Just breathe.

'I need an ET tube. And a laryngoscope. And get a drip going into that vein.'

They are there. In the crash cart. All the things that I want. Laryngoscope. Tube. Oxygen line.

But I haven't done this. Ever.

'Steff, I can't do it. I don't know how.'

'You're the doctor, woman. If you can't do it, nobody else can.'

I have never done this. Never. But I have been to the lectures.

Tip the head back further, shine the light from the 'scope on the vocal chords. Remember, too late, what they said about not levering the scope against the teeth. '*Shit.*' She will smile now with a chip in her left upper incisor. If she ever smiles again.

Shine the light in, spray the local, slide the tube in. Fail. Breathe. Try again. Slide the tube in. Watch it go somewhere.

'Is it in?'

'It better be. Give me the oxygen. And the bag.'

My hands know how to do this. Two nights ago, I did it for a dying foal. Last night it was a cat that may have lived. I didn't know I was practising for the real thing. Squeeze. Pause. Squeeze. Watch the chest rise and fall. Watch the lips change from lilac to pink. Watch

colour come back to skin that was not yellow by a trick
of the light.

Keep squeezing. Don't stop squeezing.

Look up and see an ECG trace run; slow; rhythmic,
but slow, across the monitor that's built into the crash
cart. Because Steff, who is not weeping now, has a clean
drip running into the line and has had the presence of
mind to set up an ECG. And to count the heart rate. And
to start drawing adrenaline into a syringe, ready for injection. In case the drumming stops.

And then I think we have done all that we can do.
Except to pray for the ambulance. And a clear bed in a
ward. And a consultant who knows what they're doing.

They listen, sometimes, the gods of the ben. We got an
ambulance faster than I've ever known one to come. We
got a sane team who accepted the drip line and the ET
tube and the oxygen and didn't ask stupid questions
about who was qualified to put what where. We got a
clear ride to the Western with the sirens blaring and the
lights flashing and not one single Glaswegian driver
found it amusing to get in the way. And we got Eric
Dalziel. Big Eric. Eric the Climber with his red hair like
the colt and his dark eyes like the mare and his sense of
humour that would strip the paint from a whore and
leave her standing, naked in the street. Except when it
matters. When it matters, Big Eric has an understanding
of the technology of medicine that would rival Matt Hendon's and a body of knowledge locked away in his mind
that would fill textbooks if he ever had the time. And he
has compassion. When it matters Eric Dalziel will work
through the night and out the other side to keep someone alive and there aren't many who will do that when
they've signed up beyond senior registrar. He was in the

year below me when I sat my finals. He climbs with Lee whenever they're both not on call. He was a friend of Malcolm's and he spoke for Bridget when we finally got ourselves together to hold a service. And he was waiting for Nina when they carried her upstairs to the wards.

They gave her a room of her own, which is more than she got the last time. A pale room, one shade pinker than white, with scattered rosebuds across the curtains and a salmon-rose blanket on the bed. The air was conditioned and dry. It smelled of violets, aerosol violets, cloying and sweet. I would have handled phenol better. They laid her on the bed; a pale plastic, slack-lipped doll with threads of saliva drooling round the tube in her mouth. Without that she could have been dead. The dead don't dribble. Not for long.

Then they started on the high technology. They didn't shave her head. Not yet. But the rest was the same as the last time. Multiple drip lines adding scars to her arms and to her neck. Monitors muttering electronic threats whenever they got numbers they didn't like. The ventilator. The dead-whale gasp of the ventilator. Gasp-in. Whistle-out. Repeat, once every twelve seconds. More than anything else in the wards, I hate the noise of the ventilator. I stood at the end of the bed wearing Steff's white coat and with Steff's stethoscope round my shoulders and I watched them set up more monitors than I knew you could fit on a human being. I thought Branding Iron was overwired. On Nina Crawford, I stopped counting when the lines reached double figures.

They let me stay and watch them. The nurses. The house officer. The registrar. The myriad other white-coated people who ran at the double doing efficient things to keep her alive. They let me stay because I shared the uniform and a clinical coat still carries you a long way in a hospital. But more, they let me stay because they had seen Eric greet me when I followed her in. They saw him come over and put one huge bear-muscled arm around my shoulder and they saw him show me where to stand, out of the way but not out of sight. He didn't say anything and he didn't ask questions. But it told them I could stay.

But they still watched me, sideways. In the gaps between the arterial pressure lines and the blood samples and the urinary catheter, they asked silent questions and gave each other silent answers. And when they undid her gown to place the leads for the ECG and they found the bite marks on both her shoulders and another on her breast, their eyes danced faster and their brows rose higher and they nodded to themselves in the corners.

Only Eric didn't join in. Because Eric is a friend and he knew most of the answers anyway and he knew that he'd get all the rest when he asked.

He came over and stood beside me, at the foot of the bed, the case notes hanging loose from his fingers.

'She was your friend, yes?' And with Eric, because he is Eric, these things are not ambiguous.

'She is my friend. Yes.' Then, because I have to tell somebody sometime, and Eric, of all people, is safe: 'She was a client.'

'Oh. I see. Bad luck.' And from Eric, there is no judgement.

But I want to be judged.

'Until Friday, she was a client.' He needs to understand. Whatever made her do this, I was part of it. 'I didn't get her a referral.'

'Kellen . . .' He put his arm round my waist. Slid me back into a chair. Out of range of the whispering ears. '. . . Sit down. It's history now.' He crouched in front of me. Not all doctors stand at bedsides. In his hand, hidden beneath the case notes, was the drip bag. The lethal, yellow drip bag. Flaccid now because half of it was in her body and half of the rest had gone off in bottles to be analysed.

'They said there was pentobarbitone.' He watched my eyes. 'Do you know if there's anything else?'

'I don't know. I think there could be. She was hellish bradycardic when I found her. She put morphine and ketamine in it the last time. They blew her mind . . .' You can come round from the pentobarb. Chew it up with the liver. Pee it away. Clean out your system. Learn to breathe. Repair the mess on your arm. Grow the hair on your head. But a 2 g dose of ketamine opens the doorways to hell and I don't know if we could ever have closed them completely.

'Kellen . . . keep a grip . . . don't go out on me now.' Eric. Shaking my shoulders. Eric, who is still not judging. 'What do you mean, "the last time"?'

'She was in here before. Seven years ago.'

'The same thing?'

'More or less. Things die. She doesn't cope.' Although I thought she had reasons, now, to cope. 'You'll have the records somewhere.'

He made a note on the file. A house officer came to his beckoning; an Asian lass, slight, with shining, dark hair and dull, dark eyes. Eyes that said she'd been on her feet for at least the weekend if not most of the previous week and wasn't expecting to see sleep for another month or so. She took the note, read it and vanished.

Eric still had his arm round my shoulder. 'We'll get the records,' he said.

The registrar was looking in her eyes with a 'scope. Looking past the walnut of the iris, through the wide, round window of her pupil to the scattered brightness of her retina and her optic disc. He didn't like what he saw. He called Eric and Eric looked too, for longer. He didn't like what he saw, either. He called a neurologist and, in time, the neurologist came. A wiry, hook-nosed Aberdonian with lasers for eyes and no small talk. They both looked at her retinas with the 'scope. They tested reflexes on her hands and on her feet. Then they shaved her head. Little bits of it, carefully, where it wouldn't show. They ran an EEG and printed it out. Put their heads together over the squiggles and lines. Eric came back to me, running tight-corded fingers through the red waves of his hair. I have seen him hang his full weight off those fingers, halfway up a hundred-foot cliff. And then, the next day, slide an arterial line into a pre-term infant and get it in first time.

'Was she breathing, Kellen, when you found her?' There are tight lines round his eyes. Tighter than his fingers. This is not a casual question.

'No.'

Laser-eyes joined him. 'How long was the period of apnoea?'

I was a student, once, of men like this.

'I have no idea. She was blue. That is, she was severely cyanotic with a marked bradycardia. I initiated artificial respiration and then intubated and ventilated with a hundred per cent oxygen.'

'Did you indeed?' The lasers flashed. 'How long between finding her and ventilating? How long before she got oxygen?'

'I don't know.' Time goes very fluid in a crisis. 'Mouth-to-mouth straight away. Not more than five minutes till the oxygen.'

'Good lass.' He patted me on the arm. 'Very good.'

They went back to study her eyes. The neurologist wrote in the notes and left. Eric gave orders. More drugs went into the lines.

Eric came back to me. Crouched down again. Put his hand on my knee.

'Eric . . . I don't want to know.' My voice is far away. Very faint. Like a child, in the morning, halfway in the dream.

'It's better than evens,' he said. 'You need to know that much.'

'How much better?'

'I don't know. She was lucky. Pentobarb's neuroprotective. It gives us more time. We'll blast her with Lasix. Mannitol if we have to. Run the trace again in the morning. Alec's hopeful.'

Hopeful. Hopeful. The man with no small talk is hopeful that Nina Crawford might still have a mind. That she might be able to walk. To talk. To laugh. To hear. To see. To remember.

To know who she is.

'She was a surgeon,' I said. Because I had to say something.

His fingers curled tight round my knee. 'She might still be again,' he said, and it was the compassion in his voice that made me weep. 'We'll do what we can.'

████████

Later, he came back and sat with me by the end of her bed. Brought sandwiches and coffee to share. It was quiet then. Beyond the rush of visitors in the other wards. Beyond the late evening flush of cisterns and the gush of water in ward-end sinks and the rattle of plumbing laid two hundred years ago and still in use. We sat in our oasis of electronic rhythms, hypnotised into silence

by the twelve-second hiss of the ventilator and the inter-
mittent whine of the indirect pressure cuffs on her arm
and the minute-on-minute tick of the fluid pumps.

'You'd think they'd have invented something quieter
by now.' He stared forward, focused on nothing. As if
there were only two of us in the room.

'They think there's no need. Patients on this much
technology can't hear it anyway.'

'Maybe.' He nodded. 'They hear more than you
think.'

I'd like to think so.

He pulled a piece of paper from his pocket. 'I just got
her blood results from toxicology,' he said. 'You were
right.'

'What about?'

'Ketamine.' He passed me the sheet. 'There was
ketamine in there with the pentobarbitone.'

'Shit.' I looked at the report. Three sections were
ringed in red: Pentobarbitone: 0.15 mg/ml. Opiates:
00.00 mg/ml. Ketamine 0.98 g/ml.

'How much is 0.98 g in real money?' It's a long time
since I did pharmacology.

'I don't know. Enough to bring the big green monsters crawling out of the walls, big time, but I don't think
it would have been enough to knock her out.'

'Would it be enough to make a difference to the
odds?'

'No.'

'Thanks.' I sat for a while, in the warm and the dark,
staring at the numbers until they blurred on the page.
'Why, Eric?' I said it into the darkness. Not expecting an
answer. Just trying to make sense of the senseless.

'I don't know. Maybe it makes the going easier. It
would be painless, anyway. You wouldn't feel much on
ketamine.'

'She wasn't running from pain, Eric, not physical pain. She was running from what she saw in her head. The big green monsters. Except hers were horses with teeth like mink and cats with maggots crawling out of their eyes. It took her years to recover after last time. She's had nightmares and flashbacks that would make your skin crawl on and off for the last seven years. It was the ketamine that did it. She knew that. She hated the stuff. Why would she call it all in again?'

'Some of us climb when we're terrified of heights. It's something about facing the thing that scares us most. To prove that we can.'

'But, when you climb, you're not trying to die.'

'I don't dream of patients with teeth like mink.'

'No.'

I gave him back his sheet of paper and watched him slide it to the back of her notes and I sat there thinking of ketamine and of pain and of what it takes for anyone to want to die that badly.

Eric stood up after a while. Crushed the paper mug in his hand and threw it in the clinical waste bag. 'Are you staying?' he asked. 'Are you in for the night?'

'If you don't mind.'

'Whatever.' He thumbed a button on the wall by the oxygen inlet. Somewhere in the staff room at the far end, a buzzer sounded. 'I'll get them to bring you an airbed.'

'I wasn't planning to sleep.'

'No.' He smiled, all red hair and dark, sparking eyes and the shoulders of a bear. 'But you'll need an osteopath in the morning if you spend the night in that chair.'

He stopped at the end of the ward. Turned round. Pitched his voice to carry down the ward. 'Better than evens, Kellen. You should sleep on that. It's the best we've got.'

I didn't sleep on it. I didn't sleep much at all. But the thought was there.

Steff came to visit with the dawn. They shouldn't have let her in any more than they should have let me stay. But she wore theatre greens, with her hat poking out of her pocket and the blood-stained mask round her neck and there's no night sister in the world that would argue with a surgeon, even if she wasn't six foot two with blonde spikes and a nose stud.

She stood over the bed for a while, inhaling the ward-smells of night-sweats, unwashed skin and stale urine, taking in the monitors, the drips, the urine bag filling slowly on the floor. She put out a hand and touched the unmoved, unmoving skin, seemed surprised that there was no response. She ran her fingers up a cheek and lifted an eyelid. Looked in at nothing. Nobody. Laid a hand on her chest and felt the steady, rise and fall of the ventilated lungs. She shook her head, slowly and then came to stand by the edge of the bed; a still, sober, giant with the patchwork of half-held feeling still running fresh beneath the surface. She smelled of straw and horseshit and artificial milk replacer and if she had any news at all she would have told me. I didn't ask.

'She looks just like your mare,' she said. 'Except the mare knows who I am.' Which was what I needed to know. 'How is she?'

'She's alive. She's ticking. She has cerebral oedema. They've pumped her with IV Lasix and mannitol and they'll re-evaluate at morning rounds.' I have been in hospital too long. I can say this now almost as if it is yet another clinical read-out.

'Shit.' She sat carefully on the edge of the bed.

Pressed her fingers lightly to her forehead, running circles above her brows and across to the temples. The kind of thing that might keep the headaches at bay if you were running low on coffee. Or trying not to think.

We said nothing for a while. She sat on the end of the bed with her chin on her hands and she watched me. I would have done a lot, then, to avoid the wide, grey stare of her eyes.

'Did you talk?' she asked eventually. 'After Saturday?'

And I was the one who wanted to be judged.

'No.' I shook my head. 'We didn't talk.'

'Mmm.' She nodded slowly. Took her eyes and directed them somewhere less painful. 'That's too bad.'

I said nothing. Because there was nothing left I could say.

Around us, the wards began to wake. Cisterns flushed again with increasing regularity. Somewhere, a television blared early-morning breakfast TV until an earphone plug in the socket silenced it midsentence. In our room, the staff changed shifts. Junior clinicians began to filter in, swinging their hands in the pockets of their white coats, brandishing stethoscopes like badges of office. Reading the case notes, looking at the monitors, looking at me. And at Steff. Working their way up to asking difficult questions.

Steff stood up. She tore the mask from round her neck and threw it in a waste bucket beside the bed. Then she pulled something small and weighty from her pocket and passed it to me. A mobile phone.

'It's hers,' she said. 'She left it on the table in the Lodge. I don't know who we should tell but we have to start telling folk soon, before the shit hits the fan. All the numbers you need will be in there.'

'That *I* need?'

'I'll tell the Dean,' she said. 'I figured you could do the rest.'

Thank you so much.

'I could call her mother, at least.' I opened the directory and found the number. Under 'M' for Marjorie. Just above four separate entries for Matt.

Strangely, through the night, I managed not to remember that man. The thought of calling him did nothing to improve the morning.

I turned the phone so that Steff could see it. 'I suppose we should call?' I suggested. We. One of us. Not necessarily me.

Steff brought her eyes back to mine, level and clear. 'Matt's on holiday,' she said. 'You won't get him now.'

'We can try.'

'The only person who knows where he's gone is Nina,' she said. 'We aren't going to find him before she wakes up.'

'He went to his parents,' I said. 'She told me.' I tabbed through the listings. Two numbers with Glasgow dialling codes, a third called his mobile. The fourth read 'MH (A)'

'Arisaig.' Somewhere, a long time back, she'd told me. 'His parents live in Arisaig.' On the west coast, half an hour's drive from Mallaig, on the mainland opposite Skye.

Steff had her car keys in her hand, ready to leave. She stood over my chair with her hand on my shoulder, the way surgeons do with the grieving relatives.

A balding man in a white coat changed his mind and turned away. Found it necessary to fiddle with the ECG settings instead.

I stood up and walked with her to the door. She leant against the wall of the corridor, taking two inches off her height. 'I'll call Matt if you want,' she said. 'He'll hear from the Dean soon enough but I think it would be better coming from one of us.'

'I think it would be better coming from me.'

'If you say so.' Halfway down the corridor, she turned. 'I'll be in the clinic if you change your mind,' she said.

14

At seven o'clock, I called her mother. At five past, I called the machine at work and cancelled my appointments for the day. Shortly before ward round, I pulled myself together and called Matt on his parents' number. A machine answered, its older Morningside accent blurred by age and technology. I left a message for Matt to call me back on my mobile. On the spur of the moment, I called MacDonald, who wasn't in. The clerk at the station said that he was on the night shift, that they were expecting him in at lunchtime and that if it was personal, I could leave a message. It's the first time I've ever called the man at his work. I didn't leave my name.

The ward began to fill. Professionals in clinical coats filtered in, in ones and twos, responding to the bush telegraph of the hospital. Eric arrived, hot and damp from a morning run, and he brought with him a miniature travel toothbrush, a thumb-sized tube of toothpaste and a white NHS-issue towel.

'Showers are on the third floor at the far end of the corridor,' he said. 'Ward round starts in ten minutes. She's today's star case. They'll have everyone in here from the porters to the Prof. You might want to stay.'

And I might want to be clean if I do. This man thinks of everything.

The neurologist led the ward round. He gave a summary of her previous admission in slightly under three minutes and then a somewhat more detailed account of her current status, including the neurological findings, that had the students, the house officer, the SHO and the registrar taking notes. The professor accepted the loan of an ophthalmoscope and examined the patient's retinas. He queried the doses of diuretics and had the house officer demonstrate a Babinski reflex, for whatever good that might do. She surprised everyone by performing it correctly, a feat which probably passed her through the entire medicine internship in one move. The students took more notes. Eric queried the presence of ketamine in the cocktail and the neurologist proposed an elaborate theory suggesting that the presence of ketamine would increase blood pressure and heart rate thus increasing the blood flow to the brain and enhancing cerebral uptake of other, concomitantly administered drugs. It was, he suggested, a particularly effective addition to a potentially lethal cocktail and would significantly speed the onset of cerebral and cardiac failure. We were given to understand that, should he ever be inclined to go, he might well try the same himself. There was a general murmur of admiration for the patient's grasp of pharmacology. No one took notes. The registrar was required to give an estimate of the likely time for the patient to regain consciousness and was unable to do so. Neither Eric nor the neurologist was able to offer anything of any accuracy. The Professor demanded that the remains of her yellow cocktail be produced for his inspection and when it was, he held it up to the light, dipped his finger in, tasted it, did some rapid arithmetic on the back of the case notes, and pronounced that, in the light of his experience of pentobarbitone as a battlefield anaesthetic, she was unlikely to recover consciousness within the next twelve hours. At the very least. Possibly twice that. All further neurological and psychiatric examinations should be deferred until that time. The round moved on to the next ward.

Eric stayed behind.

'He's not old enough to have battlefield experience,' I said, as the dust cloud settled.

'He was in Africa in his youth. As a volunteer. If you listen to him, the place was one big battlefield experience zone.'

'And they still use pentobarbitone?' Even on horses, they don't use pentobarbitone any more. Except when they want them to die.

'Apparently so.'

'So he might be right?' I asked.

Twelve hours. Another whole day.

'Hard to say.' The bear-man shrugged. 'Most of the time, he just asks difficult questions. He doesn't usually commit to anything unless he knows he's right. That's why he's the professor.'

'Thanks.'

Twelve hours. At the least.

One of the fluid pumps sounded an alarm. A nurse ran to check it and between them, she and Eric decided it was faulty. The nurse was volunteered to go and find another one. We stood by the bed and waited while she ran through to the next ward. 'You can stay if you want to,' said Eric. 'But I think you should go home and get some sleep. You heard the Prof. We can't do anything except keep her ticking over until the pentobarb wears off.'

'And then?'

'And then we'll know if Alec was being optimistic.'

Then we'll know if she still has a mind that works. Maybe. If she has any mind left at all.

'I want to be here,' I said.

'I know.'

The nurse returned. Replaced the pump. Rethreaded the fluid line and set a new rate. Warm, sweet, salt water ran, a drop at a time, through the giving set. Because that's all that can be done until her liver chews through the yellow death and throws it out. And then we will know.

I was never any good at waiting.

'Come in at seven,' Eric said, when the nurse had gone. 'If she looks like she's going to wake up before then, I'll call your mobile.'

———

The vet school is quite different during working hours. Even at eight o'clock in the morning, midway through the Easter break and with half of the clinical staff away at Congress, the place was teeming. Lights were on in places I had forgotten lights could go on. Nurses in green dresses wheeled dogs on stretcher trolleys across the yard. Academics in white coats and loud ties peered into their personal organisers and spoke into mobiles and bumped blindly into cars as they made their way to laboratories tucked away amongst the rhododendrons. Catering staff emptied Transit vans full of prepackaged food into handcarts and pushed them down a ramp into the bowels of the canteen. The car park was packed.

For the first time in my life a man in dark green uniform stopped me as I tried to park my car and asked me to describe my business. He thought seriously about ringing the front desk for confirmation when I told him I was a client. He changed his mind when I told him that my horse and my foal were under the care of Dr Nina Crawford in the horse ward. It was the name that made the difference.

The horse ward was a haven of quiet. Hard to remember it any other way. It was the smell that brought it to life. A mixed flavour of milk-replacer and calf-scour and late-night gnome flowed from the calf pens, the ones down at the bottom end of the ward, round the corner from the empty row of loose boxes. The place where Sandy Logan spent the night with his future stallion. A buoyant, optimistic kind of smell. Infinitely better than the aerosol violets of Nina's room. Beneath it, the reek of rancid faeces wafting down from the ICU boxes said that Rain was alive, at least, if not necessarily well.

In the interests of basic hygiene, I visited the calf pens first.

Calf pens are small. Eight of them fit into a room the size of two full-size loose boxes. The pens curve round three sides of a rectangle, all facing inwards to keep company and to keep in the heat. Radiant lamps hang from the ceiling, throwing red light and heat more or less equally on to the straw and the inmates below. The walls are low and rounded so that a man, a tall man, could step over from one pen to the next but high enough so that a day-old calf could not, for instance, lean over and suck raw the ears of her neighbour.

The foal was there, in the third pen along. Two pens away from a black-and-white calf with ringworm scales round her eyes and next door to a tan-on-white weanling goat with dark eyeliner and the beginnings of a beard. The goat had its forelegs over the wall and was halfway into the next pen, doing its best to wrap its teeth round the hem of Sandy Logan's jacket.

The foal stood with his back to the door, sucking noisily from the teat, butting the bottle with his muzzle and flagging his tail in frustration at the slow flow of milk. His coat shone the way it did when he was born and his belly was tight with milk.

'He looks better,' I said, from the doorway. He wasn't the only one. Sandy glowed. Unshaven, unwashed and on less sleep than me, he still glowed. Fatherhood would have suited him.

'He's a cracker, so he is.' The old man let his attention wander to the goat. The foal bit the teat. Twisted and pulled, spraying milk at the walls and then choked on the backwash. They squabbled, briefly, for possession. Sandy won. He scratched the child gently on the new moon of his star and then moved them both out of range of the goat. He offered the teat again, changing the angle. The foal curled his tongue round the base of the bottle and settled back into sleepy greed. 'Aye. Cracker,' said the old man softly. The foal blinked as if he'd heard it before, often, during the night. 'Do you not think it suits him?'

'As a name?'

'Aye.' He remembered a propriety that was never there. 'If you don't mind?'

'Sandy, he's your foal. If he lives, you can call him what you like.'

The foal finished breakfast. Sleek and sated. He lifted his tail, flattened his back and strained to pass a small,

round ball of dung. Good, firm, foal dung. Sandy
scratched the stubble on his chin, kneading the flesh
into new shapes with square-ended fingers. 'Oh, he'll
live,' he said. 'We're not letting this one go.'

Steff would have said the same about the mare. But Steff
would have known she was lying. I stood by the tray of
disinfectant and looked over the door. Rain lay flat out
in the straw. If you didn't know her, you might think she
was sleeping. New-foaled mares are known to sleep lying
down. But her eyes held more pain than they ever had
when she was foaling and runnels of black sweat ran free
in the shadow of her mane. And there was a catch to
each breath as it came. A small catch, not yet a grunt.
But it was there if you listened for long enough.

Steff stood just inside the door, her face set in stone.
'She wasn't down when I came out to the hospital this
morning, Kellen. I would have told you.'

'I know.'

She knelt down by the mare, a full syringe in her
hand, and began to inject into one of the catheters. If it
was dark and if it was raining, she would look not unlike
Ruaridh Innes. Ruaridh Innes, a man with compassion
who knew when to stop. A man who saved his sentiment
for children and pocket pets and gave adults the dignity
of adults.

I waited until she had finished the injection. It's not
generally a good idea to interrupt a professional in their
work. 'Steff . . . do you not think we should call it a
day?'

She didn't look up. 'Not yet.' She didn't sound ready
to compromise.

'Steff. How often have you been through this before?

We can't fight it. There's no point. Not for me. Not for you. Not for the mare.'

This time she looked up. 'I'm not doing it for you. Or for me. Or the mare,' she said, shortly. 'I'm doing it for her.' She stood up, brushing invisible straw from her hands and turned to face me. 'We might never find out what kicked her over the edge, Kellen, but I saw her face when they brought in the news about Rain. I don't know how long we've got before she wakes up. But when she does, I want her to hear that your mare is alive and that she'll stay that way.'

'They said tonight. That she might wake up tonight.'

'Right. Then I've got the rest of today to turn your mare round.'

She let herself out of the box. Fluid as before, but with the pressure of containment straining at the edges, the way it does in a spring coiled too tight.

I stood back to let her out of the box.

'How, Steff?' I asked. 'How when all the others have gone the same way? What is there left to do that might make a difference?'

She walked past me. I followed her into the drug store and watched from the door as she washed her hands three times in iodophor wash. It stinks and it stains your skin brown. But nothing lives through it to pass on to someone else.

'I spoke to the microbiologists,' she said. 'They've got some results back on Branding Iron's cultures. The ones we took before he died. They got enough of the endo- toxin to run some assays. It cross-reacts with one of the human sero-types. We didn't know that before. There are human drugs we haven't tried. I'm going into town to the Medical Library and I'm going to go through every reference on Med-Line until I find the right answer.'

'They don't all work, Steff, the human drugs. People

die, too.' Everyone else must have said this. Or perhaps they have more tact.

'Not all of them,' she said. She pulled a paper towel from a wall-cylinder and scrubbed the water from her hands, screwed the paper up and threw it in the waste bag. I thought she was going to leave. So did she. But she turned, suddenly, and sagged back against the wall. As if the enormity of it had finally hit her.

'Kellen . . .' she let it out like a sigh, '. . . she's your mare. If you want her dead, I'll shoot her now. There are a bunch of guys in white coats in the labs over there who would say you were right. But I think there's a bigger picture than that. And I think we have to try.'

It's not a very big room, the drug store. More of an oversized broom cupboard with a sink set into one corner and too many shelves for the wall space. We were less than two feet apart and I could see every one of the lines around her eyes. She's too young, yet, to have lines like that. Or to carry this much weight on her own.

'I'm sorry,' I said. And I meant it. 'She's your case. I'm not going to tell you how to run her. Do whatever you need. If there's anything I can do, call me at the farm. Otherwise I'll see you at the hospital at seven.'

'Thanks, Kellen.' She smiled and we had a deal, of sorts. Some kind of acknowledgement that we were both on the same side.

If I was Sandy, I would have spat on my hand and shaken on it. If she was Nina, I would have hugged her.

But we are who we are.

I put my hand on her shoulder as I walked out of the door.

15

At home, the kitchen smelled of hot toast and fresh coffee. A plate and the coffee pot stood upside down on the draining board, wet and warm, all of them. The red kittens curled together round a chewed-up straw dolly on one fireside chair. A dark towel lay on the other chair. And one on the window-seat. There were collie hairs and blood stains on both of them. The dog was nowhere in sight. An 8 × 10 close-up of a black greyhound lay on the counter. Long-nosed with rheumy brown eyes and flecks of white growing like mould through the black of his muzzle. Underneath, a photo-copied cutting from the *Racing Post* showed a dog and a man and a trophy, claiming to be Gary Mitchell, Jupiter's Joy and the Waterloo Cup in more or less that order. The man looked a great deal more impressed than the dog. The pedigree traced back to Ireland on both sides within two generations. I know about greyhounds. Bridget's father had one. She had nine pups.

I found a pad of Post-it notes in a drawer, wrote: *'Who's going to take the other seven?'* on the top sheet and stuck it across the eyes of the dog. Blinkers improved him no end.

I was asleep within ten minutes of hitting the bed. Sometime later, the dog joined me. Sometime after that, she left. I woke around four, thick-headed from day-time sleep and found that I had, after all, remembered to put a towel on the bed. Some things just happen by instinct.

Downstairs, the prints of the greyhound were still on the counter. A second Post-it lay across the first. It read: *'Six. You. Me. Duncan. All the rest spoken for. £150 each.'*

Are they indeed? Bastard. He's been planning this for months.

And I already told him I didn't want another dog.

Underneath, at a different angle, the note said, *'Taken Tir to the Forge. 4-ish. Tea?'*

I pulled the bike down from the rack in the shed. Spun the chain and sprayed it with lube. Sprayed more on the chainwheel. Made myself a peanut butter and marmalade sandwich and set off down the lane towards the forge. To clear my head.

<hr>

Duncan MacDonald's forge lies four miles away, on the far side of the village, a mile past the kirk and another mile down a dead-end lane, which is much like the one to the farm although in rather better repair. It's a quiet, mellow, understated place built of local stone with walls two feet thick, with windows you could cover entirely with your two palms laid together and with a shallow-pitched roof that was once covered with a thick layer of peat from the moors but has since been reroofed in black

Coniston slate on the basis that smiths like to play with fire and that stone is, generally speaking, less combustible than peat. It was built around the same time as Nina's cottage but by a family who understood the essence of practical aesthetics. The forge and the byre and the home that goes with them are all built as one unit, set into a bend in the river with a stand of alders on the far bank giving cover from the sea-blown westerly winds and a low hill that offers shelter to the north. There are walls of dry stone around the home fields with hand-cut water troughs set into them at right angles so that each trough supplies stock in two fields.

The river itself is broad and fast flowing. It splits in two about five hundred yards upstream from the forge; divided by a dam and a set of man-made sluice gates that control the flow of the water. Except in particularly dry weather, half of it continues down the natural riverbed to feed the trout pools below. The other half is channelled into an artificial tributary, cut deep and lined with massive, moss-covered flags, that runs under the western wall of the forge. The tributary drives a wooden water wheel that is easily twice my height across and the wheel, in turn, drives ox-hide bellows that blast air into the furnace. It's original hydrothermal power and it's deeply impressive to watch. If I was a child, this is where I would spend my time. Watching the magic of blue steel turned to white, flowing wax and back to steel again. Because I am not a child, and my free time can be measured in minutes per month, I come here on my rare Sunday afternoon off and I drink Duncan's tea and watch him mending the water wheel, which is what he does with his free Sunday afternoons. I can't think of a better way to switch off and forget.

I cycled into the yard and flicked the pedals round so
that the bike stood upright against the mounting block.
A smooth-coated tan and white collie bitch lay in a patch
of sun on the flagged stone outside the forge watching
me through eyes made white with cataracts. She's been
blind for as long as I've known her. She still recognises
the squeak of the bike chain and the sound of my feet on
the flags. I knelt down to scratch behind her ears. 'Hey,
Mags. It's me. Where's the grandchild?' The collie
pushed her nose, warm and dry, into the palm of my
hand. Said nothing useful.

'She's away up with Stewart to see The Lad.' A voice
from the gloom of the forge. 'He thought she could
maybe do with a walk.' He speaks like his brother,
Duncan MacDonald, low and soft with rounded vowels
and that odd gravity that makes it difficult to tell when
he's being serious and when he's not. I suspect that the
younger MacDonald has an even more warped sense of
humour than his law-keeping brother but I've rarely seen
it in full flight. In most other ways, he's not like his
brother at all. Built more along the lines of Sandy Logan,
dense and compact, but taller and with black hair that's
thinning from the front rather than on top. And his eyes
are brown. Like Nina's.

He moved out into the light, rubbing his palms
down the sides of his apron. 'Come on up,' he said, 'It's
time we brought him in.'

We walked up to the back fields and found Mac-
Donald sitting on the dry stone of the wall with the
dog standing beside him, balancing delicately on the
sharp stones of the top like a cat. She wore a broad
leather collar and a lead. Both of them a novelty. Anti-
insemination insurance.

He moved over to make space in his patch of sunlight and the two of us watched Duncan go out into the

field to catch his horse. Or, rather, we watched him go out into the field with a head collar and saw the stallion trot over to his call and follow him back with its nose on his shoulder, or in his pocket, or in the crook of his arm. The head collar, I would say, was more a formality than a necessity.

They were halfway across the field when MacDonald spoke.

'Sandy called Duncan at lunchtime,' he said. 'Told him about the mare and the foal.'

'I know.' He said he would.

'I'm sorry.'

'Sure. Thanks for taking care of the dog.'

'A pleasure.'

They reached the gate. The stallion spun on the end of the rope and danced in the sunlight. The image of the colt. Except that this one's star is less of a new moon and more of a comet trail, flaring up from his left nostril to explode in a great scatter of white between his eyes.

MacDonald opened the gate to let him out. We followed the two of them, man and horse, down towards the forge.

'I gather the insurance people were looking for your friend this morning,' he said. 'The vet school wouldn't say where she was. I wondered if you ought to go and check she's all right.'

And so it's not a good idea, after all, to go out in the fresh air and forget for a while.

And maybe I don't, after all, have what it takes to see this through to the end.

We stopped outside the forge. Duncan opened the door to the stable and let his horse put himself to bed. He bolted the door. MacDonald handed me the dog's lead and tugged at the sleeve of my fleece. 'Maybe

Duncan would lend us the van and we'll pop the bike in the back and take you home,' he said.

The ward was different. Even from the corridor, it was different. Quieter somehow. The air-conditioned violets had gone. Instead, the air was light with peppermint. Sharp. Fresh. Scented with toothpaste and early mornings and all the hope for the day ahead. The technology ranged around her bed seemed pleasantly less intrusive.

There was a woman sitting by the bed, holding her hand, talking to Eric.

Her mother. Clearly her mother. There is a way of sitting, a way of holding a hand, that speaks of ownership.

It's a long time since this woman had ownership of her daughter.

I stopped in the doorway. We've never met, her mother and I. Before this morning, I had never heard her voice. In many ways, it would be easier to keep it that way.

The young house officer paused on the way out of the door. All the better for half a night's sleep. She smiled at me brightly. In the face of strangers, those who spent the night together become part of a team. She tilted her head back, nodding towards the bed. 'It's all right,' she said. 'She's not a bad old stick.'

'I'm sure she's not.'

I am sure she's not. She is sixty-seven years old and she has lost a husband at fifty-two of prostatic carcinoma, a son at twenty-eight in a midair collision on a training flight and three times already, she has come close to losing her daughter. The world is not a gentle place and Marjorie Crawford has learned the hard way that only the ungentle survive. But there is more to life than simple survival and one could choose, now and then, to be gentle with one's only remaining child. It is not a gentle act to threaten legal action against one's daughter for breach of contract on the termination of her engagement. Nor is it an act of simple survival. There is a lot under the surface of Marjorie Crawford and there is very little of it I would choose to meet.

Eric saw me coming before she did and reached out a hand, smiling, to draw me closer to the bed. 'Mrs Crawford, this is Dr Stewart, Dr Kellen Stewart. If you remember? It was Dr Stewart who found your daughter.'

Eric. Eric who can read people from three beds away and who thinks he can keep peace at the bedside. Perhaps he can.

'Dr Stewart.' Her hand was dry, like chromed leather. The grip was solid, practised, firm. Flawless, vermilion nail polish shone on flawless, tailored nails. Matched exactly her lipstick and the scarf at her neck. And her voice. A flawless, vermilion voice. Resplendent colour and no warmth at all. 'We are in your debt,' she said.

'It's all right. I did it for Nina.' This may not have been the right thing to say. Almost certainly not. But I wasn't thinking of Marjorie Crawford. In that moment, I couldn't think of anything but her daughter.

'Eric! She's off the ventilator.'

And this is why it was quiet from the doorway, why the technology seemed less invasive. The twelve-second hiss of the ventilator has gone. She is breathing on her own. And there is colour in her face and her skin is warm to the touch and when I pick up her hand and feel her wrist, a pulse bounds; regular and rhythmic and healthy. And Eric is standing there beside me with a big bear-grin stretched wide across his face as if he has made miracles all on his own. Which he has, more or less.

'Oh God, Eric . . .' I wrapped my arm round his

waist and I hugged him. Because I still was not thinking.
Because I had forgotten that, in front of Marjorie Crawford, JP, one refers to Dr Dalziel by his professional title
and one does not display excessive physical affection.
'When did you take her off?'

'About four o'clock.'

'Has she said anything yet? Has she been conscious?'

'Not yet. But she's coming up. Prof was right.'

'You could perhaps, explain?' There was frost, now,
on the vermilion of her voice. Neatly dusted frost, taste-
fully done, but frost all the same. It froze the beginnings
of dangerous euphoria.

I sat down quickly on the other side of the bed.
Looped my fingers through Nina's. Left Eric to melt the
frost.

'Professor Russell considered it likely that Dr Crawford would begin to regain consciousness around now.
The capacity to breathe is one of the first signs of recovery. We should, shortly, be able to assess her neurological function.' Dr Dalziel can be impeccably professional
when he chooses.

'And then you will know if the brain damage is permanent?'

'We will.'

'Thank you.' She turned to me. 'Apparently, Dr Stewart, my daughter may have succeeded in—*Matthew!*'

I never heard him. I never saw him. Just felt his
hand, hard and tight on my shoulder.

'Mother.' He leaned in across me and kissed her on
the cheek. A solid, filial kiss.

'Matthew. It's absolutely wonderful to see you.' She
was glowing. Warm above the cold of her scarf. Her
voice became velvet. Soft, vermilion velvet. 'It's very
good of you to come.'

'You couldn't keep me away.' He wasn't looking at

her. Wasn't interested. He had his hand tight on my shoulder, crushing into the scars of an old-mended collar bone, as if all of the grief had moved down to his fingers and had nowhere else to go.

'I called your mobile,' he said. 'It was switched off.'

Oh, hell. 'Matt, I'm sorry, I forgot you were . . .'

'So I called the Dean.' His eyes were dry. It was his voice that wept. 'He said it happened last night.'

'Yes, I know. But . . .' His fingers ground tighter; bone on bone. Something deep down registered the pain and complained. I shut up.

'You promised me you wouldn't let her down,' he said.

'And she promised me she wouldn't do this.' It was a long time ago. But she still promised.

'You believed her?' He sounded too tired to be truly surprised. Just a faint, weary incredulity. 'You should have been there, to take care of her.'

His hand moved, finally. Relaxed its grip and fell to his side. A slow throbbing heat filled the place where it had been. I flexed my arm and found, oddly, that it still worked.

'She's a grown woman, Matt. I can't watch over her twenty-four hours a day.'

'Then you should have left her with me,' he said, 'because I could.'

He was more exhausted than anything. As if the drive down from Arisaig had taken all his energy and left him drained, like a husk.

And then, as if his mind was very slightly out of synch with the rest of him, he asked: 'What brain damage?'

'It is possible that Dr Crawford may have suffered some damage—' Eric can read people, but he doesn't know their history.

'She was apnoeic when we found her,' I cut across him. Matt Hendon the ex-partner might have wanted the pap but Matt Hendon the clinician needed the un-sanitised version. 'She had cerebral oedema on admission, Matt. They don't know how much function has been lost.'

And now, with practice, I can say it with less feeling than even the neurologist.

Matt Hendon moved blindly to the end of the bed. There was a dullness to his eyes. A man looking, but not quite seeing. We sat still, all of us, and let him work his way to the truth.

'My God,' he said, and he said it so very quietly. 'What have you done?' and because he was looking at me and I was sitting very close to Nina, it is conceivable that Marjorie Crawford may have believed he was asking it of her daughter.

The woman stood up, offered him her seat. When he accepted, she stood behind him with her hands on his shoulder and watched as he looped his fingers through her daughter's, as I had done.

'I'm so sorry, Matthew,' she said. 'I wish it didn't have to be like this.' And then to Eric, who hadn't quite caught up. 'He was going to marry her, you see.' She smiled, a smile of pure vermilion regret. Marjorie Crawford, a woman in control, who understands that those who control the present control the past.

Which Matt Hendon does not.

'I don't think so. Not really. Not even then.' He shook his head, slowly, his mind caught somewhere in the shared memories of their past. 'All you had to do was let her give up work, Kellen. It shouldn't have been that hard . . .'

A random bleep from the ECG brought him back to the present. His eyes came back to mine, held them across the bed. 'You haven't told her, have you?' he asked, softly.

If Matt Hendon knows, then by tomorrow, the whole world could know.

Or simply her mother. Which would be enough.

Suddenly it is hard to breathe.

'It's not up to me to tell anyone, Matt. It's up to Nina.'

Eric stood behind me. Put his hand on my shoulder. A bear standing over its cub.

'Tell me what, Matthew?' There is steel in the flawless voice. This woman doesn't like being a side-show in someone else's drama.

Somewhere, in the background, the young house officer returned. Spoke to Eric, showed him a sheet of paper. He tapped my shoulder, twice, and left.

So now I am alone, sitting opposite Matt Hendon, who is watching me and slowly shaking his head.

'Matt, think. She may never come round.' Even in the vacuum, there is hope. 'Is it worth it?'

He is two feet away from me, across the bed. Unreachable.

The world is a tunnel of pressing darkness.

The world lives in Matt Hendon's eyes.

'Matthew? What is it? If it's about Nina, I need to know.' She is a Justice of the Peace and she is not stupid. If we give her enough time, she will come to this on her own. Unless he stops her.

He is not unintelligent and he knows her mother, probably better than I do. There are limits, there must be limits, to the damage he needs to inflict.

'Matt. Please? For Nina?' There have to be limits.

There may have been limits. I think there were limits. But then Nina Crawford, who has a sense of timing all her own, moved her head and coughed into the pillow.

'Nina!'

Three of us. One voice.

Her hands clenched tight. In mine. In his. Her head turned. Her eyes flickered. She breathed in, a series of gasping, gagging breaths and then she coughed again, harder, through the tube in her throat.

'Matthew, take that out, she'll hurt herself.' Her mother, a woman in control. 'Nina, sweetheart, we were so worried . . .'

It all happened very fast, then.

Matt stood up, to do as he was bid and pull the tube from her throat. Not, strictly speaking, his prerogative at a human hospital but I would have done it if he hadn't. For Nina. Not for her mother.

Marjorie Crawford, the picture of the grieving parent, leaned forward in that moment, to wrap her arms around her daughter.

You can't fit two people in the same place at the same time.

Matt Hendon lost. He spun sideways, off balance. Grabbed for the nearest thing that could hold him up and found the fluid pump, standing free by the bed. They're not the most stable of things, fluid pumps. Top heavy. Ungainly. It rocked backward, teetering on the brink of a fall. He swore, violently. No Morningside at all. Caught the stand and spun further with the momentum. Jerked it to a stop that tugged, too hard, on the fluid line in her arm. Swore again when he saw what he had done. And then over his, the sound of her mother's voice, raw and ragged and stripped of all colour:

'Nina! No! . . . Oh God, no. Matthew . . . do something!'

Because, suddenly there is blood on the sheet. Heavy, venous blood. Leaking from the open end of an eighteen-gauge catheter in a broad, spreading stain. Crimson on the white of the sheet. A dark, sticky dampness on the pink of the blanket. And her mother is white, shocked white, in a way you wouldn't expect from a Justice of the Peace with this much steel in her. And so, perhaps, after all, she does care. Perhaps, after all, she has her own nightmares. Because the last time, the third time, after the death-wish cocktail and the injection of air, and with her hands strapped by Velcro ties to the bed, when she was still desperate to die, Nina Crawford leaned forward and pulled out a fluid line with her teeth and then she lay back on the pillows and watched herself bleed steadily out through the catheter on to the sheets.

And her mother was there when they found her.

Matt was closest. He spun full circle, pulling the drip stand back on its feet and sticking his thumb over the catheter, to block the flow. He fumbled out with the other hand, reaching for the free end of the drip. His eyes caught mine and held them, all anger gone. The eyes of an anaesthetist in a clinical emergency. The eyes of the man who saved the life of my foal. 'Kellen. Get that woman out of here. And get the medic. Now.'

Just once in a while, I can do as I'm told.

<hr>

People gathered in the ward. The air prickled with the scent of peppermints. White-coated clinicians circled the bed. A dim light shone on the woman propped up on the pillows. Nina; paler than the rose of her sheets. But her eyes were open.

One of the white coats leaned forward.

'Dr Crawford. What was your mother's maiden name?'

'Morrison . . .' A whisper. Dull with the aftereffects of pentobarbitone and hoarse from the tube. '. . . I think it was Morrison.'

'Yes, it was Morrison.' Matt. He knows these things. 'Thank you.'

Almost everyone was there. Me. Matt. Eric. Professor Russell. The Aberdonian neurologist. The registrar. The SHO. The house officer. The nurses.

Peacefully, Marjorie Crawford had left. Gone because Eric and Matt between them committed elaborate clinical perjury and convinced her that a full neuro test was no place for the immediate relatives. Matt lent her his mobile phone and promised to call her with the results. She left with well-voiced reluctance and promised, three times, to return at first light. No one particularly believed her.

'And can you tell me what day it is today?'

'No idea . . . doesn't matter . . .' She smiled, lop-sided, turned her head on one side, squeezed my finger. 'Kellen . . . tell them I never know what day it is.'

Which was hardly the point. But I was too full with the fact that she could talk. That she knew my name. That she remembered.

I shrugged and nodded.

'Well, do you know what day it was yesterday?' Neurologist's have a particularly linear sense of reality. And no sense of humour at all.

'No . . . I think . . . it must have been Monday. Because . . . we found Killer on Sunday . . .' She drifted off, half asleep. The neurologist tested some peripheral reflexes, tapped her elbow, her forearm, lifted the covers on his side and tapped her long patellar ligament. She opened her eyes. 'Do I work?'

'All except your head.' He flashed dimmed laser eyes.
'Is the pain still there?'

'Huge. Like a migraine, only worse.'

'We could give you some—'

'No. It's not that bad. I don't want any more drugs.'

'Do you remember what drugs you did have?'

'No.' Desperation and something close to panic drew
her voice above the whisper. 'I didn't do it. Kellen . . .'
She faded away on the end of the word. 'I didn't. I promised I wouldn't.' Her fingers squeezed again, tightly.

I squeezed back, more gently; reached over and
smoothed away the hair that was catching the corner of
her eye. 'I know. Don't worry about it.'

Eyes met above the bed. The clinical group retired
quietly to the staff area at the end of the room. I followed, with Matt.

'Well?' It seemed easiest to let him ask the questions.

For Matt, the Aberdonian broadened his accent.
'Clearly there's a degree of short-term amnesia. I doubt
she'll ever get yesterday back which is maybe just as
well. Otherwise, I would say she's pretty normal for
someone on their way up from barbiturate overdose.
Would you agree, Eric?'

'I think so. She looks safe enough. I'd say we can get
rid of most of the monitors.' He nodded to the house
officer, who made notes in the clinical record. 'Keep the
ECG. Keep the urinary catheter until she's ambulatory.
Pull the arterial line and the CVP. Maintenance fluids
until she's eating. Basic monitoring from now until she's
discharged unless anything else happens.'

'What about the headache?' I asked it. Someone had
to. Matt didn't seem moved to volunteer.

'If you had your brain trying to squeeze out of your
ears for the best part of a day, you'd have a sore head
too, Dr Stewart.' Professors can be so excruciatingly pa-

tronising when they try. 'She can have an aspirin if it gets bad. I wouldn't advise anything more potent.' He smiled winningly at his team. 'Maybe next time she'll try the Samaritans. I gather they leave less pressing results.'

Only the house surgeon was so junior that she had to laugh.

The team moved on.

16

It was dark in the ward. Her headache was less painful without the lights. The amber flicker of the ECG played across her face, drawing angled shadows and then smoothing them out again. She slept, mostly, when the pain let her. In between, she lay awake, her fingers relaxed in mine, her face turned from the light of the monitors. We talked, on and off; long, disjointed rambles through the pathways of her mind. We talked of her mother and what she could tell her; of work and how she could ease off the pressure without destroying her career; of the fire and the farm and the dog and the horses and whether the cat would let Steff live in the cottage if Nina ever chose to move into the farm. We talked of life and relationship and the fear of failure, and in the spaces between the talking, when she slept and the colour eased its way back to her skin, I thought of Bridget and wanted her to know.

Eric stood in the dark on the far side of the bed beyond the reach of the amber lacework. 'Can I have a word?'

'Sure.' I squeezed a hand that didn't squeeze back and followed him to the staff room at the end of the ward. 'You don't look so good. What's up?'

'This.' He lifted a laboratory printout from the case folder. 'I didn't throw it into ward round. Thought I'd have a word with you first.'

'What is it?'

'The tox. report on the contents of her drip bag.' He waved me to a chair. I sat down. Waited. Picked a softening digestive off the plate on the table. Nibbled at the edges. Half asleep.

'So?' I said eventually. 'Ketamine and pentobarbitone. Anything we didn't know about?'

'No.' He smoothed the paper on the table. Unclipped his pen from his top pocket and circled one line, halfway down the page. Turned it so that I could see it. 'Forget the rest, Kellen. Just read that one.'

I read it. *Ketamine in saline: 00.00mg/ml.*

That's not possible. There was ketamine in her blood. She has to have got it from somewhere.

'Are you sure?' I asked. 'Maybe they didn't run the assay. It's hardly on the usual list.'

'I'm sure. I got them to check it again. They stayed in late to run it through after the last batch. I just had a call with the results. There was absolutely no ketamine in the bag.'

'So then she must have slammed it in before she started the drip.'

'Maybe.' He doodled in the bottom corner of the report. A heart with a spiralling series of pipes flowing out of it, like a small radiant sun. Very decorative. 'I spoke to the anaesthetists,' he said. 'We did some basic maths. Worked back from what she had in her blood on admission to what she must have started off with.'

There was a pause. He drew a cross through the heart.

'So?' I asked.

'So, if you were trying to kill yourself, Kellen, would you piss about with half of the anaesthetic dose?'

I don't know. I've never thought about it. 'She put two grammes in it last time.'

'Right. That's more like it. That's twenty times the induction dose. This time, if she put it in just before the drip went up, then she used somewhere around fifty milligrams. That's half a ml. You'd barely notice it.'

'Would you get any analgesia?'

'I don't know. Not much. I'd need to go and check. You'd get a fair tachycardia and I think you'd still get pretty spectacular hallucinations. But I can't think why you'd want to see things just before you were going to die. Not the kind of things she was seeing, anyway.'

No. I can't think why either.

'So then why, Eric?' An echo of earlier.

He shrugged. Big and expansive. 'I don't know,' he said. But he said it so that both of us knew that there were things he wasn't saying. Things he thought I wasn't ready to hear.

I laid my head on my arms. Stared at the white melamine of the table. Turned sideways and stared at the sterile white of the wall. 'Eric. She's not stupid. She had access to a library full of pharmacology texts and she'd read most of them. She knew everything there was to know about ketamine. She hated the stuff. She wouldn't piss about with it at all. It doesn't make sense.'

'I know. That's why I didn't bring it up at rounds.'

I sat up. 'I guess we need to talk to Nina.'

'We do. Later.' He stood up and laid his hand over mine, his voice quieter. 'Just now, you have a visitor.'

'Oh, bloody hell.' That's all we need. 'Don't tell me it's her mother.'

'No. It's your friend with the hair.'

Steff, back in her scrub suit and a blood-stained mask. She leant against the doorframe, a tired smile somewhere round her eyes. She shrugged an apology. 'I seem to keep breaking up the party,' she said.

'Not this one. We'd broken up anyway.' I stood up. Introduced her to Eric and the other way around. Because, this time, she had a right to be there.

Eric shook her hand, raised an admiring brow at her theatre kit. 'Did you want a job in surgery? There's usually a junior Reg. post free.'

'No.' She smiled a washed-out smile. 'I just want to know I'm not too late.'

'You're not.'

We walked together across to the bed. Steff leant over and put a hand to Nina's forehead. 'She looks better.'

'She is. She was conscious earlier on.' I spoke it softly, not to wake her. 'How's Rain?'

'The same.' She slid papers from a bag at her shoulder. 'But I found out what we need. There's a human anti-endotoxin on the market that cross-reacts with the one we found in Branding Iron. I had a word with Sean in Microbiology. He thinks it might work in horses if we get it in early enough. We could be too late but it's worth a try.'

'Have you got any in pharmacy?'

'No.' She looked sideways at Eric. 'We need to get it from a human hospital.'

'Get what?' A voice from the bed. Sleepy and pushed

through the crashing pain in her head. 'What are you doing to my cases now, Stephanie Foster?'

There was a smile on both of them you could have seen even without the monitor light.

I lifted the papers from Steff's fingers and tugged at the sleeve of Eric's white coat. 'Let's go somewhere else and have a look at these.'

━━━━━

You have to believe everything they tell you about the hell of hospital bureaucracy. All of it is true. But when you get to be senior consultant, most of the rules begin to flex. We went for a walk and a coffee and talked about horses and infected theatres and about what it is that drives surgeons to the brink and residents to spend their days wired up to the internet and when we came back to the ward half an hour later, I had the entire hospital stock of E. coli strain 1507 anti-endotoxin tucked away in a specimen bag with someone else's name on the front. It wasn't much. Just three vials. And all of them ten days past their shelf date so that, technically, they should have gone down to the incinerator anyway. But just enough, according to Steff's notes, to bring a horse back from the dead. If you got it in soon enough.

Nina was asleep. Steff was sitting where I had been, watching her as if she might never get another chance. I palmed the bag and slid it into her pocket. 'You found these in the skip outside,' I said. 'You didn't get them from here.'

She smiled. Sniffed and shrugged in her best imitation of an East-End trader. 'Fell off the back of a lorry, mate.' She fished in her pocket and checked over the goods. 'How much is there here?'

'Enough.' Eric stood behind me, his hand on my shoulder. 'If you get it in fast, there should be enough.'

She bounced her car keys on the palm of her hand, buoyant, full of hope. 'I'll let you know,' she said.

████████

I heard his footsteps before I felt his hand on my shoulder. He treads softly for someone so big. 'It's after eleven, Kellen. You could go home, you know.'

'I know.' I am becoming nocturnal. I sleep by day and by night I watch the jagged edge of an ECG count out someone else's life. 'I'm still trying to figure out the ketamine.'

'Me too.' He held a paper mug in either hand, waved one of them under my nose so that I could catch the smell and nodded his head back towards the staff room. 'Fancy something to wash down another biscuit?'

'Sure.'

In the staff room, he handed me a lukewarm coffee and sat me down opposite yet another sheaf of scribbled notes. 'I've been to the library,' he said. 'Read some stuff about the sub-anaesthetic effects of ketamine.'

'And?'

'And it's weird stuff. What happens depends how much you take. At the kind of doses we're talking about, you'd get some analgesia. Nasty hallucinations. You might be verging on the catatonic but you'd probably need a tad more than she had on board. Apparently it also induces a state in which the subject no longer cares whether they live or die, which is an interesting one if you're contemplating suicide.'

Thanks.

'Eric, you've read her notes from last time. She didn't need Dutch courage if she wanted to go.'

'No, I know. I'm not suggesting she did.'

'So?'

'So, I think you're right. I don't think she was using it

to help herself die at all.' He doodled again; a series of interlocking Celtic spirals, working himself up to something he didn't want to say. 'Kellen. Suppose she had it on board before she ever put in the catheter?'

This is what he wouldn't say earlier. Now, he is more sure.

I looked at him warily. 'Why would she do that?'

He sighed. Tilted his chair back and stared at the ceiling. Brought it back to a place where he could look me in the eye. 'Ketamine's a pretty common drug of abuse, Kellen. "Special K", huge street value. Creates God-awful paranoid hallucinations but it doesn't stop folk using it. Repeatedly. It's incredibly addictive stuff.'

He let it hang. I listened and heard and failed to understand.

'Are you trying to tell me that Nina Crawford was a junkie? On *ketamine?*' It's amazing how much feeling you can get into a whisper. 'That's insane. She loathed it, I told you.'

'And she was having God-awful hallucinations the day before she died. Cats and maggots and horses with sharp teeth. You told me that, too.'

'But that was hypoglycaemia.'

'How do you know?'

'She said so.'

'You'll believe anything when you're paranoid, Kellen.'

'And it got better with food. I saw it.'

'How long did it take? How long to come round after food?'

'I don't know. Ten minutes. Quarter of an hour, maybe.'

'The half-life of ketamine's twelve and a half minutes, Kellen. I know. I just looked it up in the library.'

'That's coincidence, Eric. Pure coincidence.'

He picked up his pen and drew savage lines across the page. 'Kellen, think. You were a doctor once. You get ratty when you're hypo. You get sleepy. You might pass out. If it's really bad, you could start convulsing. But whatever else you do, you don't start seeing things. You know that.'

He said it gently. With compassion. And he kept his eyes somewhere else.

Because he was right.

Absolutely right.

I stacked the biscuits into a tower. Knocked them down again. Made damp circles with my coffee mug and rubbed them in long, off-white smears across the table. Stared blindly at the far glimmer of the ECG and saw nothing. Looking, but not seeing. Listening, but not hearing. Thinking, but not understanding. A pattern of years.

Voices, other voices played out in my head. Me . . . Steff . . .

Was Nina seeing things before she walked out of theatre?

Kellen, she couldn't tell the difference between the needle holders and the scissors by the time she left.

And Nina . . .

It thinks . . . the world would be a better place if I joined the cat.

What do you think?

Just at this moment, Kellen, I couldn't care less.

And again. Much further back . . .

I can feel it coming, sucking me in. Like gravity. I can't fight it . . . I'm scared, Kellen.

A warning. But I didn't hear it as a warning. Because I wasn't listening for a warning. I finished the coffee. Screwed up the mug and threw it in the bin.

'How badly would she have been hallucinating, Eric? With the ketamine?'

'Put it this way, I'm amazed she managed to get an eighteen-gauge catheter into her arm. I'm completely astonished that she was together enough to put up the drip and get it running.'

'No.' *I took every drop we had in the dangerous drugs cupboard, signed it all out and pumped it into a 500 ml bag of dextrose-saline. That bit was easy.* 'She's been planning this for long enough. She probably had it made up and waiting.'

'And you didn't see it coming?'

I don't want to die now, Kellen. Of all people, you have to believe me.

'No. I didn't see it coming. Not now.'

'I'm sorry.' He pushed his half-finished coffee across the table towards me. We shared it in silence. Worked logically to all the obvious endings.

'How was she getting it in? Did she have needle marks on her arm and I missed those too?'

'I don't know. I haven't looked yet. And her arm's that much of a mess at the moment, I think you'd be hard pushed to find any normal skin anywhere. But she could have drunk it. It works orally in kids. I expect it works in adults if you want it to. Saves having to explain away those inconvenient bruises round the veins.'

'Great.'

The ghosts of past conversations marched in ranks through my head. The afternoon just gone, sitting by her side in the ward. Saturday night in bed. Every therapy hour we've ever had. All of it based on fiction.

I believed her because I wanted to believe her.

Matt Hendon knew better.

I stood up. 'Now, I think we need to talk to Nina.'

'Do you think she's up to it?'

'You're the doctor. But I'd have said if she can talk to

Steff Foster, she can talk to us. And better us than the hospital cyclist. To begin with, anyway.'

'Go easy, huh.'

'Trust me.'

We sat by the bed. One on either side. The ECG chirruped. Steady. Rhythmic. Stable.

Nina Crawford slept. Sound and deep. We couldn't wake her.

'She's gone back under, Kellen. It happens like this with pentobarb. Leaks back out of the tissues and the blood levels go back up for a while. You should sleep. Talk to her in the morning.'

'Maybe.'

I sat on her left side. Ran my fingers up and down her arm. Searching. Feeling for marks to show where she'd slipped in the drug.

I thought I knew this arm.

I thought I knew all of her.

I traced the scar, long and sinuous, from wrist to elbow. And the small, finer, horizontal scars of Matt's sutures. Twelve of them. I never spotted those, either.

I traced on. Up along the scarred and knotted tracks of veins ruined by the first, catastrophic mistake.

. . . *It's more difficult than I thought. I don't have veins like a horse. And there's only one vein on my left arm that's worth going for. All the rest were shot to bits after last time.*

I never thought to ask her how she knew.

I ran my fingers up the thin, blue line of that one, remaining vein.

Stopped.

Traced back.

I used a twenty-three-gauge cat catheter because I

thought it would be easier to get in. Even so, it took me two tries.

'Eric, where was the catheter? The one she put in herself?'

'Here.' He lifted the arm on his side and jiggled the end of the fluid line. Carefully, not to disrupt the skin. 'This is it. We didn't move it. Right antecubital fossa. Very neat. Doubt if I could do better myself.'

'What size?'

'Eighteen, I think.' He checked the hub. Nodded. 'Eighteen gauge.'

I rolled up my sleeve. Had a look at my veins. Worked it through. Stood up and hunted through the drawers of the monitor trolley for a catheter. A big, eighteen-gauge catheter.

'Here. Try something for me. You're right handed, yes?'

'Yes.'

'So's she. Try putting that in your right antecubital the way she's done it. Don't do it for real. Just see if you can.'

He rolled up his sleeve and mimed a swab of the site, out of habit. He looked up, amused. 'I've got a pressure cuff raising the vein, have I?'

'Whatever you need. Just go for the vein.'

He started to mime the catheter. Stopped.

'I can't. If I was putting it in, I'd use my right hand and put it in my left arm.' He looked at me. Shrugged. 'Maybe she's ambidextrous, Kellen.'

'No. But pretend she was. Try putting it into your right arm with your left hand. Just lay it on. Where does it go?'

'Like this?' He was playing along. Humouring me. 'Lying along the vein like this.' He held the catheter flat to his arm, along the line of the vein.

'Good. So where's the tip and where's the injection port?'

'Tip's pointing down. I couldn't get the angle otherwise.'

'OK. Now put it in me. Like you would if I was a patient.'

He did. Swabbed the site and laid the catheter on my skin. Neatly up the line of the vein.

Up. Not down.

He noticed it, too. 'It's the other way up. The tip's pointing up. The usual way.'

'Right. Now which is Nina's?'

We both looked. Eric leaned over to the head of the bed and switched on the light. Bright and intrusive and exactly what we needed. She lay calm on the bed. An angelic, sleeping doll. Free of vice. There was more colour in her face than I'd seen in weeks.

He lifted her arm and looked at the catheter. Laid her arm back down on the bed.

'It's the same as yours,' he said. 'Right arm. Pointing up the vein.'

'Exactly. And she was so high on the ketamine, you were amazed she got it in at all. Never mind the wrong way up.' I followed the logic. 'If she was that far gone, Eric, could someone else have got it in, without her fighting?'

'On half of the anaesthetic dose?' He shrugged. 'It's possible. If they took it gently and fitted in with whatever it was she was seeing.' He closed over the case notes and laid them on the floor. 'But if it was someone else, we're talking murder, Kellen. Attempted murder, anyway.' He picked up her wrist and felt her pulse. For something to do. 'Don't start clutching at straws, Kells. You'll need a lot more than a dodgy catheter before you can make that one stick.'

'No.' I sat in the light and watched the sheen of damp on her forehead as it caught the wavering light of the ECG. 'I don't have to make anything stick. That's not my problem. I only have to work out who it is and make sure they don't get a chance to try it again.'

'Or talk to Nina and find out what actually happened.'

'If she ever remembers.' And then, because there was something about her colour and the damp sheen on her face that wasn't right. 'Eric, can you check what her temperature's doing?'

———

There are three house officers on duty in the west wing of the Infirmary at that time of night. None of them knew me or Nina. All three of them knew Dr Eric Dalziel and were prepared to run circles for the sake of his newly pyrexic patient. Within ten minutes we had blood samples run through the lab and a printout with full haematological and biochemical results.

'PCV's up. Plasma proteins are up. White cells are crashing.'

I don't believe I'm hearing this.

A gaping hole opened in my solar plexus. Gravity sucked.

'She's septicaemic, isn't she, Eric?'

'Looks like it.'

'Can you run her bloods through for circulating E. coli?'

'Sure. Why?'

'They've had a whole run of horses die of E. coli endotoxaemia at the clinic. Every one of them started like this.'

He picked up the phone. Gave orders. Came back to the bedside. 'It's on its way,' he said.

There is something particularly efficient about a teaching hospital, even at night. The gram stain took less than five minutes and most of the time was lost running the sample to the lab. Somewhere in the middle, they set up a new drip bag and loaded it with cephalosporins.

Nina Crawford lay, sleeping the sleep of the dead, her colour rising with her temperature. An electronic thermometer fed data back to the monitor and the monitor plotted it, dot by minute dot, to the screen. Core temperature in degrees centigrade expressed to the nearest one hundredth of a degree: 38.74°C and rising. A steady, unwavering rise.

The sheen on her forehead beaded; became sweat and ran in runnels down her temples to the pillow. She sighed and turned in her sleep.

A lad with black corkscrews for hair ran in with the last set of results. Remarkably awake for the time of night. Another nocturnal soul. Hospitals gather them.

Eric took his offering. Read it. Dismissed him with a nod. Waited till he had left. Handed me the readout from the gram stain: 'No micro-organisms visible. Advise aerobic and anaerobic culture on other tissue samples.'

'There's no E. coli.' I felt oddly deflated.

'Nope.' He shook his head. 'But that doesn't mean she isn't endotoxic.'

'Doesn't it?' It's a long time since I did clinical medicine at this level but I thought that was impossible. 'How would you get endotoxaemia without circulating bacteria?'

'I'm not sure.'

The lad with the corkscrew hair came back with packs of fresh plasma. Between them he and Eric set up a transfusion.

I sat on the end of the bed, sidelined, inactive and helpless, and watched clear yellow plasma drip into the vein on her arm. It's taken a lot of abuse over the past few days, that vein.

The houseman left. Eric came and sat down opposite me. 'Tell me about the horses,' he said.

'They were all surgical cases. They started symptoms of endotoxaemia within forty-eight hours of surgery.'

'And they all had E. coli on blood smears?'

'Yes . . . no . . . Not all of them.' I remembered Steff.

The blood smear's clear but that means nothing.

'All except the last one. Except Rain. Our mare. She's the one that started the night Nina . . . on Monday night. The smear was clear when we brought her in. I don't know if anyone's looked since.'

'Uhuh?' He pulled a pad from the pocket of his clinical coat. Made notes. 'So, in five out of six cases, you have endotoxic signs in the presence of an E. coli. That's fair.' He nodded. 'Did they run sensitivity tests on the bugs?'

'Yes. They were useless. They all tested sensitive to basic penicillin. As far as the microbiologists were concerned, they killed off all the bacteria in the first couple of hours after treatment.'

'And the animals still died?'

'Yes.'

'And nobody thought that was curious?'

'Only the microbiologists. Everyone else was too busy trying to keep the horses alive.'

'And blaming the micro crowd for being useless.'

'More or less.'

'Sounds familiar.' He made a steeple of his fingers, rested his chin on his thumbs and tugged at his upper lip. 'What about your mare? When did she have surgery?'

'She had a caesar Friday night. We took her home on Saturday to try and keep her clear of infection.'

'And she started clinical signs of infection on Monday night. That's seventy-two hours after surgery. I thought they all started at forty-eight hours post-op?'

'So she was different.'

'She was, wasn't she?' He drew a line, hard down the pad. Wrote at the head of it. 'Did anyone else go near her after you took her home? Anyone from the vet school?'

'Nina. She gave me a hand with morning treatments on Monday. Nobody else. Why? Does it matter?'

'I don't know.' He scribbled Nina's name in his new column. 'This is pretty vicious stuff, Kells. You'd think your mare would show signs a lot sooner than Monday if she picked something up in theatre.'

'Maybe. We hit her pretty hard with the antibiotics. I came home with half the vet school drug store in the back of the lorry. It could have delayed the onset.'

'It might . . .' he nodded slowly. 'Or then again, it might have done just the opposite. If you think about it the other way round . . .' The nod turned to a shake. He chewed his lip. Chewed the pen. 'And that would be nasty. Very, very nasty . . .'

'Eric? Try that in English?'

'Just because it says penicillin on the bottle, doesn't mean that's what's inside, Kellen.'

'You can't put E. coli in neat penicillin, Eric, however armour-plated it is. It would die off in seconds.'

'True. But then maybe you don't need the bugs . . .' He drifted off, floating in some internal world.

'Eric?'

'Sorry.' He smiled at me vaguely, as if he had forgotten for a moment that I was there. He stood up and pushed his pad back into his pocket. Nodded again. 'Give me a minute, Kells. Just let me check I'm not telling fairy stories.' He walked up the ward to the staff room at the end and made a brief, animated phone call.

I sat on the bed watching plasma drip into a vein and followed the rising graph of her temperature step up towards 40°. Tried to remember how high it can go before organs start to disintegrate. Tried to remember what we could do to bring it down if the antibiotics didn't work. Symptomatic treatment. All you can do in the absence of a definitive diagnosis. When I was a student, it was iced-water enemas. No doubt there are better things now.

Eric came back. Sat down again on the end of the bed. 'Right.' There was something new in his voice. Urgent. With an undercurrent of excitement. Like the dog when she's hunting. 'How serious were you about someone else putting in her catheter, Kellen?'

'Fairly.'

'To make it look like suicide?'

'Yes.'

'OK. I've read her file from last time. As far as they were concerned, she cracked because she'd had a run of cases that died. As her therapist, would you say that was right?'

'Yes. That and about a week on no sleep trying to keep the last one alive.'

'Fine. Who else knows that?'

'Me. Matt Hendon, probably—she told him most things. And Steff Foster. She worked it out for herself.'

'So if we were working backwards, from a suicide that wasn't a suicide, either one of those two could, potentially, have set up a series of deaths to follow the same pattern as before?'

'Maybe.'

But if I'm right, Kellen, then we aren't too far off a repeat prescription. I don't think she'll blow it a second time.

'Make that definitely, Eric. How would they do it?'

He smiled. Tight-edged and hard. 'Injectable endo-toxins. Things have changed since we were in college, Kellen. I just called a friend in micro. If you have a valid research grant number, you can buy neat endotoxins off the shelf. They come dried. All you need to do is add water and inject.'

'Without any bacteria?'

'You've got it. The bacteria were a blind, a red her-ring for the micro team. Your horses weren't infected in theatre, Kellen; it's probably the safest place in the clinic. I think they got it afterwards. By injection. You can kill mice in hours if you get the dose right. Horses won't be any different. You just decide how fast you want them to go and then you slip the right amount of junk into a vein when nobody's looking . . .' he leant forward and wrapped one big bear paw over both of my hands, '. . . which is exactly what they've done with Nina.'

His face was different. Grim. Hard. Like gritstone. The house officers might see him like this. Possibly his registrar. I never have. 'She's got about four hours, Kel-len,' he said. 'If we don't get some anti-endotoxin into her by then, she's finished.'

And we just gave it all away.

I stood up. Headed for the staff room. 'I'll call Steff. She might not have put it into Rain yet.'

He caught me. 'No you won't, Kellen Stewart. That woman's just run off with the only thing we had that would work. If you're calling anyone, it's the police. I'll start ringing round the other units. Someone else will have some.'

They might not.

I pulled free. Kept going. 'The vet school's closer than anywhere else, Eric. And it might not be her.'

He followed me in through the door. 'Who else has been alone with her, Kellen?'

'Matt Hendon. And he has a reason.'

'And you think your blonde friend hasn't?'

'Of course she hasn't. Why should she?'

We were both in the staff room by then, beside the phone. He caught my arm. Not hard. But enough to stop me reaching for the receiver. 'Try watching her sometime, Kellen. She looks at Nina the same way you do. I'd say she has as much of a motive as he does.'

'That's unnecessary, Eric.'

'Maybe, but it's true. The only person who hasn't seen it is you.'

'Bullshit.'

My bag was beside us, my mobile somewhere in the bottom. It rang, loud in the space we left.

I reached for it on instinct. 'Hello?'

'Kellen? It's Steff. I've got some bad news.'

So what's new? 'It's Rain. Rain's dead, isn't she?'

Dead because I injected her. With drugs Steff Foster helped to pack.

'Yes. I'm really sorry. She'd gone by the time I got back.'

Just now, this is not the worst news I could have.

'So you haven't given her the stuff?'

I put a thumb up for Eric and tilted the phone his way. He leant over and put his ear beside mine.

'No,' she said, 'I didn't. There was no point. But that's not the problem. It's the foal.'

'He's got the E. coli too?'

Beside me, Eric made eyes. Big, wide I-told-you-so eyes.

The voice carried on in my ear. Smooth Chicago with three years of Glasgow overlaid. 'No. At least, I don't think so. You remember he was straining to pass dung this morning?'

'Vaguely.' At this moment, I can't remember past the last half-hour. Nor do I care.

'Well, he wasn't straining to dung, he was straining to urinate. He can't. He's got a ruptured bladder.'

'So?' Do I really need to know this?

'So we need to cut him, Kells. Now. Matt's here. He called in on his way home and he's offered to stay and help. He can gas him, I can cut. I just need your consent.'

Eric shook his head. Mimed a cut to the throat and shook his head again.

'No . . . Not yet. Hang on for ten minutes. I want to see him first . . .'

Eric's head swivelled through a single, emphatic 180 degree arc. He mimed a shot to the temple.

'Kellen, we haven't got . . .' She sounded frustrated. 'OK. Just don't hang about. I'll get everything ready to drop him.'

'I'm on my way.'

Eric stood blocking the doorway.

'You're not going, Kellen. It's madness. One of those two has just tried twice to kill Nina. They're not playing games.'

'Or both of them together.' At this stage, anything is possible. 'But we need the anti-endotoxin. I'll go in. I'll get it. I'll come back. I won't take any risks.' I gave him a squeeze round the waist. 'Just keep her going till I get back, huh?'

'All I can do is keep her cool, Kells.'

'I know. It's three miles. I'll be back in under an hour.'

17

It was warm outside. A low cloud layer caught the fuzzed glare of the sodium lights in Bearsden and reflected it down through the trees of Garscube so that the shadows were sharp-edged and the ground was full-moon bright. The wind came from the south. Warm and damp and clinging. The air smelt of rhododendron and the slow-moving river and exhaust fumes from the traffic on the switchback.

I stopped the car at the top of the drive, just outside the cattle grid and called MacDonald on the mobile for the second time in half an hour. The duty clerk was less cordial the second time around. Repeated the fact that Inspector MacDonald was out and unavailable but that my message, my urgent and personal message, would be passed on and that she had no doubt that he would call me as soon as he could. She hung up before I could thank her.

The car rolled on down the hill. I switched off the lights as I crossed the cattle grid. Switched off the engine halfway down. Coasted silently to the space behind the unloading ramp. Invisible from anywhere but the back of the ward. To my left, a hound yodelled a greeting from the small animal ward. Somewhere down in the medicine byres, a cow lowed. No sound of a foal. Or a surgeon. I pushed the mobile into my hip pocket and followed it with the cigarette lighter from the glove box. Left the car door unlocked behind me.

Inside, the ward smelt of death. Death and disinfectant. As if there had never been anything else. I slid in through the upper doorway. The way we had brought Rain in. As far from the calf pens as possible. Rain lay in her box. Flat out. Rigid. At peace. The drip lines were gone. And the spider's-web leads of the ECG. Someone had brushed her mane and tail into smooth sheets of dark silk. If there were new scars on the wood of the walls, I couldn't see them. Perhaps it was peaceful after all. A note on the door read: *'Await permission for PM.'*

Maybe.

But then again, why bother?

The door to the drug store hung open. The lighter flickered, shielded by my palm. Shadows loomed, leering across the walls. Bottles glinted on the shelves. Antibiotics, anti-inflammatories, steroids. Cardboard boxes packed with drip sets and fluids sat squat in the cupboards. Plastic bottles of liquid paraffin ranged along the floor, sharing space with the bandages, VetWrap, cotton wool, gamgee. I moved them all, quietly, furtively, searching. Listened to the sound of my own breathing, too loud in the hollow darkness. An audible counterpoint to the incontinent flame of the lighter. I don't have the stamina for this. Not now.

I found no vials of anti-toxin.

The door squeaked behind me as I left.

There were lights in the calf pens. Lights and noise and people. A combined assault on the senses that hit me as I turned the corner. Sandy was waiting for me at the bend in the corridor. Sandy, leaning half-asleep against the wall, with a black woollen cap pulled down over his bald head and a good two-day growth of stubble showing speckled white against the wind-blown brown of his skin. I tapped him on the shoulder. 'Hi. I'm here.'

'Kellen . . .' His eyes were yellow for lack of sleep. The relief was raw in his voice. 'It's Cracker. He's—'

'I know. I heard. Shall we go and see?'

'They said they could fix him. As soon as you came—'

'I know. Let's have a look first.' He shuffled after me, lame from too long spent on his feet. I reached the door-way to the calf pens before he was halfway down the corridor.

The ringwormed calf lay asleep in the centre of its pen, directly under the heat lamp, nose under tail and eyes tight shut to keep out the noise and the light. The goat leaned sleepily over the door and made a half-hearted grab for my fleece as I walked past. The foal lay flat out in the straw, straining and swatting his tail to the floor like a bad-tempered cat. A urinary catheter stuck out like a thin, white straw from the end of his urethra. A drip line already ran into his jugular. A route-way for toxins.

I could already be too late. For him. Not for Nina.

Steff knelt at his head, her hand on his mandible, counting a pulse. Matt leant on the wall outside the pen, just out of range of the goat, filling a twenty ml syringe with something the colour of skimmed milk.

'Kellen.' He put down the syringe. Put a hand on my shoulder. Smiled welcome. Fatigue had etched new lines on his face. Fatigue and emotional burn-out. The smile looked real enough. 'You made good time,' he said.

'No traffic,' I said.

I looked at Steff. 'How is he?'

'Grim.' She kept her eyes on her watch until she'd finished the count. Of the three of them, she looked the most rested. And the most stressed. 'Blood results are real crap. Urea's up, potassium's up, pH is down. He's uraemic, hyperkalaemic and acidaemic. And his pressure's falling. If we don't cut him soon, he won't stand the anaesthetic.'

Quite.

Sandy caught up with us. 'But she's here now. You can go ahead.'

'Can we?' Matt. Filling another syringe.

'In a minute.' I stepped over the door into the pen and knelt down by the foal. Cradled his head on my knee. Felt the soft velvet of his nostrils pushed against my hand, flaring tight with each breath.

'How do you know it's a rupture?' I asked.

'Signalment. History. Clinical signs.' Steff. Frustrated. Very frustrated. Time ticks with the pulse of her patient. Both of them running out. She is, after all, a surgeon.

'And what are they? The clinical signs?'

'Oh, for God's sake . . .' She reined in. Pressed her lips to a hard white line. 'He's a three-day-old colt foal with a history of a prolonged foaling. As far as I know, no one has seen him urinate in a complete stream since he was born, certainly not since he came in here and he has an abdomen full of fluid. It's classic, Kellen. What more do you want?'

'Answers. I want answers to questions I can't afford to ask. And I want three vials of anti-endotoxin. Now.

The foal's skin was damp under my fingers. I leaned forward and felt the tight, round drum of his belly. Tapped fingers on one side, felt the ripple of fluid on the other. Watched his tail swat the straw.

I looked up at Steff. Hot, grey ice-eyes. 'Have you tested the fluid?' I asked. 'Are you sure it's urine?'

'Kellen, what is this? Of course it's urine. What else would it be? I'm not sticking needles in there blind unless I absolutely have to. I don't want to spend half the night repairing a puncture wound in his small bowel on top of everything else.'

'The lass is right, Kellen. The wee lad's not fit for more than he's got.' Sandy stood outside, leaning on the top of the gate to take the weight off his hips. Worry and pain dug deep into the lines of his face. 'You have to let them have a go.'

'If you want confirmation, we could ultrasound his abdomen.' Matt, from the other side of the pen wall. Leaning back with his hands in his pockets and his eyes half shut, tired beyond caring. 'It's fast and it's non-invasive and it'll give you a positive diagnosis. Would that help?' He is humouring me and it is obvious to all of us.

'How long will it take?'

'Minutes. Less than five.'

'Right. Thank you.'

'I don't believe I'm hearing this.' Steff pushed her way out of the pen, pulling a fistful of keys from her pocket. 'What I don't need in my life right now is an obstructive owner.'

We watched her go. Sandy played with the goat, ran his gnarled fingers along the top of the gate and then trapped its lip as it tried to eat his thumb. Matt laid out a row of neatly labelled syringes in a rectangular metal tray. Arranged them in order of size. Rearranged them in order of use. He sat down outside the pen, folding up his jacket inside out to make a cushion and then picked a piece of straw from an empty pen and began weaving knots.

I left the foal and sat opposite him, watching.

'How is she?' he asked finally.

'She's fine.' I practised this lie all the way down from the hospital. I will tell it until someone else tells me differently. 'She's had some soup. She got halfway through writing a letter to Marjorie.'

She talked about it, anyway.

'Did she, by God?' Amusement lightened the dark thumbprints under his eyes. 'Is there all-out war?'

'I think if she sends it, she'll be disinherited, but I gather that's no loss.'

'Hmm.' He smiled a mirth-free smile, the closest he could come to a vermilion sneer. 'Depends if you think a couple of hundred grand is no loss.'

I wouldn't. But it's not my inheritance.

He knows more of her finances than I do. To him, these things matter.

'Is that why you said nothing this morning?'

'No. Did you think I would?'

'It crossed my mind.'

He made a loop of the straw, neatly tying off the ends and tossed it into the pen beside the sleeping calf. It fell against one flank, a lover's knot, perfectly circling a round patch of ringworm. We watched it rise and fall to the rhythms of sleeping calf breath. Slow and restful.

'She needs peace, Kellen,' he said eventually. 'It's all she's ever needed. I'm not going to be the one to bring her war.'

'Thank you.' In that moment, I was grateful.

A trolley clattered on the concrete. Matt levered himself to his feet and helped Steff lift the scanner over the drainage gutter that runs along the doorway.

They were busy, both of them, for a few frantic moments, running the extension lead to the nearest socket, clipping a hand's span of hair from the colt's belly and then covering the dark skin with gel. In the space afterwards, the scanner whined, right at the borderline of hearing and fell back into silence.

'OK.' Steff. Tight-clipped and tight-jawed. Kneeling in the straw by the foal. 'Watch the picture. Black is fluid. White is tissue.' She moved the probe of the scanner across his abdomen with one hand, using the other to move a pointer on the screen. 'Abdominal wall at the top. Fluid . . . all the way down here . . . and right back here . . . we have this useless blob of tissue floating in the breeze.'

I moved back into the pen for a better view. Lifted the foal's head and held it on my knee, scratching softly at the place where the moon rose between his eyes. Snow storms raged briefly across the monitor like white noise on the television when the signal goes down. The snow gathered, became a solid white streak that waved in a flowing sigmoid curve at the far right of the screen. 'That's the bladder?'

'I expect it is.' She looked at Matt, not at me. 'Got some saline?'

'Sure.'

'Shake it up.' He filled a syringe. Shook it hard, like you would shake a bottle of penicillin to get it mixed. Passed it over. 'Here.'

Still not looking at me, she fitted the syringe to the urinary catheter and moved the pointer on the screen until the tip lay over the end of the curving white blur. 'Watch.'

I watched. She pushed the plunger, hard and fast. A blizzard of white snow scattered across the screen and then cleared to nothing. She did it again. Made another, smaller, snow storm.

'There's a free connection from the catheter to the fluid in his abdomen. Straight through the bladder wall. Satisfied?'

She was very, very angry.

Or acting very well.

I have been sworn at by worse things than Stephanie Foster.

'I'm satisfied it's a ruptured bladder.' I looked over her head at Matt. 'Surgery's the only option?'

'It is. I'm sorry.'

'Kellen . . . what's your problem? We have to cut. It isn't ideal but you've got two horses dead already. It'll be three by morning if we do nothing.' She stood up and pulled a plastic bag from her pocket; a small zip-sealed specimen bag with three glass vials chinking gently in the bottom. It hung two feet from my eyes. Spun everything else out of view. 'Look, I can premed him with the anti-toxin now. That way the only thing we have to worry about is getting him through the anaesthetic.'

Or not. As the case may be.

'No.' I stood up. Lifted the bag from unprepared, unresisting fingers. 'They need this back at the hospital. It's why I came back.' There was a short, painful pause. I felt the foal, warm against my shins. Rain's colt. Breathing in the way she breathed the night he was born, grunting low on the outbreath. Raw, ugly noises.

I watched Matt, watched Steff. Looked for changes. Saw none. 'I really think there's no point in operating,' I said quietly. 'Without this, he'll go the same way as Rain did in the end.'

Three people stood quite still in the hush that followed. One of them understood what was happening. I had no way of telling which.

Steff recovered first. She stood up. Smoothly. Very slowly. All the way up.

Her voice wasn't quite as smooth. 'Fine. So we've been wasting our time.' She threw the scan head into the bracket. Jerked the lead from the socket. Reversed the scanner out of the box. Touched Sandy once, on the shoulder on the way past. 'I'm sorry. You did your best.' Nodded to Matt. Curt. Functional. 'I'll see you in the morning.' No love lost, still, between these two. The scanner clattered back down the corridor. Twice as fast as it came up.

And then there were two.

Sandy Logan stood in the doorway. Desolate. Bereft. Speechless.

Matt Hendon gathered his tray of syringes and slung his jacket over one shoulder. 'You're going back to the hospital now?' he asked.

'Yes.'

'I'm going back up to Arisaig tonight. You've got the number. Call me, will you?' He turned, slowly in the doorway. 'I think if you want someone to euthanase your foal, Steff is probably not the right one to ask.'

'Is that an offer?'

'He's got a long way downhill to the bottom if you do nothing.' He smiled thinly. 'I believe I have a professional obligation to persuade you not to leave him like this.'

'Fine.'

'You need to sign a consent form.'

'Fine.' I checked my watch. An hour since I left Eric. 'Make it fast. I have to go.'

'No.'

He's not a violent man, Sandy. He didn't grab, he didn't shove. He simply thrust his arm out, rigid across the doorway two inches from where Matt Hendon was standing and he said: 'No. I won't let you do it.'

He was a farrier once. He still has the power when he needs it.

Matt Hendon had been on his feet for at least as long as I had. He was tired. He was planning a four-hour drive up the side of Loch Lomond and on past Fort William. He was possessed of commendable self-control.

He laid his tray of syringes down on the floor, folded his jacket and laid it squarely on top. Lifted Sandy's hand, with gentle care, out of the way. 'The Euthatal's in the drug store,' he said. 'It'll take me a couple of minutes to draw it up. I will get it and I will bring it back here. I suggest you two get your heads together and sort yourselves out. Let me know what you want to do when I get back.'

We listened to the quiet pad of his handmade shoes receding along the corridor. At the corner, they stopped. His voice carried back to the foal pen. 'If you want my professional opinion,' he said, 'you've got nothing to lose by going for surgery.'

The steady tread fell away to nothing.

The foal rocked warmly against my shins, his eyes dull, his breathing painful to hear.

Sandy Logan stood on the other side of the pen door. Sandy. The man who lives for his horses. Sandy. With the stubble standing out on cheeks so gaunt he might not have eaten for a week. With eyes red at the edges from the pain of it. With hands twisting in ways his hands should not be made to go.

'Kellen. What's going on? I've never seen you like

this. The wee lad . . . He's dying, lass. Will you not listen to the man? There's nothing to lose.'

In two minutes, the man will be back. Possibly less.

I have three hours to get three vials three miles back to Nina.

Three.

'Sandy, come with me.'

I took him outside, to the car. Through the pool of the external light and into the sodium-darkness of the night. When we stopped, I turned in a circle, listening. The woods spoke. And the river. I could hear no people.

I opened the car door and let the light from inside spill out on to his face. My face leered at me briefly from the wing mirror as I leant back against the unloading ramp. Another one in need of sleep.

I took his hand in mine and squeezed it. To make contact.

'Sandy, listen to me. Rain didn't die by accident. She died because someone filled her up to the eyeballs with toxins. Nina Crawford is lying in the Western Infirmary three miles down the road with exactly the same stuff on board.'

He looked at me, fuddled. 'I don't understand.'

No. Neither do I. And time is running out.

'This is not an accident, Sandy. Someone is doing this. They did it to Rain. They did it to Nina. They will do it to the foal if they haven't done it already. There is no point in drawing it out.'

He is old and he is so very tired.

His fingers cramped in mine. 'But you've got the jags. The lassie told me. You can stop him getting what the mare got.'

'No. You're not listening. We need them for Nina. It's the foal or Nina, Sandy. That's not a choice I can make. You can't expect me to make it. I'm taking the drugs back to the hospital. They should never have been taken away.'

'Then let them operate, woman. Why not? If you're that worried, you stay and watch. Nothing'll happen with you here. You owe it to the mare, if you don't owe it to the wee lad.'

'No, Sandy.' I owe that mare all kinds of things. But I owe Nina Crawford more. And with her, I might not be too late.

'Then do you not think you might owe it to me?' He spoke more quietly now. As if there was more hope in quiet. 'I've never asked anything of you before, Kellen, but I'm asking this. Will you not do it for me? Please?'

He sagged at the knees and for one ghastly moment, I thought he might be going to kneel. He caught the car door, held himself upright by the handle. The door wavered in his unsteady grip. The interior light flickered, flashing on and off across his face. Even without it, I could still see him clearly. The red of his eyes. And the desperate pleading.

Obligation is a strange and very onerous beast.

Like gravity, it has its own laws.

I took his hand and pushed him round the edge of the door. Manoeuvred him gently, unprotesting, until he was sitting in the driving seat of my car. I laid the specimen bag on the passenger seat beside him. Took the phone from my hip pocket and slotted it into the holder on the dashboard.

'What are you doing, lass?'

'I am making you an offer, Sandy. I will stay here, and watch them while they operate on the foal. I will do my best to see that he doesn't die on the table. I will do this if, and only if, you will take these to the Western. Will you do that?'

Hope gave him more than a night's sleep could ever have done.

'And you'll stay here with the foal?'

'I don't guarantee it'll save him, but I'll do what I can.'

He smiled. The first smile I'd seen all night that I could really believe in. He wrapped one swollen hand around my shoulder. 'I'll do it,' he said. 'Anything you want.'

'Fine. I'll hold you to that.' I found my notepad in the glove compartment and wrote on it two names; Eric Dalziel and Stewart MacDonald. Handed it to the old man and watched his eyes widen slightly as he read the second name.

'It's that serious?'

'It is. I am. Stewart is supposed to be calling me on the mobile. If he hasn't called by the time you get the drugs to Dr Dalziel, then you call him and you keep calling him until you get hold of him. Then you give the phone to Eric. After that, you do whatever he or Stewart tells you to do. Does that all make sense?'

'No. Not a bit of it. But I understand what you're saying if that's what you mean.' He turned the keys in the ignition, kicked the gas, played with the lever until he found reverse gear. He did it like he does everything else, slowly and with limitless care. When he was ready, he wound down an inch of window. 'You'll see him safe, won't you, Kellen?'

'I'll do my best.'

He didn't smile. 'Do better than that.'

He reversed slowly out of the space beside the un-loading bay.

Matt was standing inside the pen when I got back. 'I've paged Steff,' he said. 'If you give me a hand to clip the rest of the abdomen, we'll be ready to go in to theatre by the time she's scrubbed.' He had changed into his theatre greens. There was no sign of any Euthatal.

'Am I that predictable?'

'No.' He smiled, a man who knows people. 'You're not predictable at all.' He lifted the clippers from a hook by the door, plugged them into the coiled-up extension lead. 'Sandy Logan, however, is absolutely one hundred per cent reliable. He wouldn't have left if he wasn't absolutely certain we were going to cut his treasure. What did you promise him? Eternal life for all colt foals?'

'Just this one.'

'Fine.' The flex uncoiled at the flick of his arm. 'So let's make it happen.'

I sat in the straw with the foal's head on my knee. Stroked the short, curling strands of his mane. It was straight last time I saw it. He's curling under the heat of the lamp. I dragged my fingers through and through, straightening it out. Watched it all spring back into waves again. Ran my hand down the side of his face instead. He blinked dreamily under my hand. Lipped at my fingers. Made a pink loop of his tongue and sucked the end of my thumb. Chewed in frustration with the first edges of new-cut teeth and then fell slowly back into a dull, uraemic stupor.

The clippers buzzed. Ran in broad, straight bands, along and along, carving race tracks in the hair of his belly. Underneath the hair, the skin was black. Coal black. The foal lifted his tail to strain. Grunted into the palm of my hand. Four nights ago, his mother did much the same thing. A lifetime ago. Time does odd things sometimes.

'Why did you send him away?' It came quietly. A question hidden in the buzz of the clippers. From Matt.

'Sandy?'

He nodded.

'I promised I'd give Eric a lift home. He stayed late to be with Nina.'

Thin ice. I am always on thin ice when I'm lying. I never quite had the knack.

'So Sandy's gone to take him home?'

'Right. One of us had to be here with the foal. I doubt if Sandy's ever been in a theatre. He'd lean over and cough on the sterile field. Steff would kill him.'

He smiled. A wry smile. Like Nina's. 'Tonight, she'll kill anyone who gets in her way.'

'Thanks.'

The buzz of the clippers died into silence. Syringes rattled in the metal tray. A stretcher trolley rolled across the concrete.

'Want to give me a hand to get him over to theatre?'

'Sure.' What else am I here for? I have a promise to keep.

18

████████I am losing my fear of theatre. When every other sense is stretched to breaking point, the smell of surgical spirit and volatile anaesthetic is perversely comforting.

Matt waited while I changed into the thin, green scrub suit and then, together, we carried the colt into the small animal theatre. The place where, two nights ago, I stood squeezing life into Nina Crawford's cat.

Sleep comes between breaths to a half-dead foal.

I held his head. Matt Hendon slid a tube up one nostril and down into the windpipe. The air filled with the heady, sweet smell of isoflurane; a glue-sniffer's paradise. The foal breathed deeper and his head lay heavy on my elbow. The tube was changed for a bigger one, through his mouth and down into his airway. We laid him on his back on the operating table and piled sandbags along his side to keep him straight; a living sculpture in copper and burnished coal stretched out under the white heat of the operating lamp.

Monitors whined through their start-up routine. Tedious now. Background noise. Irrelevant unless the rhythm changes. Drip lines went up and antibiotics went in. Because you need these things in surgery. Any one of them could be lethal and I wouldn't know.

I have a promise to keep and no way of keeping it.

I sat on a stool, out of the way and thought about what I could tell Sandy Logan if his foal died.

Your horses weren't infected in theatre, Kellen. It's probably the safest place in the clinic.

There is always hope.

Steff backed in through the doorway, masked and gloved, her hands in the air, her gown untied. 'I can't get hold of Mo.' She looked at me. 'Will you do the running?'

'Sure.'

'Thanks.' It came out without warmth. A curt functionality. Yesterday, we were part of a team. This evening, we shared hope. Now, we can't even share grief at the loss of the mare.

I tied her gown. Watched her lay drapes on the shaved belly of the foal, locked in her own world, halfway to the bladder. Like Nina with her cat's ruptured diaphragm.

'How's Killer?' I asked.

She smiled at that. Even behind the mask you could see it. 'He's cool.'

'He's the Cat from Hell and Jason is going to find a shotgun and blow his head off.' Matt smiled too. A different smile. Exasperated. He looked at me for sympathy and support. 'She has him in the Lodge,' he said. 'They

won't have him in the ward in case he eats the nurses.
Jason had to sleep on the mattress in the feed-room last
night because she had him roaming loose and he
wouldn't let the lad in the door.'

'He's a guard cat. It's his job.' She looked down the
table towards us. There was less ice in her eyes than
before. 'OK to cut?'

'He's a monster and he needs shooting for everyone's
safety.' He laid a finger on a pulse. 'We're ready this end.
Don't hang about.'

It was never like this in the Western.

Theatre is hot. Hot and tedious. A foal laparotomy is not
a complicated procedure. The running is minimal. Maureen, had she been found, would have wasted her trip.
Twice, I changed the suction jars. Switched the end of
the hose from the full jar to the stand-by. Emptied a litre
of foal urine down the drain. Put the empty jar back on
the machine, standing by for the next time. Once, I rifled
through the cupboard for a set of retractors. Matt found
them in the end, in a drawer in the other theatre.

In between, I sat on the high stool where I had been
put and watched the foal breathe. Watched the irritating
rhythm of the ECG. Felt the beginnings of greasy sweat
trickle down between my shoulder blades. Found a bottle of Nina's Highland cow water on the anaesthetic machine and drank half of it. Revolting stuff. It wasn't a
patch on coffee but it pushed back the beginnings of a
headache.

I watched Stephanie Foster operate with exactly the
same degree of care and precision as Nina had done with
her cat. Watched the concentration on Matt Hendon's
face as he fine-tuned his patient's sleep to the rhythm of
the monitors. Decided, as Steff found and began to close

the defect in the colt's bladder, that paranoia can only go so far. There are rational reasons for everything. Even E. coli infection. It's simply a question of attitude. Hospitals breed paranoia.

I thought about Nina and about the farm. And sleep. Deep, dream-filled sleep.

'Kellen, can you get me some 3/0 PDS? It's in the suture rack beside the scrub sink.'

'Sure.'

The world is an odd place at 2 A.M. The air becomes thicker. Flows like water. Long rippling waves of water. The solid boundaries of metalwork sway in time with a drumbeat. I hadn't noticed the drumbeat. Soft and distant, like waves on a shore. But fast, like a horse, running flat to the ground for the finishing line.

The suture pack is blue. Bright, Mediterranean blue. Brighter than the sky over Skye. The numbers dance from pack to pack. Threes to fives to twos. A long, rippling, dancing line. If I close one eye and think hard, I can stop them long enough to find a three.

'On the left. Second row up. Bring two.'

Two is harder than one. For two, they dance faster. The drum beats faster. It's easier, if I'm honest, with both eyes shut. In the world of my fingers, the lines are straight.

'Where do you want them?' My voice is out of rhythm with the drumbeat. This is not good. I need to work on that.

'On the trolley. Sterile.'

But the trolley is not sterile. The trolley is foul. Putrid. Purulent. Pestilent. Crawling with vivid, nameless things that drop out of the sky, the savage fall-out from the tension in the air around us. Anger made manifest. It could kill us all.

The blue of the suture pack floats outwards and is eaten alive by the chaos.

'Thanks . . . Are you OK?'

'Fine. Just tired.' I can lie about this, because lying is easy. Lying has always been easy. I just prefer to tell myself otherwise.

I am not tired at all. I could run marathons and not be tired. I could climb mountains with Eric and beat him to the top.

Or I could sit on the stool where I was told to sit and watch the world flow in past in rippling, waving lines.

The ECG runs in rhythm with the drumbeat. This is good. If I hold my breath, the drum beats louder. If I hold my breath and stare at the ECG, I can keep them in absolute synchrony. Very beautiful. Except that the ECG is changing. Waving. Wavering. Writing lines across the page. Lines of past lies, easily told. In time to the drumbeat. This is not good.

I should look at the foal. The foal can't lie. But the foal is angry. With me. I can see it in the way he is watching me, in his fiery, incandescent, hate-filled eyes. He is angry because I sent the three vials away with Sandy and there is nothing else that will do. His anger feeds the things that breed on the trolley. They could kill us all.

'Kellen . . . ? Matt, is she all right?'

'She'll be fine. She's in caffeine depletion. Her blood levels are probably the lowest they've been since she qualified.'

I resent that remark.

'Here. Drink this. It'll keep you hydrated if nothing else.'

The bottle is green. An ugly, translucent, green. Like the fire in the foal's eyes. The water inside it is green too.

'Drink it, woman. Don't wash out your eyes . . . Here. Like this.'

It's cold, too. Icy cold. In the desert, ice is good. I could drink this for ever.

'Are you sure she's OK?'

'No. But there's nothing we can do about it now . . . Kellen. Lie down . . . here . . . along the wall. Shut your eyes. You'll be fine.'

I can still see the foal. Even with my eyes shut, I can still see him. He floats above me. His eyes are green fire. He hates me. Wants me dead. Because I let his sister die. Because I wanted her to live. Because I let his mother die. Because I am going to let him die, too. Because I don't care enough to save him. He can spin in the air, in time to the drumbeat and he can spit bottle-green poison straight at my eyes. And there is nothing at all I can do . . .

'Matt? I'm coming out. I need some more PDS for the midline and then some nylon for the skin.'

'Will he do?'

'Probably better than she will. What's up?'

'Water overdose? How should I know? I expect she hasn't slept since Sunday night and probably hasn't eaten since before that. It had to hit sometime.'

'That figures. Is your anaesthetic stable?'

'Very.'

'Do you want to scrub in for a minute and follow me up the midline? I'll do the subcut, you do the skin.'

'If you like.'

They hate each other, these two. You can feel it in the air. But they are so excruciatingly polite about it.

So excruciatingly polite.

She didn't have him. He had her. There's a difference.

Isn't there just?

She doesn't even listen to Steff any more.

But did she ever?

They hate each other, these two, with the same kind of passion that they both love Nina and for exactly that reason.

They could hate me too. Either of them. Both of them, possibly.

But you'd never know.

Kellen? If I said that the walls of the incubator were on fire, what would you say?

I would say you were mad.

Nina? If I said this colt was spitting bright green fire, what would you say?

I'd say it's hypoglycaemia.

You'll believe anything when you're paranoid . . .

The man's right, you know.

She could have drunk it. It works orally in kids. Saves all those nasty needle marks.

So very easy.

Bastards.

Breathe. Listen to the drumbeat. The heartbeat. Make it slow down. Don't watch the green fire.

Just keep breathing.

Walls should be straight.

Floors are flat.

Foals don't fly.

'Kellen? Just stay where you are. We'll sort you out in a bit. Don't try to sit up. It won't help.'

And how the hell would you know?

I can sit, if I try to. I could probably stand if I had to but I'm not about to try that now.

My heart is hammering as fast as the foal's. It shouldn't be that fast.

You'd get a fair tachycardia with that much ketamine on board.

Wouldn't you just?

████████

'OK, we'll stick on a stent and then you can wake him up. How's the patient on the floor?'

'I'm fine.'

I can speak. Over the drumming of my heartbeat, I can speak and sound normal.

The half-life of ketamine is twelve and half minutes. But I don't know how much I've had or how much is still floating round. I could ask them. One of them will know. But just now, that would not be wise. Later maybe. If it still matters.

'OK. We're done. Let's wake them both up. Foal first.'

'I'm awake.'

'All things are relative . . . Matt, can you get the foal out on your own? I'll help Kellen.'

'If she's awake, she can push a trolley . . . Can you push a trolley?'

Floors are flat.

'I don't see why not.'

Walls should be straight.

'Good. You take that end. We'll put him on oxygen when we get him to the calf pen. He's not very deep. He'll be awake in ten minutes.'

'Fine.'

Foals don't fly.

'You look grim.'

'Caffeine deficiency. Like you said.'

The floor is flat. The walls are straight. The foal is asleep, breathing slowly, on his own. His eyes are dark, like his mother's. Flickering already with the beginnings of waking.

'Where's Steff?'

'Getting changed. She'll be over in a minute.'

███████

Outside, it was warm and dark and the air was fresh.

Under the heat lamps, in the calf pens, it was warmer and the air was damp and smelled of calf and goat, evenly mixed. The calf still slept. The goat raised its head but didn't make the effort to stand. We lifted the foal from the trolley and sat him on his brisket, like a dog, with loose straw piled under his shoulder to prop him up. There was an oxygen cylinder on the trolley. We slid the tube gently up his nose and taped it in place with zinc oxide wrapped around his muzzle.

My foal, the pipe-dreamer. At least he is still alive. I have kept my promise. So far.

'Are you all right if I go and get our jackets?'

'I'm fine.' This kind of lie, I can manage.

'OK. I won't be long. If he wakes, try not to let him stand up.'

'I'll do my best.'

███████

I could so easily sleep. In the warm, ruminant air of the calf pens, I could sleep and not mind if I never woke up.

I am Alice and I have eaten once more in the company of the White Rabbit.

Or, alternatively, it is three o'clock in the morning, I haven't had a decent night's sleep for as long as I care to remember and someone, somewhere, has doped me up to the eyeballs with ketamine. Which is dangerous. And a very good reason not to sleep. A very good reason, in fact, to be somewhere else. Now.

I can move. It is not a lie. I simply can't do it very well.

Standing is easy. The walls make a good lever, the gate a useful prop. Walking is more difficult. Without the trolley to hold on to, directional control is not quite what it could be. Action does not necessarily follow intention. Intention is hard enough. It would be so much easier simply to sleep.

I step out of the foal's pen and remember to shut the gate. I would have liked to go out through the door and into the corridor. Instead, I lean over a different gate and commune, briefly and very personally, with the goat. Both of us are surprised about that. He is more pissed off about it than I am.

If I half shut my eyes and run my fingers along the wall, I can walk in a line for the door. It's all to do with balance. I don't have any. But my fingers have lots. As long as I don't think.

Beyond the doorway, the corridor is light. Too light. To hide, one must be in the dark.

I follow the line of the corridor, all the way along to the end. The ladies' toilet is on my left. A dead end. But useful in a hurry, I should remember that.

In the corridor, there are noises. If I stop and listen, I can hear the goat. Far in the lower byres, the cow is still lowing. She must be calving. Or sick. Or both. Outside, the wind whispers through the trees. Tonight, if I listen, I will know what they say. She never mentioned that, the talk of the trees.

Probably just as well.

I am listening for people. There are none. Unless they walk more quietly than the trees.

The door screams as it opens. A loud, jagged noise thrown out into the dark. The trees fall to a whisper. The night is black with sodium-orange tints. The things that walk through the trees are tall and wisped and they smile with Nina's eyes. Walnuts amidst the rhododendrons. I have to ask their permission to move on. It is not certain that they will give it. I have lied too often to too many people.

But I have never lied to the trees.

This is true.

I can pass.

There are no walls in the dark of the car park. There are also no people. Still. No Matt. No Steff. This is surprising. One or other of them should be back by now. I could try to run. While the coast is clear.

Running is not good. For emergencies only. Now, I am missing some skin on one knee and the palms of both hands. There is no pain. There has never been any pain. Not physically. All the pain is on the inside, trying to get out.

The walls to the clinic are straight, very rough but straight enough to move with. I run my finger along the brickwork, feeling the rough cast of the bricks. Mountains and valleys of baked clay. Man-made geology. I had no idea the surface of things could tell stories like this. My fingers are a new window on the world.

There is a doorway ahead. Beyond it, a corridor. Inside, it is totally dark. No windows. No lights. Perfect.

On my left, is the silent, swinging door to the small animal ward. It opens, hissing a greeting, like a snake. Snakes are small animals too. I fear snakes more than

anything else in this world or any other. If there are
snakes in here, I will turn round and give myself up.

I see no snakes. I hear things breathe. Things that are
not snakes. A cat sings, quietly, a song of welcome. A
dog bays. More dogs join him. A cacophony of baying
dogs and singing cats. A betrayal in sound.

'Kellen? Are you there?'

A perfect betrayal. Her voice. The tall one. The one
who so carefully kept me away from Nina while she was
dying.

No. I am not here. I am nowhere.

I shut the door, back out, feel in the dark for a wall
to walk with. There is no wall. But there is a banister,
smooth, warm, peaceful wood. Upstairs there is a haven
of hiding places. And the Lodge. Where she lives. Bad
idea.

'Kellen?'

No. I am not here.

There is a wall if you know where to find it. Straight
and smooth. Like the floor. On this floor, I can walk, fast
and silent. MacDonald taught me how to walk in the
woods. Part of my education. Heel and toe. Soundless. If
you can walk soundless through a beech wood with
fallen twigs and beech nuts underfoot at every step, you
can walk soundless along a tiled corridor. I am not here.
There are ghost-forms here, all around. But not me.

'Kellen? Are you there? It's me. I'm safe. I promise
you.'

The other one. Him. The one who thinks he can give
Nina the peace she needs.

Why is he whispering? Come to that, why have they
not switched on the lights? Their loss. My gain. In the
dark, I have the advantage. Because I can see and they
cannot. I can see the bends in the corridor. I can see the
doorways, turn the handles, feel them locked. I can see

her, or him, one of them, standing in the dark at the far end of the corridor, looking the wrong way. I can hear the other one walk into the ward. Hear the hissing door and the cacophony of greeting. I should have stayed there. You can hide in a jungle of sound.

There is a door that opens. Here. On the right. Well used and well oiled. It opens as silently as the one to the ward although, at this moment, it could creak like the barn and you wouldn't hear it over the baying of the dogs. There is no light in here. The darkness is perfect. My fingers are windows on the world. There are shelves. Right from the doorway, there are shelves. Long, long shelves reaching high up the walls, stacked with glass bottles and cardboard boxes. So many different sizes. So many different shapes. There is a geometry here, if I had the time to work it out.

There is no time. The dogs have stopped. There are footsteps in the corridor. Difficult to tell if they are coming or going and either way I must hide.

There are boxes on the floor. I hadn't thought of that. My feet are windows on the world too, it's just that they have the curtains drawn so I can't see what's there. Now I know, I can step round the boxes. Silently.

Further round, shelves jut out into the room. Like a library. Except it isn't a library. But it is a good labyrinth. Lots of places to hide. All I have to do is to find one my size. I need to find it soon because the footsteps outside have stopped by the door and the door is not, after all, silent. When the dogs are not barking, it makes a faint, serpentine hiss.

'Kellen? Are you there?' A whisper. Without accent or gender. Frustrating. But it makes no difference. The footsteps are steady, even and long-striding. It could be either of them. I need to hide. Soon.

This is a big room. There is a corner ahead. A bench-

top, covered in smooth, cool plastic. And a sink. The
water drips, very, very slowly, very softly, on to the cold
metal of the sink. Like a drumbeat, a long way off. Calling.

To my left is a smooth, metallic chest. To the right of
that is a filing cabinet. Between them both is a space. My
size of space. The drumbeat calls. Soft. Insistent. A song
of safety and of peace and the need to sleep. I can fit in
here and I can sleep. As soon as the footsteps leave, I can
sleep. Just me and the drumbeat.

And the footsteps.

Stopping.

'Kellen. It's me.' Matt. Crouching in front of me.
Shining a light on my face. A small, bright, circle of
amber light. He flicks it away when he sees that it hurts.
I can live in the dark. In the peace. He knows that. 'It's
all right. I'll look after you. Steff's upstairs. She won't
find us here.' He crouches beside me in the way he
crouched by the injured German shepherd. The consum-
mate professional. Bringing help.

The light swings, slowly, in time with the drumbeat.
The soft, slow call to sleep. A slow, swinging circle of
amber light, spiralling in towards a centre that is me.

'Kellen? Can I hold your arm? Just for a bit? It won't
hurt. The light will move again if I can just hold your
arm for a bit.'

'Sure.' Why not? His voice is warm in the way a cat's
coat is warm. Soft and silken and pleasant to feel. Very
safe.

'Not that one. The other one.'

Fine by me. Have them both. I don't need them.

There is cold in my arm, just for a moment. In time
with the drumbeat. And then warmth, a slow, spreading
warmth.

The light is moving again. Shining upwards. Up to

the sky. The sky is blue, like the sky over Skye. And in the corner is a fat, bloated sun. A clear sun. Absolutely clear, with strange, viscous swirls spiralling upwards through it. Clear, translucent raindrops fall from the sun. One at a time. Falling. Towards my arm. A long river of rain running into my arm. Rain. From the sun. This is good. I would never have thought of that.

'Rain.'

'What? Oh. Yes. I'm sorry she had to go. One of the innocent bystanders. Don't worry, we're on to the real thing now. It'll be very peaceful. Better than the mare. All you have to do now is let go and watch the drops.'

And I do. I watch slow drops of colourless rain, falling in time with the drumbeat. I can hear them. Each of them. Falling softly. Calling my name.

▬▬▬

'Kellen.'

'Kellen.'

'Kellen.'

▬▬▬

There is light. Too much light. Bright, white light. And the clear sun has set. Driven away by the light.

There is pain in my arm. A sharp, shooting pain. Spreading upwards and outwards all through me to my head. Mother, my head hurts. I need to sleep. To escape from the light and the pain.

'Kellen!' A sharp, stinging pain on the side of my face. Better than the pain in my head. 'For Christ's sake, woman, will you wake up?'

'No . . . can't . . .'

'You bloody can.' Another rush of cold pain in my arm. 'Jesus . . . Why did you have to use Immobilon? Where's the bloody data sheet? How am I supposed to know the dose without the data sheet? Where's the effing anaesthetist when you need him . . . ? Kellen . . . Can you hear me? Have you seen Matt? . . . Oh God. No . . . Not there. If you're going to be sick, do it in here . . . here . . . like that. Shit . . . this is why I never did medicine . . .'

The pain came in waves and consciousness with it. Steff Foster pumped dextrose-saline and neat naloxone into the catheter in my right arm and held a leaking cardboard box on my knees and, in between the coughing, retching bouts of nausea, she read me the riot act. A constant stream of muttered invective laced with unanswerable questions.

'Why, Kellen? Why now? She's getting better, for God's sake. She's not going to die. You don't have to play the guilt-stricken lover. All you have to do is wait till she's well enough to talk and then go and sort things out. It's not that difficult.'

'I didn't . . .'

'Right. Sure. If you say so. But that's not the point, is it? . . . You wanted to. Come on. You're not going out on me now. Have some more Narcan . . .'

The nausea passed. We changed to another cardboard box. One that smelt less bad.

The world began to focus. Became straight more often than not. The drumbeat drew back into the distance.

A collapsed, clear sun lay on the floor at her feet leaking rainwater drops in a puddle all over the grey plastic tiles of the floor.

'Not yellow.'

'Yes. Very good. It's not yellow. Half the contents of the Dangerous Drugs Cupboard are 'not yellow', Kellen.

You're bloody lucky I found the bottle or you'd be dead
by now. Why Immobilon, of all the stupid, fucking
things to use? You don't get second chances with this
stuff, Kellen. You could kill a horse with the amount you
put in here. Stone dead. Bang. Gone. Faster than a gun.
That's overkill, you know? It's not good for making a
point to the rest of the world. If you want to make state-
ments, next time use something peaceful like pentobarbitone where there's a chance of bringing you back in
the first five minutes. Or if you really want to go, put in
something we can't reverse, then we won't even think
about pulling you back. Jesus, even Nina had more sense
than this . . .'

'I didn't . . . She didn't . . .'

'Kellen. I don't care what you did. It's none of my
business. You could be having a ménage à trois with the
cat for all I care. Just get your act together and talk to her
and stop pissing about with the happy juice, right?'

'No . . . I mean, I didn't put up the rain . . . the
drip. It wasn't me.'

'Of course it was you. Who else would it be?'

'Matt. It was Matt. Ketamine . . . in the water, first
. . . then this. Like Nina . . . Matt.'

There was silence. Blessed silence. I focused on eyes
of puzzled ice. Blurred. Not understanding.

Waves of iced water flowed up my arm. The pain in
my head was worse than anything I have ever known. To
speak was to invite the Inquisition to visit the interior of
my skull. I ground my teeth and fought to find words in
the mess of my mind.

'I couldn't do this on my own, Steff. I've never heard
of . . . the rain . . . I don't know what it is.'

The eyes unblurred. Sharp, grey ice-in-fire. 'Matt. He
knows . . . ?'

'Yes.'

'And Nina?'

'Nina's got endotoxaemia . . . He injected her this afternoon . . . through the line . . . neat stuff . . . No E. coli. That's why I . . . took the anti-toxin.'

'And the horses? Did he kill the horses too?'

'I think so . . .' Fragments of memory returned. 'Innocent bystanders . . .'

She stood up, then. Turned to the wall. Lifted a phone. Punched in a number. Hard, vicious stabs at the key-pad. Hung up. The phone rang again before she had a chance to sit down again.

'Matt? It's Steff. Yes, I found Kellen. She's in the pharmacy . . . On a drip . . . Can you? Thanks.'

I'm dead. This time, I really am dead. She could just have let me go on the rainwater tide. It would have been so much easier.

'Why . . . ?'

She smiled. Not the kind of smile I'd want to meet often. Pushed me back into the space under the fridge. Put the half-empty drip bag back up on the stand and laid the drip line across my palm.

'He's on his way up. Play dead, huh?'

Some things are easier than others. This is so close to the truth, it is effortless.

'Why . . . ?' I sound like a jammed record. But I have no strength for anything else.

'Can you move?'

'No.' Not for anything or anyone.

'Right. So I can't leave you. He has to come to us.'

'Why . . . ?'

'I called the hospital. To let Nina know about the foal. They said Dr Dalziel was coming here with Sandy. I'd like your foal to still be alive when they get here.'

'But . . .'

'Not now, huh? We can talk about it later.'

If there is a later.

Footsteps sounded in the corridor. Running. Steff stepped back into the labyrinth of the shelves. Put a finger to her lips. Smiled again. A slow, leonine smile. The nose-stud winked erratic morse-code as she leant on one shelf, breathing unsteadily.

The footsteps reached the door. Came through it without pause. He stood in front of me. He's tall, Matt Hendon. Not as tall as Steff and not as broad in the shoulder as Eric but he's bigger than I am in both dimensions. And fit. Very fit. I don't notice these things until I have to.

'Kellen . . . you're . . . you   look   dreadful. Where's Steff?'

'Gone . . .'

'Has she? Good. She'll be back soon. Do you know where you are?'

'Pharmacy.' I knew that before. It didn't matter then. It matters now. 'Where we found Nina . . .'

'Exactly.' The bottle came from a cupboard, high up on the wall. A small, anonymous steel box. One amongst the many. You wouldn't see it if you didn't look. 'I didn't choose it, though, Kellen. For her or for you. The dream wasn't mine.'

The syringe came from his pocket. And the needle. A 20 ml syringe. He filled it. Held it out in front of him, as if even that close, it might be dangerous. 'You should have left her with me, Kellen.' He said it gently, in the same, cat-warm voice as before. I didn't hear the venom behind it, then. 'She would have come back, you know, if you'd left her alone. After Branding Iron, after the fire, she would have come home.'

'Give it up, Matt. She'd have gone to her mother before she ever went back to you.'

Steff. Behind him. Stepping out from her space between the shelves. Steff, who is taller than he is and who moves with the grace of a tiger. But it was what she said that hit him, more than her being there. It showed on his face, the sudden, cracking anger as he spun round and then backed away, slowly, the full syringe held up like a knife, his thumb on the plunger, ready to push.

'No.' A single word, spoken as if the intensity of it made it so.

Steff stood in front of him, just out of range, both hands spread wide, swaying rhythmically, the mongoose before the swaying cobra. He swayed with her, the snake, coiled to strike.

'I don't think so, Matthew.' She crooned it, smiling. 'Nina didn't leave you because there was too much work, whatever she said. She left you because she didn't like being owned. There's no way she would have come back to you. Ever.'

'No.' He said it thickly this time, as if he couldn't think past the word. 'She would have come. She had nowhere else to go.'

'Oh, but she did, didn't she? She had us. She's always had us. And there are more of us than there are of you, Dr Hendon. Even now.' She held out her hand, a teasing invitation. 'Give me the needle, Matthew. You can't fake both of us.'

'I don't have to fake anything. No one's going to find you here before morning. I'll be out of the country by then.'

'No, you won't . . .' I spoke with care. Because words were still difficult. 'Eric's on his way. He knows about Nina. He'll find us . . . you.'

'Sorry, Kellen.' He smiled. A smile not unlike Steff's.

Cold-cooled poison. 'The posse's been and gone. I met
them in the car park on the way up here. Told them
you'd gone back to the farm and taken young Stephanie
with you. They seemed in something of a hurry to follow.' The smile grew broader. Warmer. A winning smile.
Scoring points to even the balance. 'You thought it was
her, didn't you?'

He was talking to me. But the points were all sharpened for her.

I said nothing. But it hit home, just the same.

'Kellen . . . ? You didn't seriously think I
would . . . ?'

He struck then, as a snake strikes. The needle
flashed, quicksilver under the bright ceiling lights. A
curving arc, downwards. Straight for the mass of her
body.

Which wasn't there.

She swayed, side-stepped, kicked, all in one smooth
movement. The side of her foot connected somewhere
high on his body, punching him sideways. In all of the
motion, there was only one noise; the solid thud of a
Nike trainer on flesh. And then a tumbling, gathering
cascade of sound as he stumbled against one shelf and
the one beside it, knocking bottles and boxes and plastic
tubs to the floor in a flailing mess of glass and tablets and
intra-mammary tubes.

But he didn't fall. Not all the way. And the floor was
as lethal for her as it was for him. Like stepping on
marbles, rolled in oil. A pungent chemical stench choked
the air.

Matt pulled himself upright and they circled, warily,
half an eye on the floor, half an eye on each other. No
eyes at all for me. She didn't need one. He did. They
circled past. I kicked out, as she had done. Not as hard
and not as accurately, but enough to push him off bal-

ance. He spun out. The needle flashed, still aiming for her. She chopped down, hard, with the edge of her hand. Bone connected on bone. And then bone cracked on metal as he hurled forward on to the steel drugs cabinet, flung by the floor as much as her hand.

The world disintegrated. Shelves, flesh and drugs spun randomly to the floor. Silence strayed in the spaces between until everything stopped.

'Shit.' It was Steff. A sick, half-dazed expletive in the quiet.

Matt Hendon sprawled like an unstrung puppet, against the wall. The syringe jutted upwards from his thigh, the plunger halfway down the barrel.

She's uncommonly fast in a crisis, that woman. She had the needle out of his leg and was already grabbing his ankles before I was halfway out of the hole by the filing cabinet. She was stepping back, ready to jerk him clear of the wreckage, just as I stepped upright.

'No!'

I clamped a hand on hers, just in time.

'Kellen! That's Immobilon. He needs—'

'Don't move him. Look at his neck.'

'Oh, fuck.'

And the rest.

You only need to see a cervical fracture once to know it again for the rest of your life. Steff Foster must have seen them often enough in the wards. Animals are not that different to people, she just needed to see past the lethal column of the syringe.

Very, very slowly, she let go of his ankles. Leant forward and laid two fingers to the inside of his wrist. I did the same on the other side, felt the pulse. Not as strong as it could be, but a good, steady rhythm. Alive, if not necessarily well.

The syringe lay beside him on the floor. Half-empty.

'Has he got enough of the happy juice on board to kill him?'

'Easily. But it's gone intra-muscular. If we can get the naloxone into a vein, we can bring him round.'

'With a fractured C-spine?'

'That's his problem.'

She stood up. Stepped over me. Pulled a bottle from the steel cabinet and started filling another syringe. Smooth. Efficient. Sure of her choices. 'Can you find a vein without moving his neck?'

'I don't know.'

'Try.'

I didn't move. Waited until she had finished loading her gear and was kneeling down where I could see her, where I knew she could see me.

'Why, Steff?'

'I have a career, Kellen. A murder charge doesn't look too good on the résumé.'

'It was self-defence. On top of two attempted murders. You're water-tight.'

'It isn't self-defence if we sit here and do nothing.'

'Maybe.' But there are ways and ways of doing things and not all of them would bring him back. We both know that.

She looked away, a thin, tight line drawn down between her eyes. Matt Hendon's pulse fluttered under my fingers.

We are not so very different, she and I.

And for both of us, I think, in the world of all possible nightmares; to live, to breathe, to think, to feel and not to be able to move, is by far the worst.

One of us needed to say it.

'He might prefer it if we let him go, Steff.'

'I know.' Her eyes came back to mine. Clear, untroubled ice-in-fire. 'I didn't say we were doing him any favours.'

She slid the needle up the inside of his forearm towards the blue shadow at his elbow. 'Raise the vein for me, can you?'

Epilogue

There are three magpies spread out around the Hawthorn field this morning.

The first one's sitting beside us on the hedge, close enough for me to reach out and touch it. The next one is high up in one of the hawthorns at the top of the hill, dropping curses on the horses below. The last one hopped all the way along the roof ridge behind us as we brought the mare and foal to the field. It's there now, clinging to the tiles at the gable-end as if it doesn't know how to let go.

Three. Not the easiest of numbers.

'Kellen?'

Nina is here, leaning on the gate beside me. She half turns, running one hand up through hair the colour of chestnuts, straight from the shell. You have to look quite hard now to see the line of the old henna, close to the ends.

'Problem?' She asks it quietly. So that it doesn't matter if I have no answer.

'I was counting the magpies.'

She turns full circle, finds them all.

Three. For a girl.

'Megan?'

'Yes.'

'Do you still mind?'

'No.' I shake my head. 'No, I don't mind.' I really don't. And that surprises me more than all the rest put together.

We lean together on the gate, watching the morning.

The sun lifts higher over the ben, burning the last of the dew from the grass. The breeze lifts with it, carrying the smell of seeding grasses down from the hill. In the far distance, Kate leads an early ride of English tourists on the long route past the loch. Somewhere, up beyond the village, Gordon Galbraith and his lads load pigs on to a lorry.

The birds change places in the field, finding new vantage points as the horses move. The mare ambles down the hill towards us; a battered bay, long past her days as an athlete, with splints on both fore limbs and a spavin behind that you could see from across the field and a set of feet about which even Duncan had trouble finding something good to say. But she has plenty of milk, which was all Sandy looked at when he paid for her and she took kindly to the foal after the first day of temper and frayed nerves which is just as well, if you think about what she cost.

The foal trots down the hill behind her; a bright, shining chestnut with long, gangling legs and the new moon rising clear between his eyes.

The dog squirms under the gate to greet him. He props, makes wild eyes and spins on his quarters. She waits for him to settle. A week ago, he wouldn't have let her near. By next week, they will herd each other into the far corners of the field. She has more time to play with him, now that the youngsters have gone.

She had five pups in the end. Three dogs and two bitches. The biggest of the bitches came first; an odd pale colour with marbled streaks of copper and tan through the white and you could believe that, when she opened them, her two eyes would turn out different colours. She went to Stewart MacDonald, for a promise.

After that, the dogs all came in a jumble: one black with a single white paw like his sire and the other two tan and white collie-marked after their great grand-dam. The white-pawed black went to Duncan. Steff and Sandy Logan each had their pick of the tan and whites. Sandy's would be here now, if he hadn't gone off down to Ayr to see a man about a mare and taken the pup with him for the ride. Steff's lives with her in the cottage and has, strangely, not been eaten by the cat. I am grateful for that, more than most things. Living with Nina is more peaceful than either of us imagined but living with Killer could well be the prologue to a very messy divorce.

The last of the bitches came two hours after the others. She's solid tan, all but a white flash on her left fore-leg and a narrow lightning strike that zig-zags across her muzzle. She fed badly the first few days and we took turns holding her on the teat every two hours overnight until she was strong enough to fight the mewling mass of her siblings in her own right.

She was Nina's without question, from the moment she first came out. We called her Megan after Duncan's

old bitch who started the line and I spent a string of
summer evenings teaching her not to eat ducks and how
to stay on the right side of the cats so that she would fit
in with the rest of the family. It wasn't until they were
seven weeks old and almost ready to go that Nina first
suggested that the pups might not be staying at the farm.

To say that nobody thought much of the idea would
be a huge understatement. MacDonald thought she was
mad and said so, but then he was still sore that, after
three months of police time, nobody had gone ahead
and pressed charges. Sandy and Steff and Duncan threw
in their ha'pence-worth when they were asked and then
had the good sense to stay quiet. No one else had an
opinion that counted.

So it came down to me and Nina, as we all knew it
would. We put it off as long as we could and then on
Monday, the day after the last of the other pups had
gone, we took two of the ponies and headed out past
Galbraith's and up over the moors to the ben. We took
the longest route. Two hours out and longer back with
lunch up by the loch in the middle and most of it spent
talking through the tangled circles of her reasons for and
my reasons against and somewhere in the middle, a fuzz-
coated pup with bright amber eyes and a way of answering back that reminded me, stupidly, of Bridget and
didn't help the logic at all.

Nina got her way in the end, of course. There was
never really any doubt about that. I just wanted to make
sure we were doing it for the right reasons.

And so, yesterday, eight weeks from the day she was
born, we put Megan in a van with one of Sandy's friends
and sent her up to Arisaig, to live with Matt Hendon, to
hunt rabbits with his father along the side of Loch Morar

and to sit by his chair in the evenings looking out over the Sound of Sleat towards Eigg and the south tip of Skye.

It was odd, letting her go. She's left a gap that the rest of them don't quite fill. But no, when I think about all of the possible ends to the nightmare, I don't begrudge him her company at all.

If you enjoyed Manda Scott's NIGHT MARES, you won't want to miss any of the titles in this series.

Look for DEATH, SANG THE RAVEN, coming in paperback from Bantam Books in summer 2000.

And don't miss HEN'S TEETH, available now at your favorite bookseller's.

ANN RIPLEY'S

The Gardening Mysteries

"This hybrid of traditional whodunit and up-to-the-minute gardening guide is certain to appeal to mystery readers with a green thumb."

—*The Denver Post*

Mulch
___57734-4 $5.99/$7.99

Death of a Garden Pest
___57730-1 $5.99/$7.99

Death of a Political Plant
___57735-2 $5.99/$7.99

Ask for these books at your local bookstore or use this page to order.

Please send me the books I have checked above. I am enclosing $____ (add $2.50 to cover postage and handling). Send check or money order, no cash or C.O.D.'s, please.

Name _____

Address _____

City/State/Zip _____

Send order to: Bantam Books, Dept. MC 21, 2451 S. Wolf Rd., Des Plaines, IL 60018
Allow four to six weeks for delivery.
Prices and availability subject to change without notice.   MC 21 1/99